To Win a
LADY'S HEART

To Win a Lady's Heart

An unforgettable tale of honor and love

SIAN ANN BESSEY

Covenant Communications, Inc.

A delightful read full of adventure, intrigue, and romance. Its combination of charming characters, rich setting, and medieval heroics make this book impossible to put down. Expertly researched, To Win a Lady's Heart *brings history and romance alive in a book readers will want to enjoy time and time again.*

—JUILE DAINES

Cover image: *Medieval Woman with Chestnut Horse* © Nikaa / Trevillion Images

Cover design copyright © 2016 by Covenant Communications, Inc.

Published by Covenant Communications, Inc.
American Fork, Utah

Printed in the United States of America
First Printing: November 2016

22 21 20 19 18 17 16   10 9 8 7 6 5 4 3 2 1

ISBN 978-1-52440-152-8

For Emily Manwaring and Samantha Millburn,
whose encouragement and expertise are unfailing

Acknowledgments

I'D LIKE TO GIVE SPECIAL thanks to my husband, Kent, and my children for their unwavering support. Throughout all the writing deadlines I've put them through, they've never once complained—even when dinner has meant foraging for leftover food in the fridge or eating a bowl of cold cereal.

Thanks also to my parents, Noel and Pat Owen, who are (and always have been) my greatest fans. They were the ones who took me to Beddgelert as a child.

I appreciate the love and support of all my siblings but especially my sister Emily Manwaring, who willingly reads all my first drafts and consistently gives me constructive suggestions.

I'm grateful for my friendship with the remarkable people at Covenant Communications. I truly appreciate all their efforts on my behalf. My editor, Samantha Millburn, is a gem, and I'm so glad she's willing to take the journey from manuscript to published book with me.

And then there are you readers, who pick up my books and write to tell me that you stayed up late into the night reading them. Thank you for sacrificing your sleep and for letting me know how much you enjoy my novels. I hope this one will keep you up past your bedtime too.

Glossary

Addlepated—confused, stupid, or befuddled.

Antechamber—a small room that serves as a waiting room or entrance into a larger room.

Archery butt—a mound of earth on which targets are placed.

Bowyer—a person who makes or sells archers' bows.

Carrack—a three- or four-mast sailing ship developed in the fifteenth century.

Charger—the name given to a medieval English warhorse.

Crenellated walls—a serrated or notched pattern built on the top of castle walls that enabled guards to protect their heads from incoming arrows while defending the castle.

Fletching—the feathers on an arrow.

Grand chamber—a large room in the keep used by the lord of the castle for private business.

Great hall—a large room in the center of the keep where the public would gather for meals, entertainment, and business transactions.

Hauberk—a shirt of chain mail.

Inner bailey—sometimes known as an inner ward. It was the fortified enclosure at the center of a medieval castle. It surrounded the keep, where the Lord and his family resided, and was usually the location of the well and the most important defensive elements of the castle.

Keep—a fortified tower built within castles during medieval times. Traditionally this was the residence of the lord and his family, along with knights and other visiting nobility. It was often the location of the castle kitchen, which gave the cook easy access to the well in the inner bailey.

Landwaiter—a late-medieval customs official who watched over the loading and unloading of boats from foreign ports.

Outer bailey—sometimes known as an outer ward or base court. The outer portion of a castle, separated from the inner bailey by a defensive wall. This was the location of most of the buildings and facilities necessary to maintain the castle, such as the stables, brewhouse, bakehouse, workshops, and granary.

Pell—a wooden post planted firmly in the ground and used as a target when practicing swordplay.

Plainchant—sometimes known as plainsong. A form of medieval music sung within churches. The words were chanted with no accompaniment.

Searcher—a late-medieval customs official whose job was to ensure that the boat's cargo tallied with what was on the receipt.

Tidesman—a late-medieval customs official who stayed with the boat until the unloading of cargo was complete.

Tidewaiter—a late-medieval customs official who boarded boats at high tide to ensure that they docked and unloaded their goods at the designated quay.

Waghalter—a rogue; one likely to be hanged.

Prologue

SIR EDWYN LEANED FORWARD IN his saddle, studying the surrounding trees. All was quiet. Too quiet. There was no birdsong, no rustling of small creatures in the fallen leaves. It was as though the very pulse of the forest had been suddenly extinguished. He turned his head. In the hushed clearing, a dozen of his fellow knights and their squires sat silently astride their horses, awaiting Lord Gilbert's signal to begin their annual hunt in Langston Forest. But the exuberance that had been present among the men only an hour ago was gone, replaced by a disturbing sense of unease.

From his position at the head of the riders, Lord Gilbert motioned Edwyn forward. "What do you make of it, Sir Edwyn?" Lord Gilbert spoke softly.

"I cannot tell, my lord," Edwyn replied, his horse shifting nervously beneath him. "But whatever it is, the animals feel it too."

Lord Gilbert spared a glance for the his greyhounds. Only moments before, the dogs had been anticipating the upcoming hunt with frenzied excitement. Now they were huddled together within the protective circle of the mounted knights.

"What's out there?" Lord Gilbert said, frowning at the trees as though he were deeply displeased that they were keeping secrets from him.

The forest did not answer, but a whisper rippled through the waiting men, and Sir Maynard, one of Lord Gilbert's most trusted knights, broke away from the others to approach him.

With an acknowledging nod toward Edwyn, Sir Maynard faced Lord Gilbert. "If I may be so bold, my lord," he said, his voice low. "It has just come to the attention of your men that Gelert is missing."

Lord Gilbert's frown deepened. He looked to the place at his right where his faithful wolfhound, Gelert, always stood guard. The spot was empty. An unidentifiable emotion flitted across the lord's face but was gone almost as quickly as it had arrived. "Return to the lodge," he ordered with sudden urgency.

The knights needed no second bidding. Moving as one, they wheeled their horses around and cantered after Lord Gilbert as he pressed his horse to greater speed along the narrow path that took them back to the outskirts of the forest.

His lordship was the first to reach the lodge, but Edwyn was out of his saddle before him. As soon as his feet hit the ground, Edwyn ran to the side of the young guard who was lying on the ground clutching a blood-soaked thigh.

"Who attacked you?" Edwyn said, crouching down and grasping the young man's shoulders tightly.

"He came out of nowhere," the guard gasped, his eyes glazed. "There was no time to draw my sword before he attacked."

"Who? Who did this?"

Edwyn's insistent voice must have finally penetrated the young man's fog of pain because as awareness returned, his expression changed to one of panic. "Lady Joanna," he gasped and began clawing his way across the ground toward the lodge's open door. "He's gone after the baby."

Edwyn jumped up. Behind him, knights were dismounting and drawing their swords as their squires readied their bows, but Lord Gilbert charged into the lodge alone, not waiting for his men. Edwyn pulled his dagger out of the scabbard on his belt and raced after Lord Gilbert.

If Lord Gilbert's cry of rage hadn't stopped Edwyn in his tracks, the sight that met him when he crossed the lodge's threshold would have. The cradle where Lord Gilbert's infant daughter, Lady Joanna, had been sleeping was upturned, the bedding strewn across the room. Pools of blood stained the shredded woolen blankets and the wooden floor. And in the midst of the chaos, with bloodstreaked teeth, face, and fur, stood Lord Gilbert's wolfhound.

"Gelert!" Lord Gilbert roared, his face ashen. "What have you done?"

Seemingly oblivious to his master's fury, Gelert gave an answering bark and bounded across the room toward him. Lord Gilbert drew his sword, and with an agonized cry, he plunged it into the dog's chest. For a second, time froze. Then the awfulness of the situation hit with full force. Gelert's limp body fell to the floor, and his master dropped to his knees beside him, his sword clattering to the ground as he buried his face in his hands.

As the other knights arrived at the doorway, Edwyn moved into the room. Lowering himself onto one knee beside Lord Gilbert, he picked up his lordship's sword and wiped the blade clean. Unwilling to view the lifeless body of the once-beloved guard dog, Edwyn kept his head bowed and simply waited. One by one, the other knights filtered into the lodge and moved cautiously about the room, but still he waited.

Finally Lord Gilbert lowered his hands. "Where is the nursemaid?" he asked, his voice harsh with emotion. "Where is the woman who pledged to care for my child?"

"I do not know, my lord," Edwyn said, a knot of dread forming in his stomach.

"Find her!"

"Yes, my lord." Edwyn rose quickly, knowing he had to locate the nursemaid before anyone else joined the search.

To his right, Sir Maynard and Sir Thomas were raising the cradle. He heard their collective gasps moments before Sir Maynard's shout reached them.

"Lord Gilbert, she lives! Lady Joanna is alive and unhurt."

Edwyn swung around, and Lord Gilbert stumbled to his feet. Sir Maynard reached down and raised a small bundle from the ground. It gave a high-pitched wail, and Lord Gilbert stepped forward, snatching the baby from Sir Maynard's outstretched arms. He pulled back the swaddling clothes and stared into his daughter's bright-blue eyes. She reached out a chubby hand to him.

"But how?" He looked over at his men. "How can she be unharmed? You see the blood in here. The blood on Gelert."

"Lord Gilbert." Sir Thomas's voice was strained. "It seems that Gelert may have been the guardian, not the villain."

Three grave-faced knights moved back, and Sir Thomas tossed aside the blanket lying next to the cradle. An enormous wolf with savage claws and vicious fangs lay in a pool of blood, his curled-up lips and glassy eyes still menacing in death. Edwyn turned away from the hideous sight, nausea assailing him as he considered the brutal battle that must have taken place only minutes before the men had arrived. And to have it end with the tragic death of Lady Joanna's solitary and valued defender made it all the worse.

Hurrying to the door, Edwyn paused long enough to take three deep breaths before scouring the area outside the lodge for a clue as to the whereabouts of the nursemaid. Even though his mind was still reeling over what had just happened, he had to keep his wits about him. There had been enough tragedy for one day. The nursemaid's fate could not be another.

He ran to his waiting horse and swung himself into the saddle. With a quick glance behind him to be sure he was not being followed, he chose the path that led to the river. The leaf-covered ground masked the sound of the horse's hooves, and the dense foliage soon completely concealed them.

Pausing only long enough to get his bearings, Edwyn headed toward the sound of running water. He rounded a bend in the path and almost ran into a young woman holding a little boy's hand.

"Katherine!" Edwyn dismounted immediately and stood before her. "Where have you been?"

"To the river, my lord," she said, concern filling her eyes. "Didn't the guard explain? Lady Joanna was fast asleep, and I told him I would not be gone long." She looked slightly uncomfortable. "It was a necessary trip."

"The guard could not tell me," Edwyn said grimly, "because he was attacked by a wolf."

Katherine's eyes widened with shock. "A wolf?"

"Yes," he said. "And you are fortunate it did not come upon you and your son out here in the forest."

His rebuke had little effect. The nursemaid was not thinking of her own well-being. "The baby," she gasped. "Did it find the baby?"

Edwyn quickly rehearsed what had happened at the lodge, and Katherine's complexion became more and more pale as the story unfolded.

"I must go to her." She moved away from Edwyn as she spoke.

"No!" Edwyn had not intended for his voice to sound so harsh, but as Katherine halted in her tracks, he realized that it had given him the outcome he'd desired.

"You must not go back to the lodge," he said.

"But Lady Joanna . . ."

"You do not understand," Edwyn said. "Lord Gilbert is distraught. Only moments ago he thought he'd lost his only child. By some miracle, she's been given back to him, but the faithful guard dog who has been by his side for years and saved his daughter from a ravaging wolf was killed by his own hand mere minutes ago. He is not thinking rationally. If you return, his wrath will be heaped upon you, just as it was upon the healer Agnes when Lady Anabel died. There is no telling what he might do."

"But surely Lord Gilbert would not blame me for what has happened," she said.

"You were not where you should have been," Edwyn said. "You did not protect the child and were not there to defend Gelert's role in the attack when Lord Gilbert entered the lodge. Those things alone are sufficient for him to remove the culpability for what has happened from his own shoulders onto yours."

As the truth of Edwyn's words registered, Katherine began to tremble. "What am I to do?" She clutched the toddler's hand more tightly. "I am all that my son has left. If something were to happen to me, what would become of him?"

Edwyn was well aware that Katherine was alone in the world. Until his death less than a year ago, her husband, Nicholas, had been Sir Edwyn's squire, and after the man's passing, Edwyn had remained mindful of Katherine's difficult situation. It was he who had suggested bringing Katherine in to help when Lord Gilbert's wife, Lady Anabel, had died in childbirth a few weeks after Nicholas's death. Lady Anabel had left behind an infant daughter who had needed a wet nurse, and Katherine's son had reached an age that he could be weaned. Having his squire's widow take on the role of the baby's nursemaid had seemed a perfect solution for everyone involved. Until today.

"Where are you from, Katherine?" Edwyn asked. "You do not speak like the local women."

Confusion crossed the nursemaid's face. His question was doubtless not the response she'd been expecting.

"I grew up in Cornwall, my lord," she said. "Not far from Launceston Castle."

"And can you ride?" Edwyn asked.

"Yes," she said.

"Then you must take my horse." He extended the horse's reins to her. "Take him, and return to your people in Cornwall. You will be safe there."

Katherine stumbled backward. "I cannot take your horse, Sir Edwyn," she said.

"Katherine." He spoke urgently. "Nicholas was my squire. He gave his life for me. You and I both know that if he had not taken the arrow intended for my heart, he would have been knighted for his efforts on the battlefield. I cannot, in all good conscience, sit back and allow harm to come to his widow and son. You will take my horse because I will not let you accept an unjust punishment."

Tears pooled in Katherine's eyes. "And I must leave now?" she asked.

"Yes," he said. "Before anyone else comes looking for you."

She took a hesitant step forward, and without another word, Edwyn helped her into the saddle, then lifted her son up to join her. The little boy's questioning eyes were the image of his father's, and Edwyn felt his chest tighten at the sight.

"You should be well on your way by nightfall," he said, handing her a small leather purse. "Then find an inn where you and the boy can rest. A stableman will help with the horse."

A tear rolled down her cheek. "I will not forget your kindness, Sir Edwyn," she said. "And my son will know of it too."

Edwyn gave an acknowledging nod. "Godspeed to you both."

He watched until they disappeared through the trees, then he turned back toward the lodge. He would not dwell on the loss of his horse and saddle or the fact that he was acting expressly against his lordship's request. He was a knight with a code of honor to uphold, and he'd made this commitment the day Nicholas had died in his arms.

Chapter 1

Eighteen years later

RAISING THE TORCH IN HER hand, Lady Joanna peered into the darkness. Shadows cast by tall barrels, wooden crates, and lumpy sacks flickered across the walls, adding to the eeriness of the vast cellar. She shuddered, trying to ignore the sound of scurrying rodents as she moved across the dank room.

"If you get too close, I'll step on your tails," she said. It was a vain threat, but it helped remind her that even though she was outnumbered, she was bigger than any rat in the cellar.

The rats' answering squeaks echoed off the walls.

Joanna kept her eyes off the movement on the floor and hurried to the far corner of the room. She placed her basket on top of the nearest casket of ale, then she reached out her free hand and ran her fingers along the stones, carefully counting the slabs: four up and six over. She recognized the indentation in the stone as soon as she felt it. Pushing with the palm of her hand, she stepped back, and almost immediately, a grating sound filled the cellar.

At her feet, a large block of stone shifted, and by the light of her torch, Joanna watched a hole appear. She waited until the grinding stopped before lowering her light enough to expose the first two rungs of a wooden ladder leaning against a rock wall beneath the cellar floor. Joanna reclaimed her basket, threaded her arm under its handle, and carefully stepped onto the first rung.

Rats aside, she couldn't help but smile at how accustomed she'd become to this clandestine method of leaving the castle. The first time she'd attempted to visit Agnes, it had taken her over an hour to locate the stone that hid the lever to the secret passageway. The ease with which she now descended the ladder, with a torch in one hand and a basket over her other arm, was a far cry from her initial attempt, which had almost ended in her landing in a heap on the rocks below. Even the coarse fabric of the peasant clothing she wore to protect her identity, which had felt so itchy and uncomfortable when she'd first donned it, now felt almost normal.

She reached the lowest rung and stepped into the tunnel. The limestone walls glinted in the torchlight, the sound of distant dripping water magnified by the empty passageway. Quickly, she bent over and pushed a smooth rock hidden behind the ladder. A shower of grit fell from above as the stone slab slid back into place. Then, raising the torch to light her way, she hurried down the winding tunnel.

Water seeping off the walls made the rocks slippery. Twice Joanna nearly fell as her worn shoes slid out from under her. But both times, she caught herself and continued on. She didn't have time to spare. Not only did she need to return to the castle before anyone missed her, but she also had to be mindful of the tide. Within a couple of hours, the sea would rise too high to allow her reentry into the tunnel.

At last, the passageway widened to form a cave, and Joanna slowed her steps. As the intense blackness lessened slightly, she knew she'd reached the cave's entrance and the narrow ledge that marked her path down the remainder of the cliff. The scrub bushes that clung tenaciously to cracks on the ledge blocked her view of the moon above and beach below, so she paused, listening. When she heard nothing but the rhythmic rushing of waves, she left the protection of the cave for the barely discernible rocky trail on her right.

Seconds later, she pressed her hand against her lips to prevent a scream from surfacing. Someone was on the ledge. The scraggly branches of the farthest bush concealed most of the man's head and torso, but his long legs lay directly across her path. She leaned back against the mountainside. Who was he? And why was he here? Had her secret trips out of the castle been discovered?

As these frantic questions spiraled through her mind, she hesitantly lifted the torch a fraction and forced her reluctant feet forward. The man remained silent. Why had he not questioned her sudden appearance? Merciful heavens, was he dead? She bent down, holding the light over him. Still he did not move. He appeared only a few years older than she was. His face, covered in angry scratches, was pale, and the dark hair that fell across his forehead could not completely cover the goose-egg-sized lump above his right temple. She placed her hand near his nose and felt the slight movement of air against her skin. He was still breathing.

Quickly, she moved the torch, searching for any other signs of injury. His clothing was not the simple apparel of a peasant, but his white shirt and green doublet were torn and stained. A two-inch slash through the hose on his left thigh was the center of a dark-red stain that covered half his leg. Blood coated his left hand as though he'd pressed it against his leg, and even now, more blood was dripping onto the rocks beneath him.

With shaking hands, Joanna placed her basket and torch on the ground, lifted the hem of her homespun tunic, and pulled at the lower edge of the smock beneath. The coarse, thin fabric tore easily, and within seconds, she had a ragged strip long enough to tie around the man's leg. She cinched the knot as tightly as she dared and heard a faint moan. Her hands froze, and she looked up. The man's eyelids flickered open, and for a fleeting moment, he held her gaze. Then, as though his eyelids were too heavy to keep open, he closed his eyes again.

"No!" she said, taking his arm and giving it a gentle shake. "You must waken. You cannot remain here."

He did not respond, and panic filled her. Apart from the fact that he was in desperate need of a healer's care, the man had to be moved. If he shifted any more than ten inches from his current position, he could fall to his death. He obviously could not climb down to the beach in his present condition, and he was far too heavy for her to lift. She would have to get help.

With dawn approaching, the night sky was lightening. Surely she knew the trail well enough to leave her torch behind. She glanced at the makeshift bandage she'd placed around the man's leg wound. The white fabric was now red. Tamping out the torch's flame, Joanna set the bundle next to her basket, and with a new sense of urgency, she began her descent.

Tufts of grass, rocks, and roots became her anchors on the steepest portions of the trail, and even though she stumbled, she did not stop. Her sole focus was reaching the bottom of the cliff as quickly as possible, and when her feet finally touched the loose shale of the beach, she picked up her skirts and ran.

Agnes's small cottage was tucked away between the trees where the woodland reached the shore. In years past, Agnes had lived at the castle and had served as the healer for all the knights and nobility there. But when she'd been unable to stem Lady Anabel's bleeding at the time of Joanna's birth, Lord Gilbert had blamed the healer for his wife's untimely death and had turned Agnes out.

Unwilling to let Lord Gilbert's bitterness define her, Agnes made a new life for herself, living quietly in the woods outside the town walls, treating the townsfolks' various ailments whenever called upon to do so and making her cottage a sanctuary for the less fortunate.

Joanna had first learned of Agnes through her maid, Eva. She'd been twelve years old when Eva had discovered her sobbing in her room with Grey, her lame puppy, on her knee.

"Why, whatever's the matter, my lady?" Eva had asked.

"My father says that Grey cannot be my guard dog because he's crippled," she responded through her tears. "He's going to have one of the stable hands dis . . . dispose of him."

More tears fell, and Eva knelt beside her, running a gentle hand over Grey's small back.

"Take him to Agnes," she said softly. "Agnes will care for Grey. I'm sure of it."

"Who's Agnes?" Joanna asked, not sure if she could trust in the glimmer of hope Eva was offering.

"The healer, of course," Eva said.

Joanna's brow puckered as she tried to understand. "But I thought Beatrice was the healer."

Eva shook her head. "For those in the castle, maybe, but most of the commoners still seek out Agnes if they're needing a curative." She bent a little closer as though imparting a secret. "She lives in a cottage down by the seashore."

Joanna immediately sought out Sir Edwyn, whose expression clouded when he learned of Grey's impending fate, and he wasted no time in saddling his horse and Joanna's pony for the dog's rescue attempt.

Just as Eva had supposed, Agnes willingly took in the puppy. But as Sir Edwyn was disinclined to do anything more against Lord Gilbert's wishes, he refused to facilitate repeated meetings with Agnes, and Joanna did not see either the banished healer or the lame dog for another four years. Then, on a rainy day in the spring of her sixteenth year, Joanna found an old map inked on parchment in a trunk that had belonged to her grandmother. The map outlined the way in and out of Moreland Castle through a long-forgotten tunnel beneath the cellar. This remarkable discovery had suddenly provided Joanna a way to leave the castle unattended and had enabled her to come to know and appreciate the kindly healer as a friend.

Now, as the outline of Agnes's cottage came into view amongst the tall, shadowy trees, Joanna heard Grey bark, and a chink of light appeared from within the house as the front door opened and someone stepped outside.

"Garrick!" Joanna tried to shout the young man's name as she ran toward him, but it came out as only a breathless whisper. She tried again. "Garrick!"

Grey barked once more and trotted toward her with his distinctive three-legged gait. He was old enough now that he rarely left Agnes's hearth, but he still recognized and welcomed Joanna.

The young man stopped and turned to face the beach, peering through the dim light.

"Garrick, it's me, Lady Joanna," she said, finally close enough for him to recognize her.

"Oh, hullo, Lady." Garrick smiled, seemingly oblivious to the fact that she was leaning on her knees, gasping for breath. He raised the sack he was holding. "Checking my traps," he said. "Got to get them rabbits before the foxes do."

"Wait!" Joanna tried to remain calm, knowing she desperately needed this gentle giant's assistance. "I require your aid."

"I'll help you, Lady," he said. "I'll bring back the rabbits, *and* I'll help you."

Joanna tried a different approach. "Is Agnes awake?"

"Yes," he said happily.

Even though Garrick was almost as old as she was, she grabbed his hand and drew him back toward the cottage door. "We must talk to Agnes before you get the rabbits."

Confusion showed on his guileless face. "Before?"

Joanna opened the door and pulled Garrick in after her. "Agnes?"

A woman was bent over the fireplace, stirring something in a large black pot. At the sound of Joanna's voice, she turned and gave her a warm smile. "Good morning, my lady," she said. "What a lovely surprise."

"There's an injured man on the cliff," Joanna blurted out. "He's unconscious and bleeding badly."

Agnes's welcoming expression immediately turned to concern. She took Joanna's hands in hers. "Now then," she said. "Take a deep breath and tell me everything from the beginning."

Joanna rehearsed all that had happened from the moment she'd stepped out of the tunnel until she'd arrived at the cottage. Agnes listened without interruption. Garrick alternated between staring at her and wringing the hemp sack in his hands.

"Garrick, go wake up Slip," Agnes said as soon as Joanna finished her account.

Garrick obediently lumbered over to the corner of the room, calling for the boy as he went.

"I don't think Slip will be strong enough to lift the man off the ledge," Joanna said, her anxiety rising as she realized the virtually impossible task she'd given her friends.

"I don't either," Agnes said, already bustling around the room, dropping various items into a leather satchel. "But Garrick trusts him. And I'm hoping that he can help Garrick get the man down."

Agnes hung the satchel over her shoulder and was tucking her long gray braid under her wimple when Garrick returned with a very sleepy Slip behind him.

"Why did Garrick wake me up so early?" Slip grumbled, pulling his tunic on over his nightgown.

"Because you're needed," Agnes said simply.

That seemed to get Slip's attention. "Needed?"

"Come along," she said, not elaborating any further. "We don't have much time."

Chapter 2

Dawn was painting the sky pink when the unlikely foursome reached the base of the cliff. The rising tide was lapping at their ankles, and Joanna's worry for the man on the ledge was increasing with the passage of time. Perhaps she should have returned through the tunnel to fetch some of her father's knights instead of going on to the cottage, but her focus had been on getting the man's wounds treated, and Agnes's home had been the closest.

"We're going up there?" Slip asked, his face shining with excitement as he studied the craggy rock.

Joanna wished she shared his enthusiasm. Slip was a wiry ten- or eleven-year-old—even he wasn't sure of his exact age—who had fended for himself on the streets until Agnes had rescued him from the baker who'd been soundly boxing the boy's ears for stealing a loaf of bread. Known in town as Slippery Fingers because of his aptitude for lifting coins out of purses and food items off stalls, Slip had little fear of anything.

Garrick followed Slip's gaze. "I'll wait here," he announced.

Joanna gave Agnes a worried look.

The older woman squared her shoulders. "We're all going up," she said. "Lady Joanna will show us the way. I need to see to the man's wound, and you two boys will help bring him down."

"Come on, Garrick." Slip took the young man's large hand. "It will be an adventure."

"An adventure?" Garrick repeated the words slowly, as though he were trying to work out exactly what they meant.

"That's right," Slip said with a grin. "You and me. On an adventure together."

"Together." Garrick seemed to seize upon that idea. He nodded. "I'll go with you, Slip," he said.

Agnes gave Joanna an encouraging smile. "Show us where to go, my lady."

Joanna started up the trail. Agnes followed behind her, with Garrick and Slip bringing up the rear. Joanna moved as quickly as she dared, pausing only occasionally to turn back and check on the others. She noticed that Agnes watched her carefully, using the same rocks and roots for leverage when needed. She was close enough that Joanna could hear her breathing hard, but not once did the older lady stop to rest. Garrick's and Slip's progress was also steady, but they were considerably noisier.

"Garrick, that was my hand, not a rock," Slip said. "Watch where you put your great big feet."

"Sorry," Garrick mumbled. He slid sideways, and a shower of small rocks rained down on Slip.

"A mouthful of grit to break my fast," Slip said, spitting between words. "Just what I wanted."

"Sorry," Garrick said again, and after a few minutes of silence, he added, "Are we having an adventure now?"

Slip sighed. "I s'ppose so. But next time, I'm going first."

"Right," Garrick said. "Agnes says it's good to take turns."

Joanna reached the ledge, and all she could hear was the pounding of her heart. When there'd been no sign of a body on the beach, her relief that the man hadn't fallen had quickly turned to fear that he was already dead. Now she saw him lying exactly where he'd been before, and that fear intensified. She knelt beside him and placed her ear to his chest.

"Well?" Agnes asked. She had joined Joanna on the ledge and was already pulling items out of her satchel.

"He's still alive," she said.

"Then there's hope," Agnes said. "Now let me take a look at his leg."

Joanna shifted slightly so Agnes could move closer to the man's left side. While the healer tutted over the condition of his wound and the loss of blood, Joanna leaned forward to study the large bump above the man's right eye. Gently, she brushed the dark hair off his forehead. Now that there was more light, she could see the extent of the swelling and the purple discoloration that spread around his eye and along his cheekbone.

This was not the man's first injury, she realized. A thin white scar ran through his left eyebrow, ending just above his eyelid, and his nose was not quite straight. She guessed he'd broken it at least once. He had an angular jaw, currently covered in dark whiskers. His eyes were still closed, but regardless of their color, Joanna had already ascertained two rather unnerving facts: first, she'd never seen this man before today, and second, his injuries did little to detract from his appearance.

"Move over, Garrick!" Slip's voice brought Joanna back to reality.

"I'm trying." Garrick was inching his way along the ledge, looking at anything and everything except the drop-off. "This adventure's too high," he said. "I'll go down now." Joanna rose and took his hand. It was shaking. Giving it a comforting squeeze, she led him to the cave entrance, where he could be farther from the edge.

"You were magnificent, Garrick," she said. "You climbed that cliff like a mountain goat."

"I did?"

Joanna smiled. "Yes, you did, and I'm very proud of you."

Garrick smiled in return. "Is Slip like a mountain goat too?"

Slip appeared beside them, brushing the grit out of his hair and off his tunic. "No, Slip is more like a mole," he said. "I may as well've crawled through the mountain."

"Well, don't get too comfortable," Agnes said, coming to her feet. "I've stitched and bandaged the leg as best I can, but he's lost a fair amount of blood. We must get him to the cottage right away."

"But we only just got here," Slip said in dismay. "I didn't even see inside the cave."

"That will be for another day," Agnes said, gathering her leftover bandages and thread and dropping them into her satchel. "Now we must go."

"Down there is better," Garrick said, already shuffling his way to the end of the ledge.

Agnes reached out and touched his arm. He paused and turned to face her.

"Will you carry the injured man for us?" she asked.

Garrick glanced from Agnes to the man on the ground, then back. "He's big," he said, his forehead creasing.

"Yes," Agnes said. "But you are strong."

Garrick studied Agnes's face for a moment and must have seen something in her eyes that convinced him because with an assenting nod, he crouched down beside the prone body, wrapped his large hands around the unconscious man's torso, and raised him until he was high enough to place over his shoulder. Then, clasping the man's legs with both hands and with an enormous grunt of exertion, Garrick pushed himself to his feet.

Joanna released the breath she'd been holding. "I thank you, Garrick," she said.

He didn't respond. His whole focus was on steadying the man on his shoulder and the slow and steady steps he was making toward the rocks' edge.

"I changed my mind," Slip said. "I don't want to go in front."

"You go first, Slip," Agnes said, pushing him forward. "You must guide Garrick's feet."

"Can't Lady Joanna do that?" the boy asked.

Agnes shook her head. "Lady Joanna is not going with us."

Joanna frowned. She was not accustomed to anyone other than her father telling her what she was or was not going to do. "But . . ." she began.

"The tide is already too high, my lady," Agnes explained. "If we are fast, we will get across, but you would not make it back. Besides, you have been away from the castle long enough. Your father will send out a search party if you are gone any longer."

As much as she hated to admit it, Joanna could not deny the truth of Agnes's words.

Slip must have realized it too because he walked past her, muttering under his breath. "If Garrick falls on me, I'll be flattened. Completely and forever flattened."

"I thank you too, Slip," Joanna said. "We could not have managed this without you."

"Well, we haven't exactly managed it yet, have we?" the boy said, raising his eyebrows in Garrick's direction.

"No. But we will," Agnes said, urging Slip forward with her hand. She turned and gave Joanna a brief hug. "You get back to the castle as quickly as you can."

Joanna took the apples and cheese out of the basket she'd left on the ledge and slipped them into Agnes's satchel. "Be careful," she said. "I'll return to the cottage soon."

Agnes patted her hand gently. "All will be well; don't you worry."

Asking Joanna not to worry about their perilous return trip was as futile as asking the tide not to rise. And not being there when the injured man opened his eyes felt wrong. It was wholly nonsensical. He was a stranger and was now in the hands of a competent healer. But logic did not hold sway over the pang she felt as she watched his unconscious form swinging over Garrick's wide back or the panic she felt when the big man missed his footing and slid forward until a boulder curtailed his downward movement.

With her heart in her throat, Joanna stood alone on the ledge and watched her friends' labored progress down the steep slope. She should leave, but she could not. Not until she knew they were safe.

She stayed until they reached the beach. Garrick was bowed down with the weight of his load, but he waded slowly through the knee-deep water, with Agnes on one side and Slip on the other.

"Thank you, Father God," Joanna whispered, glancing heavenward. "Please bless them for their goodness."

Then, putting her hand into the pocket of her tunic, she pulled out a small flint and used it to light the remains of her torch. With it and her empty basket in hand, she hurried into the cave and up the winding passageway to the base of the ladder. Once there, she pushed the rock lever and waited for the stone to move before climbing the rungs and entering the cellar.

The rats were still scurrying around, but Joanna did her best to ignore them. As soon as the stone slab was back in place, she tiptoed up the stone stairs. Based on the clanging and banging and talking and shouting filtering through the heavy wooden door, there would be no cutting through an empty kitchen this time. Morning meal preparations were well underway.

Replacing the torch in the wall sconce, Joanna slipped off her wet shoes and hid them in the basket. Then she pulled the hood of her peasant tunic up and over her head, making sure that her long blonde hair and distinctive blue eyes were fully covered. Grasping the door handle, she turned it slowly. It gave a high squeak, but the sound was drowned out by the other noises in the room.

Joanna peeked through the crack. The cook had her back to the door, and the scullery maids were all running around busily. This was as good a time as any. She pushed the door open, slipped through, and closed it quickly behind her. Then, keeping her head low, she walked over to the table where the food had been set out. Using a serving cloth to cover her wet shoes, she added a loaf of bread to her basket and picked up a flagon of ale. Carrying the basket in one hand and the ale in the other, she walked across the kitchen to the stairs that led to the great hall. No one stopped her. At the top of the stairs, she entered the crowded room.

Knights and their squires were preparing for the day. Pages were gathering equipment while the men sat around the long dining tables. One servant was tending the fire in the enormous grate in the center of the room, and others were hurrying from one knight to another, refilling goblets and trenchers.

Joanna kept close to the walls, hoping she could remain in the shadows as she crossed to the other side of the room and to the safety of her own bedchamber. But just before she reached the door, Sir Thomas called her over, raising his cup for more ale.

Praying that her shaking hands would not give her away, Joanna approached the table and silently filled the knight's cup from her flagon.

The golden-brown liquid sloshed over the rim of his cup, dripping onto his fingers and the table.

The portly knight frowned. "Careless wench," he growled.

As she braced herself for a tongue-lashing or, worse, her discovery, Sir William called to him from a nearby table.

"Sir Thomas! Your opinion on the matter of Sir Colin's broken crossbow, if you please."

With Sir Thomas's attention momentarily diverted, Joanna made her escape. She placed the flagon on the table and darted across the remaining ten yards to the door of her bedchamber. Knocking once in case anyone in the great hall was watching, she pushed open the door and stepped inside.

Chapter 3

"Gracious saints, Lady Joanna, where have you been?"

Joanna leaned back against the door and closed her eyes, temporarily blocking her distressed lady's maid, Eva, from view. That had been close. Too close. She took a steadying breath.

"I went to visit Agnes," she said. "I told you before I left."

Eva was the only person in the castle who knew of Joanna's secret trips to visit the healer. The lady's maid was only four years Joanna's senior, and in many respects, Joanna considered her more like an older sister than a servant. Eva was the one who had procured the peasant clothing Joanna used for her clandestine outings, but she regularly told Joanna how much she regretted it.

"You've never been gone this long before," Eva said. She waved a hand toward the door. "And with the whole castle awake, I couldn't imagine how you'd ever get back without getting caught."

"I was lucky," Joanna admitted.

Eva's forehead wrinkled. "More than you know," she said sternly. "Your father's been asking for you this morning, and I've already perjured myself once, telling his page you were bathing and would need a little longer before joining his lordship."

Joanna smiled at her maid's grumpy expression. "You are too good to me, Eva."

"Indeed I am, my lady," she said with a sniff. "I just hope Lord Gilbert doesn't ever hear of my foolishness."

"You are not foolish," Joanna said. "You are kindhearted." She fought back a smile. "But don't concern yourself unduly. I won't tell anyone that either."

Eva snorted, but her expression softened. "Well, come along, then. Let's get you out of those ridiculous clothes and into something more suitable for the lady of the castle."

Joanna allowed Eva to help her change, but things became uncomfortable when her maid noticed the blood on her tunic and the tear in her smock.

"Look," Joanna said, holding up both hands. "You can see that I am quite all right. A few small scratches from a rock and a bramble bush is all."

"That doesn't explain all this blood," Eva said, holding up the stained tunic.

Joanna shrugged. She loved Eva, but she wasn't yet ready to share her story about the stranger on the ledge. She wanted to keep that to herself until she knew more about who he was and how he'd come to be in that isolated spot with a serious leg wound. She took the cloth out of the basket and pulled out her shoes.

"These are wet," she said. "Can you have them dry and the clothes ready for me to wear again tonight?"

"Tonight?" Eva's mouth hung open. "But, my lady, your father—"

"Will never know," Joanna said. "Please, Eva. This is very important to me."

Joanna watched anxiously as Eva waged her own internal battle. "Very well, my lady," she finally said. "But I hope you know that if your father ever catches wind of this, my fate will be far worse than being banished to a cottage by the shore."

"He will not learn of it," Joanna promised.

Five minutes later, Joanna was dressed in a plum-colored silk dress, with her long hair braided and a simple gold band around her head. She wore soft kid slippers and a gold girdle that hung around her narrow waist and reached almost to her ankles.

"There now," Eva said with satisfaction. "That looks much better. Lord Gilbert will be pleased to see how well you look in your new gown."

Joanna gave a small smile. Her father treated her as though she were a prized possession worthy of occasional display and constant guard. Over the years, she'd learned to act as though his emotional distance didn't hurt. When she'd been young, her nursemaids had done what they could to comfort her. Since then, she'd relied on Eva to be a shoulder to cry on and a listening ear, and she'd always turned to Sir Edwyn to right a wrong and dust her off when she fell. But none of them had been able to truly console her when she'd plucked up the courage to ask her father for a flute or a pet rabbit or archery lessons and he'd not cared enough to even remember her requests. Instead, his gifts had always been expensive gowns that arrived a few days before she was to make a public appearance or greet distinguished guests.

She ran her fingers across the smooth silk of this new gown and wondered vaguely what upcoming event had prompted him to send it.

"You'd best be on your way, my lady."

Eva's voice startled Joanna. Her mind had been elsewhere. "Yes, of course," she said. "Come, Cona."

From his position at the foot of Joanna's bed, a huge wolfhound rose to his feet and trotted to her side. She rubbed his head affectionately. "Have you forgiven me for leaving without you, or are you still sulking?"

The dog looked at her with reproachful eyes, and she shook her head. "You're too recognizable, Cona. No one would believe that I was a servant girl if you were by my side."

"Really, Lady Joanna," Eva said, the worry back in her voice. "It's bad enough that you travel out of the castle at night, but to do so without Cona's protection is madness. Lord Gilbert—"

"Is waiting," Joanna said, cutting her off before she could say more. "I must go." She opened the door and entered the great hall, with Cona beside her. Servants were moving the dining tables to the sides of the large room. Most of the knights had left to fulfill their various morning responsibilities, but the few who remained bowed their heads deferentially as she passed, showing no surprise when she paused at the door that led to the grand chamber, the room where Lord Gilbert conducted all his private business. Joanna knocked.

"Come!" her father's voice called from within.

Joanna entered. "You wanted to see me, my lord," she said.

Her father was sitting in a heavy wooden chair on a dais at the other end of the room. A long wooden table was before him, on which sat a quill, a bottle of ink, a small pile of parchment, and a large leather-bound book. A fire was burning in the grate, and heavy tapestries hung from three of the walls. The fourth wall housed three narrow windows that were letting in enough morning light to obviate the need for candles.

Three men stood behind her father, and as Joanna moved closer, she recognized them all—Sir Edwyn, who had been a knight in her father's service longer than any other and who was more of a father figure to her than was Lord Gilbert; Sir Nigel, the son of the late Sir Maynard, who had replaced his father as chief advisor to Lord Gilbert, despite the fact that he was one of the youngest knights in the castle; and Gerard Bartholomew, the castle steward, who was responsible for the administration of the castle, its lands, and the town of Moreland.

"My lady." Sir Edwyn bowed, and the other two men immediately mirrored his greeting.

"Sir Edwyn, Sir Nigel, and Steward Bartholomew," Joanna said, bowing her head in return. "I apologize for interrupting."

"They were just leaving," Lord Gilbert said, rising to his feet. Her father was a tall man with thick, silvery gray hair and beard. His blue eyes were as piercing now as they'd ever been, and despite his declining years, his presence still commanded the respect of most and the fear of many. "I would have you look into this sheep matter with the peasants, Sir Nigel."

"I will see to it immediately, my lord," Sir Nigel said.

"Very well." Lord Gilbert turned to Gerard, his finger pounding the cover of the leather-bound book in front of him. "I want a proper accounting by the end of the week."

"Yes, my lord." Gerard waited until Lord Gilbert moved his hand, then swept the book up and clutched it to his chest. He directed a pointed look at Sir Nigel, as though he knew they would have to work together if they were to assuage Lord Gilbert's displeasure over this matter.

Sir Nigel, however, did not seem as troubled by his lordship's annoyance. He waited for Gerard to precede him out of the room, wished them all a good day, gave Joanna a particularly warm smile, and followed the steward out.

Joanna lowered her head as she felt her cheeks color. She'd begun to notice that Sir Nigel often sought her out in the great hall or went out of his way to speak to her if she was outside in the courtyard when the knights were practicing their swordplay, but she was so un-schooled in the rules of courtship, she did not know if his attention meant anything or not.

She'd tried asking Eva's opinion on the subject—Eva had fallen in love and was now betrothed to Timothy, the stable master—but she'd not been very helpful. Instead, she'd simply told Joanna that nobility rarely married for love and that it was unlikely that Joanna would have much say in her choice of husband anyway. The discouraging conversation had caused Joanna to miss her mother all the more and made her wonder if there had been any love between her parents on their wedding day.

Joanna suddenly realized Sir Edwyn was speaking to her, and she only just caught the end of his compliment.

"You look well, Lady Joanna."

"Thank you, Sir Edwyn," she said. She ran her fingers over the plum-colored silk. "I received this gown from Lord Gilbert today."

Her father gave an acknowledging nod. "It will serve you well for your appearance at the tournament," he said. "I have another one being made for the banquet to follow."

"What tournament?" Joanna looked from her father to Sir Edwyn. She'd heard rumors that tournaments involving knights from all over southern England had been held at the castle before her mother's passing, but she did not think there had been a single one since.

Lord Gilbert cleared his throat. "It is time for you to take a husband, Joanna. You are of age, and for our family to maintain its claim to Moreland Castle, you must produce an heir."

Joanna stared at him in shock, hoping the talent she'd developed for hiding her true feelings from him would not fail her now. Did her father truly believe he could order her to take a husband much as he ordered her a new gown?

"Father," she said, "you have played the part of a protective parent to a fault. A wolfhound guards me around the clock, and I have never traveled beyond the lands that belong to you." Joanna's nails were digging into her already scratched palms. "Unfortunately, such safeguarding has its consequences. Perhaps it has escaped your attention, but I have no suitors. No noblemen are vying for my hand. Indeed, few noblemen outside our own castle know I exist."

Sir Edwyn glanced at Lord Gilbert's reddening complexion and stepped forward. "Your father has given this matter considerable thought, my lady," he said. "He has determined to host an archery tournament that will bring noblemen to Moreland Castle. You will have the opportunity to watch the archers demonstrate their skills with the bow and afterward, perhaps, greet them at the banquet."

Joanna wanted to be sick. The awkwardness she'd felt when her father had presented her to past guests at castle banquets paled in comparison to the mortification she would experience this time. Every nobleman would know that she was in attendance because her father was looking to make an advantageous match. And with her lack of experience in socializing with noblemen, she had no doubt she would be assessed and found failing.

"What if I do not meet the expectations of any nobleman and receive no offers?" she said. "What do you propose to do then?"

"Becoming Lord of Moreland Castle will be incentive enough," her father said confidently. "There will be many noblemen willing to marry for that prize."

Joanna tried not to flinch at the pain Lord Gilbert's words inflicted. Was her extensive dowry truly the only thing she had to recommend herself?

Sir Edwyn looked at her, his eyes troubled. "You are a beautiful young woman, Lady Joanna," he said. "Any nobleman would be privileged to win your hand."

"Of course she's beautiful," Lord Gilbert snapped. "She looks just like her mother."

Joanna's breath caught. Her father never spoke of her mother. Ever. Sir Edwyn had once told her that her long blonde hair was the image of Lady Anabel's, but that was all she knew of her mother's appearance. She had always longed to know more, but those in the castle who still remembered her had been forbidden to mention her. "Father," she said, taking a hesitant step forward.

"You may go." He spoke before she could say anything else. "The tournament takes place eight days hence. I expect you to be in attendance when the winning archer is introduced as your betrothed."

A forbidding expression masked his face, and she knew the subject of her mother was once again firmly closed. Disappointment, like a lead weight, filled Joanna's chest. "Very well, my lord," she said. Then she bowed her head toward Sir Edwyn and her father and escaped the room before her tears could fall.

Chapter 4

Awareness returned slowly, penetrating the fog inside his head like faint pinpricks of light. He heard a clanging of metal and the scrape of something being dragged across the floor. There was the sound of voices and the smell of baking bread. Something large and furry brushed past his arm, and then came the pain. His head throbbed as though someone had taken a hammer to it, and his leg was on fire. Every part of him ached, and the simplest movement, from opening his eyes to lifting his fingers, seemed to require more strength than he possessed.

He moaned, his throat too dry and his thoughts too addled to do anything more. He heard hurried footsteps, and then a gentle hand touched his forehead.

"Well, now." It was a woman's voice. "It's about time you were waking up. Bring me a cup of water, would you, Garrick?"

More footsteps. This time slow and heavy. The woman moved her hand, placing it beneath his head and raising it a few inches. He groaned as the pain intensified. Something hard touched his lips.

"It's water," the woman said, her voice calm and reassuring. "See if you can't swallow a little."

Lukas felt the cold liquid running across his mouth and dripping off his chin. Desperately he tried to move his mouth so some of the life-giving liquid could enter. He swallowed once, twice, three times before the woman lowered the cup and his head once more.

"Why isn't he waking up?" A man spoke.

"I daresay he's trying," the woman said. He felt a cloth touch his neck where the water had spilled. "We just have to be patient."

The man grunted. "Like when I'm waiting for the rabbits to go into the trap."

"That's right."

"I don't like being patient," the man said, his footsteps moving away.

"Not many of us do," the woman said softly.

Lukas wasn't sure if it was minutes or hours later when the smell of something cooking roused him again. This time he pushed past the pounding in his head and forced his eyelids open. Blinking slowly, he tried to focus on what was visible in the dim light. Above his head, he could see the thick thatch of the roof. Bundled plants hung upside down in rows from the rafters, and smoke was spiraling upward from the fireplace below. Something was bubbling in a pot suspended on an iron hook above the flames.

Turning his head gingerly, he lowered his gaze. He appeared to be lying on a pallet in a small room. The shadowy forms of a couple of wooden chairs and a table filled one corner. A lit candle was sitting on a cluttered shelf against the nearest wall, and its light was reflected in the eyes of an enormous hairy animal that lay not more than three feet from his pallet.

Instinctively Lukas moved his right hand to his waist, groping for his sword. It was gone. He tried raising himself, but his ribs screamed in protest, and as he shifted his position on the pallet, a bolt of pain shot down his left leg. Clenching his hands, he closed his eyes and took a couple of deep breaths, waiting for the agony to subside. He had no idea where he was or how he had arrived here, but at least he knew where he must go. And no matter how severe his injuries or what the fearsome creature was that lay between him and the outer door, he needed to leave.

At his side, the animal moved, and Lukas held completely still as it rose to its full height and gave a short bark. The dog—if indeed it was a dog—was the size of a small horse, and it towered over him.

For a moment, it gazed down at Lukas, then it bent its long neck and began sniffing the ground beside the pallet. Lukas watched, barely breathing until the dog abruptly stopped and turned its nose toward the door.

The latch clicked, and a gust of cool air entered, causing the candle to flicker and the flames in the fireplace to surge. Frantically, Lukas scoured the room, searching for anything he could use as a weapon. A poker stood upright beside the fireplace, but it was a good six feet away, and he knew that in his current weakened state, even that was too far. He had never felt so vulnerable, and he did not like the sensation at all. Tensing, he watched as an older lady with gray hair and a tall, broad-shouldered young man entered the room.

"I caught three rabbits today," the sandy-haired man said, smiling proudly.

"That's splendid," the woman replied. "If you prepare them the way I showed you, we shall have rabbit stew for supper."

She handed him a bucket of water, and he placed the sack he'd been holding on the table and carried the bucket over to the fireplace. With the bucket delivered, he ambled over to the pallet and peered down at Lukas.

Lukas met his stare.

"Uh, Agnes." The man backed up a couple of steps and pointed his finger. "His eyes are open."

The woman hastened across the room and knelt beside him. "Good morning," she said. "My name is Agnes, and this is Garrick."

Lukas ran his tongue across his cracked lips. "Lukas," he said croakily. "Sir Lukas of Cornwall."

Agnes reached for a wooden cup. "You're needing water," she said.

She helped him raise his head and held the cup to his lips. He drank deeply.

"I thank you," he said when she finally pulled the cup away.

She nodded, concern lining her face. "You have a bad leg wound, my lord," she said. "Do you have any recollection of how it happened?"

Lukas lowered his hand, cautiously touching the area on his thigh where the dagger had entered. "Aye," he said, his jaw tightening as a flood of images flashed through his mind. "I remember." Then he turned to look at Agnes. "But I have no memory of getting here. Would you be so good as to tell me exactly where I am?"

"This is my cottage, my lord. It's located by the shore just outside the town of Moreland."

Lukas frowned. He'd been close to Moreland Castle when he'd been attacked, and he had fine threads of memory about what had happened to him afterward: a sensation of falling, searing pain, a girl with yellow hair and startling blue eyes, and the sound of the ocean. But no matter how hard Lukas tried, he could not weave those threads together to explain his presence in Agnes's cottage.

Suddenly the door flew open, and a scrawny boy with dark hair that stuck out in all directions walked in carrying a pitcher. "Lady Joanna's here," he called. "And I finished the milking."

The boy put the pitcher on the table and turned to hold the door open as a young woman stepped inside. Cursing the pain that kept him from moving freely, Lukas struggled to pull himself into a sitting position. Agnes leaned forward and placed a supportive arm behind his back.

"I fear you may have broken some ribs, my lord," she said.

Her words filled Lukas with alarm. He could not be bedridden now. "I pray they are merely badly bruised," he said once his breathing was under control again. "I must be to Moreland Castle as soon as possible."

The boy and the young woman had moved to stand beside Garrick. Agnes rose and put her arm around the thin boy's shoulders. "Sir Lukas, this is Slip," she said. Then she turned and smiled at the young woman. "And this is Lady Joanna of Moreland Castle."

"She's the one who found you," Slip said. "And Garrick carried you. And Agnes tended to you. And I . . ." He thought for a moment. "I brought you some goat's milk to break your fast."

At the boy's earnest expression, Lukas fought back his smile. "You are most thoughtful, Slip," he said solemnly. "For I do not remember when I last ate."

Slip beamed and ran back to the pitcher. "I'll pour you some right away, my lord," he said.

Lukas turned to Lady Joanna. He was puzzled that she was dressed in peasants' clothing, but now that he could see her azure eyes, it was hard to look at anything else. "I apologize for not rising, Lady Joanna," he said. "It seems beyond my abilities at the moment."

"It's of no consequence, my lord," she said, giving him a shy smile. "I am simply pleased to see you awake and of sound mind."

"Not completely sound, I fear," Lukas said, wondering why breathing was suddenly difficult again. "There are significant gaps in my memory, and I would be most grateful if you would tell me where you found me. And how I came to be in Agnes's cottage."

Joanna gave a small nod. "Very well," she said. "Perhaps we can share information, for I am anxious to learn how you sustained your injuries and your reasons for visiting the castle."

Slip handed him a cup of milk, and Lukas used the momentary diversion to think through how much of his story he should tell. His rescuers appeared to be good people, but he was a stranger here, and until he knew more about what was afoot, he could not risk telling them everything. He raised his hand to touch his swollen forehead. It would be far easier to think clearly if his head would stop pounding.

"Why don't you begin by telling us where you're from," Agnes suggested. She took his now-empty cup and moved to the fireplace, where she began stirring the pot.

Garrick dragged one of the wooden chairs closer and offered it to Lady Joanna. She murmured her thanks and sat down facing Lukas. The large dog lay at her feet, and Garrick and Slip remained standing, but they were all watching Lukas expectantly.

"I was trained for knighthood under Richard, the Earl of Cornwall, at Launceston Castle," Lukas said. "I had no intention of ever leaving his service until a few weeks ago when I was called to my mother's deathbed. Just before she passed, my mother told me of a great debt my family owes to Sir Edwyn of Moreland Castle." He saw Lady Joanna's eyes widen, and he paused. "Do you know Sir Edwyn, my lady?" he asked.

"I know him well," she said. "I spoke with him only yesterday."

Relief washed over Lukas. He had made enquiries among the other knights at Launceston Castle, and one of them remembered training beside Sir Edwyn three years earlier, when King Henry had requested reinforcements to defend Dover Castle from the threat of a French attack. Knowing that Sir Edwyn had been fit and able three years previously had given Lukas hope that if he traveled to Moreland he would yet find the knight alive and well.

"I am glad to hear it," he said. "I had hoped to speak with him myself by now, but by the time I reached the town of Moreland, it was late evening. I asked one of the local merchants how I could gain entry into the castle and was told that all the gates but one would be locked for the night. I was directed along the cliff path that cuts through the woodland to the north of the castle."

Lady Joanna nodded, obviously familiar with the path.

"There was very little moonlight," Lukas said. "And as it was an unfamiliar road, I rode slowly, which is probably why I heard men's voices coming from somewhere deeper in the woods. Thinking it strange that men would be gathered together among the trees at night, I dismounted and approached more cautiously.

"I was close enough to make out their silhouettes when my horse stepped on a dead branch and the sound alerted the men to my presence. One of them leaped out from behind a tree, and before I could draw my sword, he threw a dagger that penetrated my thigh. By the time I pulled out the blade, the men were upon me." The pain in Lukas's leg seemed to intensify as he thought back on those critical moments.

"At some point during the fight, I must have lost consciousness because the next thing I remember was hearing one of the men telling another to drop me over the cliff's edge so the sea could claim my body."

"Why would they do such a terrible thing?" Lady Joanna's horrified voice was barely above a whisper.

"They wanted to make sure Sir Lukas couldn't ever tell anyone they were meeting there," Slip said, his expression far too knowing for someone his age.

There was a moment of silence as the truth of Slip's words sank in.

"Could you identify the men, my lord?" Agnes asked.

"I'm a stranger here," Lukas said, choosing his words carefully. "I did not recognize any of them."

Agnes gave him a long look, then turned her attention to ladling liquid out of the pot and into a wooden cup. Lukas suspected the older woman recognized the glaring omission in his answer. He had not known the men who had attacked him, but he had a good idea of whom he'd be searching for. The darkness had prevented him from getting a good look at any of them, but during the skirmish, he'd ascertained that two of the men were French. One of them had a thick beard and an earring that glistened in the moonlight; the other had a hooked nose and was missing a front tooth. The man who'd thrown the dagger had kept his head down, but he'd been better dressed than the others, and when he had retrieved his weapon, Lukas had noticed a scar in the shape of a *C* running across his forearm. The fourth man had kept to the shadows, but Lukas would recognize his voice if he ever heard it again. And he was quite determined that he *would* hear it again, no matter how long it took him.

"I'm very sorry you were treated so brutally, my lord," Lady Joanna said. "I will be sure that Lord Gilbert hears of it."

"No!"

At Lukas's exclamation, Garrick's eyes widened with alarm, and the dog gave a startled bark.

"My apologies," Lukas said, cursing himself for his injudicious response. "I did not mean to raise my voice, and I appreciate your desire to see justice done, my lady, but I ask that, for now, you say nothing. It's imperative that no one know that I survived the fall."

"He wants the men to think they got away with it so they keep on doing whatever it is they were doing," Slip said. "That way he can catch them at it."

Lukas managed a tired smile. "You're a very clever young man, Slip," he said.

Slip stood a little taller and glanced from Agnes to Lady Joanna as if wanting to be sure they'd heard his praise. "I'll help you track them down, my lord," Slip said. "I'm good at running and hiding."

At the fireplace, Agnes rolled her eyes, and Lukas suspected Slip may have evaded being caught a few times before.

"I thank you," he said. "It's good to know I can count on your service."

Slip looked as though his narrow chest might burst out of his threadbare tunic.

Lady Joanna stood up. "I understand that a knight always wishes to avenge himself, Sir Lukas," she said, her frown suggesting that she did not necessarily agree with that age-old custom. "But your wounds may confine you to your bed for weeks. By then the men could be long gone from here. Surely it would be better to have others help rout them out than to risk letting them get away with attempted murder."

Lukas lifted a shaky hand to his throbbing head. He'd been talking for only a few minutes, but already he was weakening. "My lady," he began, "if this were only a matter of my pride, I would agree with you." He lowered his head. He could not fight the increasing pain much longer, but he had to say something to help her understand. "Please believe me." His voice was fading. "I believe there is much more at stake."

"What do you mean?" she asked.

"I cannot say," he said, wishing he could think clearly enough to offer her more.

He felt himself sway, and the indignation in her face melted into concern. "Garrick," she called.

The large man moved forward, crouched beside the pallet, and placed a steadying arm across Lukas's shoulders. Through an encroaching haze, Lukas saw Agnes approach with another cup.

"Yarrow and mint tea, my lord," she said. "It will help your wounds heal."

He let her help him drink the bitter liquid and heard her ask Garrick to reposition him on the pallet. Of their own accord, his eyes closed, and as the vision of Lady Joanna's beautiful but troubled face faded, he could only pray that she would keep his presence in the cottage a secret.

Chapter 5

JOANNA HURRIED THROUGH THE EMPTY castle kitchen, hoping to reach the floor above before the servants arrived to begin their preparations for the early-morning meal. She could not repeat the experience of the day before. Eva would likely hide her peasant clothing if Joanna risked being caught like that again.

It was a blessing that Agnes and her small household rose so early. Slip often grumbled that he did more chores before the sun came up than most children did by noon, but Garrick was happy to be catching crabs at the stand of the tide or checking his traps before dawn. For Joanna, it meant that if she timed it just right, she could visit her friends and return to her chamber before the castle residents awoke. Normally it wasn't difficult. Sir Lukas's appearance had changed that.

When the mysterious knight had lost consciousness once more, Joanna and Agnes had discussed what little they knew of his situation. The desperation in his brown eyes when he'd pleaded for secrecy had persuaded Joanna to say nothing to anyone else until he'd explained himself more fully. Agnes had agreed to share the details of his rescue with Sir Lukas when he next awoke but had promised to make no mention of the tunnel Joanna used to access the castle.

Giving her attention to this day's activities would be hard, but Joanna knew it was the only way she could keep her thoughts from returning to the wounded man in Agnes's cottage. She didn't want to be the one who compromised the fledgling trust between them. For some reason, that was important. It was yet another secret to keep, but she had a lifetime of training in how to keep her tongue in check.

Cona gave Joanna a welcoming bark as she entered her bedchamber.

Eva looked up from her sewing, relief evident on her face. "No blood or tears this time, I hope," she said sternly.

Joanna smiled, knowing that Eva's grumpiness was a manifestation of her concern.

"Not even mud today," she said, twirling in a circle to show all sides of her homespun smock and tunic.

"I'm very glad to hear it." Eva put down her needlework and rose to her feet. "And now we must hurry to get you dressed. It's market day today, and if we're lucky, we may find some ribbon for your hair that will match the gowns Lord Gilbert has had delivered."

"He sent more?" Joanna asked, her heart sinking as she remembered the reason for the new dresses.

"Yes, indeed," Eva said. "And I've never seen the like."

She led Joanna to the corner of the room where two dresses hung beside the plum-colored gown she'd worn the day before. One dress was forest green. The sleeves were long and tapered to a point. Gold trim ran along the hemline and the scooped neckline, and tiny gold bells hung from a narrow gold belt around the waist. The second dress was pale blue and shimmered when the light hit the thin silver threads woven into the silk fabric. Fine lace added elegance to the wide sleeves and neckline, and a slim silver girdle fell from the waist to the floor.

"Oh," Joanna breathed. She stepped forward and ran her fingers down the light-blue dress. It was the most beautiful gown she'd ever seen.

"Lord Gilbert ordered the fabric from France," Eva said. "They're both lovely, but the blue one matches the color of your eyes perfectly." She gave a contented sigh. "You will look perfect at the tournament and at the banquet that follows."

Joanna had told Eva of her father's plans as soon as she'd returned from the grand chamber yesterday. Eva had listened patiently and had held her while she'd cried, but that was all she'd been able to offer. They both knew that nothing could be done to change Lord Gilbert's mind on the matter.

In silence, Joanna turned her back on the dresses and walked to the window, gazing out at the inner bailey below. She could see the walls of the outer bailey and, beyond that, the roofs of the buildings that made up the town of Moreland.

"Do you remember when we went to town last month and saw old Barlow Coates grooming his prize mare for that afternoon's auction?" she asked.

"Yes, my lady," Eva said.

"A week from now, the only difference between me and Barlow's horse is that my purchase will come with a castle and land."

Eva shook her head. "You must not think that way, my lady," she said. "Things may yet work out for the best. You mark my words. It's long past time for your father to realize that he cannot keep you hidden away in this castle forever. Your beauty and goodness will attract many fine noblemen. And who knows, when all is said and done, perhaps you will have your pick of several suitors?"

"I am to be promised to the winner of the archery tournament," Joanna said. "But even if my father allows me any say in the matter, how would I choose? After doing nothing more than observe how well they shoot an arrow or whether they can eat a meal without food sticking in their teeth, I will be little closer to knowing their character than if they had just walked into the keep unannounced." She faced her maid. "Eva, I've seen the way your eyes light up when you see Timothy across the courtyard and the way he smiles when you are near."

Eva lowered her head but could not completely hide her blush. "I'm sorry, my lady, I—"

"No," Joanna said. "Please don't apologize. I find it enchanting. It's just that I had always hoped that one day I would share similar moments with the man who was to be my husband. You tried to warn me that an arranged marriage was likely in my future, but I allowed myself to dream." She gave a weak smile. "Perhaps I should focus instead on the fact that this tournament will ensure that my husband is an excellent archer."

"Love could still play a part in your choice," Eva insisted.

Joanna wanted to believe that, but it seemed such a faint hope. "How will I know if a suitor offers his hand in marriage because he genuinely cares for me rather than simply because he wants to become Lord of Moreland Castle?"

Eva stepped closer and took Joanna's hand. "You will know, my lady," she said. "Have faith in the quiet whisperings of your heart. Listen to those feelings, and you will know."

❧

Two hours later, Joanna and Eva left the castle by the south gate and took the road that led to the center of town. Horses, carts, pedestrians, and stray animals jostled for position on the narrow streets, and the closer they got to the town square, the busier the roads became. As usual, Cona was at his mistress's side, his head held high, his eyes and ears alert. The locals recognized him as Lady Joanna's escort, and with deferential bows, they made way for her despite the congestion.

The town square was a hive of activity. Merchants were clustered together on one side of the open area, each one trying to out-call the others as they worked to entice the passersby to stop and buy the wares set out on their wooden carts or rickety booths. Peasants' wives who'd come into town for market day mingled with townspeople as they made their weekly purchases.

The noise was almost as overwhelming as the smell. The pungent odor of animals and sweat mingled with the enticing aroma of baking bread and pasties. Joanna wrinkled her nose at the disagreeable blend and hoped the smell wouldn't cling to her hair and clothes and follow her back to the castle. Eva seemed oblivious to the unpleasantness, however, and she forged on through the vendors, determined to find one selling the right color ribbons.

Joanna followed more slowly, studying the vendors' wares with interest. She paused at a stall loaded with knives of all sizes and shapes.

Each handle was unique; some were of beautifully carved wood, others of metal decorated with detailed etching or filigree work.

A tall, thin man with long greasy hair was standing behind the stall. He picked up one of the knives and offered it to her. "Knives fit for nobility, they are, my lady," he said, exposing his missing teeth as he smiled. "You'll find none finer anywhere."

"It is excellent craftsmanship," Joanna said, "but I have no need of a knife today."

Not willing to let her go so easily, the man stepped forward. Immediately Cona moved to stand in front of his mistress. His lips curled back, and a growl sounded deep in his throat. The man's eyes darted from Joanna to the dog, his smile evaporating.

"Good day to you," Joanna said.

Eva was talking to a woman beside a nearby cart filled with fluttering ribbons. A little girl was hovering near the woman, and as Joanna and Cona approached, the girl quickly ducked behind her mother's skirts and peeked out at the enormous dog with wide and fearful eyes.

Joanna bent down so she was at the child's level. "He's very big, but he doesn't hurt children," she said. "Would you like to touch him?" She extended her hand to the child. "Come stand beside me, and you can pat him."

The little girl studied Joanna's face for a few moments, then took a hesitant step forward.

Joanna took her hand. "Sit, Cona," she said.

In wonder, the little girl watched as the wolfhound bent his legs and dropped to the ground beside her. Gently, Joanna guided the child's hand until it touched Cona's shaggy back. Cona laid his head on his paws, gave them both a bored look, blinked, and turned away. With her free hand, the little girl covered her mouth and stifled a giggle. Joanna smiled and rose to her feet. Cona did the same.

"Thank you, my lady. Cecily will be talking of this for days," the woman said, bobbing a curtsy.

"She's a lovely little girl," Joanna said.

"After four boys, she has been a joy," the woman said, looking down fondly at the blonde-haired child who continued to furtively study Cona from behind her mother's skirts.

"Do your boys enjoy coming to market too?" Joanna asked.

The woman's face fell. "They do, my lady," she said. "But they had to stay behind today. They were needed at the shearing shed."

"Are your boys old enough to help with the shearing, Margery?" Eva asked.

Joanna realized that Eva must already know this woman and her family.

"Not the clipping," Margery said. "They're just there to keep an eye on the sacks of wool."

"The sacks of wool?" Eva looked as puzzled as Joanna felt.

Margery nodded miserably. "A goodly portion of this year's raw wool has gone missing. The steward has sent men out to the shearing shed three times to collect the Lord's taxes, but every time, they've found the shed empty."

"How can that be?" Eva said, her expression troubled.

"Some claim a band of outlaws from Kent has been stealing from shearing sheds all along the coast, but no one's been caught yet," Margery said. "Those of us with sheep still needing to be sheared are guarding every sack of wool that's gathered. The peasants will pay what tax they can, but it may not be enough."

Joanna's thoughts flew back to the meeting she'd interrupted in the grand chamber the night before. Hadn't her father been demanding that Sir Edwyn, Sir Nigel, and Gerard Bartholomew do something regarding sheep? And the large leather book he'd relinquished to the steward could easily have been the tax ledger.

"Surely someone at the castle must have a better understanding of the situation, and things will be remedied soon," Joanna said.

"Perhaps, my lady," Margery said. But her response was more polite than hopeful. With a smile that did not reach her eyes, Margery reached for her daughter's hand. "Come, Cecily." She bobbed a brief curtsy to Joanna. "I have taken too much of your time, Lady Joanna. Thank you again for your kindness. Good day to you. Good day, Eva."

While Eva paid the vendor for the ribbons, Joanna watched the peasant woman and her daughter disappear into the crowd.

"Shall we return to the castle, my lady?" Eva asked, tucking the ribbons safely into her purse.

Joanna nodded, although her mind was still on Margery and her family's plight. "Eva, if the wool is not recovered, what will happen to the peasants who cannot pay their taxes?" she asked.

Her lady's maid looked down. "That is for Lord Gilbert to decide," she said. "He has been known to occasionally show leniency, to demand a larger portion of the summer crops instead. But if he wills it, he can evict those who do not pay or put them in the dungeon."

Joanna stopped in her tracks. "The dungeon?" She gripped Eva's hand. "You cannot mean that? Not the whole family."

Eva gave a helpless shrug. "It sends a message to others who may consider the Lord's taxation to be optional."

The thought of little Cecily in the castle's damp, dark dungeon was appalling.

"Something must be done to help them," she whispered.

Eva nodded encouragingly.

"Truly," Joanna said, her voice strengthening with her growing conviction. "Something must be done."

Chapter 6

THAT AFTERNOON, JOANNA WENT IN search of her father. He often conducted castle business late into the afternoon, so she decided to start at the grand chamber. With Cona by her side, she crossed the great hall and had almost reached the large meeting room when the solid wooden door swung open and three of Moreland's bailiffs walked out.

One glance at the men's stormy expressions told Joanna their meeting with Lord Gilbert had not gone well. She stifled a sigh. Were the bailiffs glowering because her father had secured more from them than they had hoped? Or had they been discussing something displeasing to all parties? Whatever had transpired between them would undoubtedly influence her father's current disposition.

For a moment, Joanna watched the three men walk out of the great hall, their heads shaking as they spoke to one another. Then she turned to face the door of the grand chamber. She refused to be intimidated by her father's volatile temperament. Her concerns were not for herself but for a group of people with virtually no voice of their own.

Giving a sharp rap on the door, she lifted the latch and pushed the door open. Her father was standing, his back to her, gazing out one of the narrow windows.

"What is it?" he growled.

"Might I have a word with you, my lord?" Joanna said.

Lord Gilbert swung around, surprise flitting across his face before his brows lowered in a frown. "Joanna? Why are you here?"

Joanna experienced a moment of sadness at his question. How had they come to this? During her childhood, she'd attempted to claim her father's attention and win his affection over and over again, but she'd been rebuffed every time. And finally, she'd stemmed her tears of disappointment and loneliness by building a defensive wall around her damaged heart. She'd stopped showing up at his rooms uninvited, and now an even greater distance had grown between them.

It had been a long time since she'd sought out her father without his summons, and she wasn't sure quite how to proceed. She gave him a tentative smile. "This morning, I learned of something that is of great concern to Moreland's peasants," she said. "I came to you hoping that you could shed some light on the situation."

The lines across her father's forehead deepened. "And what is that concern, pray tell?"

Joanna kept her eyes on her father. "Their wool is disappearing."

Lord Gilbert gave a snort of derision. "Wool does not simply disappear," he said. "Someone is taking it."

"There is talk among the peasants of a gang of thieves from Kent," Joanna said.

"So I've heard," her father said drily. "A rather weak ploy to remove suspicion from themselves, don't you think?"

Joanna stiffened. "Why would they do something like that?"

"Because they don't want to pay the tax they have already pledged to the bailiffs."

"The peasant woman I spoke to at the market is most anxious to pay the tax," Joanna said. "Her greatest fear is what will happen to her family if they lose the wool and cannot make their payment."

"If she has sheep, she has wool. I will accept no excuse for unpaid taxes."

"But if it is stolen . . ."

"I have considerably more experience working with peasants than you do, Joanna," he said, a hard edge to his voice. "And it would serve you well to not question me on such matters."

"I only wanted to be sure that the peasants are treated fairly, my lord," Joanna said.

An all-too-familiar thunderous look filled Lord Gilbert's face. "Oh, they will be treated fairly," he said. "If they do not pay their tax, they go to the dungeon. That is the law. That is fair."

Joanna was quite sure her horror showed on her face. "But, my lord—"

"Enough!" Lord Gilbert bellowed, dismissing his daughter and her opinions with a single word. "I will hear no more." He turned on his heel and marched onto the nearby dais, where he took his seat, picked up a quill, and began scrawling something across a piece of parchment.

Joanna stood silently until she was quite sure he had no intention of looking up. Then, without a word, she slipped out of the room. Nothing had changed. Her father still had no interest in her or her feelings.

Joanna allowed that discouraging thought entry into her heart and mind for only a few minutes, then, with an ability born of practice, she pushed it aside. No good would come from dwelling on her father's dislike of her, but her personal disappointment could do great harm if it prevented her from helping people like Margery. Joanna turned her back on the grand chamber and straightened her shoulders. As she had done so many times before, she would appeal to Sir Edwyn instead.

In the center of the great hall, a servant was replenishing the wood supply beside the enormous fireplace.

Joanna approached him. "Do you know where the knights are met this morning?" she asked.

The boy jumped to his feet, obviously startled to discover that he'd been approached by the lady of the castle. "I heard talk of 'em practicing their swordplay in the south pasture, my lady," he said, running a dirty hand across his untamed hair.

"I thank you," Joanna said.

The boy gave a fumbling attempt at a bow. "Yer welcome, my lady," he said.

She smiled at him, grateful for his simple kindness after her interview with her father.

Joanna left the keep by the main stairs that circled the external wall of the large tower and cut across the inner bailey, passing under the shadow of the crenellated walls and through the gate into the outer bailey. The castle chapel stood to her right, and behind that was the brewhouse and the castle garden. To her left was the garrison accommodation, and although soldiers stood on duty at the gates and patrolled the walls, most were obviously being employed elsewhere because the outer bailey was remarkably quiet.

She heard the sound of men's voices coming from the stables, and the ringing of metal on metal echoed from the smithy next door. Simon the bowyer was sitting on a stool outside his house, stringing a longbow with hemp. At his feet, two more bow-shaped pieces of yew at least six feet long sat waiting for his attention. He did not look up from his task as she passed, and Joanna wondered if he'd been told to ready more bows than usual with the archery tournament only a week away.

She'd almost reached the main gate when she saw Gerard Bartholomew exit the gatehouse followed by the three bailiffs she'd seen in the great hall. The tower above the gatehouse was the steward's residence, and to minimize intrusions into the castle grounds, he conducted most of his business with the townspeople there. It appeared that the bailiffs had transferred their concerns from the grand chamber to the gatehouse.

All four men looked grave and were engaged in deep conversation, and even from this distance, she could hear the low rumble of the bailiffs' voices and the steward's nasally response. These were the men charged with balancing the needs of those living within the castle with the needs of those living in the town of Moreland and on its lands. Joanna did not envy them their responsibility.

The men walked together toward the inner bailey and were soon lost from sight behind the buildings. Joanna and Cona continued through the main gate, following the dirt track that curved around the castle walls. As they cut through a small copse of trees, the sloping ground leveled off and widened into the vast grassy area known as the south pasture. Although knights occasionally used it as a place to practice their combat skills, it was better known as a quiet meadow ideal for a peaceful horse ride, a walk, or even a picnic. Which was why when Joanna emerged from behind the largest ash tree, she paused in amazement at the sight before her.

In the center of the field, over a dozen knights were practicing at swordplay. Three of them were wielding heavy wooden swords against pells, attacking the tall wooden poles as though they were battling formidable opponents. Six others were dueling, their metal swords glinting in the sunshine and the clash of blades as jarring as the sounds coming from the smithy. The remaining knights were gathered around, shouting encouraging and disparaging remarks as the combatants cut, sliced, and thrust through the air.

Some distance from the knights, a group of laborers was erecting what appeared to be an enormous pavilion. Joanna could already identify the raised platform, benches, and poles that would eventually hold up a canopy. Several men were cutting and fitting the wooden pieces together while three others were pacing the length of the field, calling out instructions to each other as they left wooden markers in the grass.

"They must be preparing for the archery tournament," Joanna said, looking down at Cona. A flutter of nervous excitement filled her. If it weren't for the husband-finding portion of the upcoming event, she would look forward to the thrill of her first tournament, with its attendant pageantry, competition, and holiday-like atmosphere. As it was, her enthusiasm at the sight of the preparations was tainted by her knowledge that her future was not her own and her life was likely to change dramatically in a very short space of time.

At the thought, a picture of Margery's worried face entered her mind. She was not the only one whose way of life was teetering in the balance.

"Come, Cona," she said and started across the field toward the battling knights.

From a distance, it was impossible to tell the men apart. Those who were wielding swords all wore hauberks and helmets. Many of the knights who were watching were similarly clad, awaiting their turn with the pell or a willing opponent. Only three knights had relinquished the heavy armor to their squires, their practice sessions already completed.

As Joanna approached, one of those knights looked her way. She knew Cona's presence made her immediately recognizable and was not surprised when she saw the knight lean closer to speak to the man at his side. Within moments, more heads turned. Word had spread.

The knight who had seen her first stepped forward. "Lady Joanna, we are honored by your presence."

Sir Thomas was obviously recovering from his recent match-up. Sweat lay beaded across his forehead, and his face was flushed. It was the first time Joanna had seen him since her misadventure at his table the morning before, and she wondered briefly what he would say if he knew she was the one who had spilled ale all over his hand.

Thinking it best not to dwell on that mishap, she smiled politely. "I thank you, Sir Thomas," she said. "I have come in search of Sir Edwyn. Do you know where I might find him?"

"He and his squire left the castle early this morning, my lady. I'm afraid he gave no reason for leaving, only that he likely would not return until week's end."

Joanna's heart sank. She'd been so sure of Sir Edwyn's willingness to aid her efforts to help Margery and the other peasants, but it seemed it was not to be. "I see," she said, working to hide her disappointment as she desperately tried to think of anyone else who might be willing to help her. "Is Sir Nigel here?" she asked before she could talk herself out of it.

Sir Thomas raised his eyebrows. "Why, yes, my lady." He pointed to one of the knights who was sparring with another a few yards away from them. "That is Sir Nigel over there. I imagine he will dispatch with Sir William quite promptly, so you will not have to wait long to speak with him."

Joanna glanced at the men who were clashing swords. Even with her limited exposure to swordplay, it appeared that one knight most certainly had the upper hand. Blow after blow rang out as the knight in question relentlessly forced his opponent backward until the other man fell upon his back and raised his arms in defeat.

The winning knight stood over him and poked the tip of his sword into the loser's chain mail. "Not good enough, Sir William," he said. "Still not good enough."

Sir William's helmet muffled his reply as he struggled to free himself from the cumbersome headwear. From the sidelines, a squire ran out to help, and the other knight turned to walk away. Joanna watched as he too removed his helmet and handed it to a second squire. The knight was indeed Sir Nigel, although she'd never before seen him with his light-brown hair in such disarray or wearing such a satisfied smirk.

She was aware that several of the nearby knights were awkwardly waiting for her to say something, but she stood quietly until Sir Nigel looked over and saw her.

His expression changed to one of pleasant surprise, and he immediately altered his course to greet her. "Lady Joanna," he said with a slight bow of his head. "To what do we owe this great pleasure?"

Frustrated that his words brought a blush to her face, Joanna seized upon the reason for her errand, glad to have a solid, impersonal excuse for her presence there.

"Forgive me for interrupting your practice," she said. "I recently learned of a serious concern among Moreland's peasants, and as you are Lord Gilbert's advisor, I came to discover what, if anything, you know of the matter."

Sir Nigel gave a puzzled frown. "Of course, my lady. Let me accompany you back to the castle, for I am anxious to hear what you have to say."

"Very well," Joanna said, more than happy to remove herself from the other knights' curious stares.

Sir Nigel unbuckled his belt and handed it, his sword, and his scabbard to his squire, who took them and then began pulling the cumbersome hauberk up and over Sir Nigel's head. Suddenly realizing Sir Nigel was wearing only a shirt and hose beneath his chain mail, Joanna swung around, turning her pink face toward the castle walls.

After a seemingly interminable wait, Sir Nigel appeared at her side, free of his heavy armor and wearing a dark-brown doublet.

"Shall we?" he said, offering her his arm with a knowing smile.

Joanna raised her head. She had no one to blame but herself for being in this uncomfortable position, but she would get herself out of it as gracefully as possible. She placed her hand on his arm. "Yes," she said.

A low rumble sounded in the back of Cona's throat, and the large dog moved closer.

"Protective, isn't he?" Sir Nigel said.

"Very," Joanna replied. She would make no excuses for her guard dog; she was grateful for his reassuring presence.

Chapter 7

To his credit, Sir Nigel paid more attention to Joanna's concerns than her father had. He interrupted her explanation to greet passing merchants and exchange a few words with some of the tradesmen they passed as they walked through the outer bailey, but he seemed to be listening as she told him about the peasants' missing wool and her unease over their future well-being. By the time they reached the castle's keep, she harbored great hope that Sir Nigel would be able to offer some viable solutions.

"What can be done to help the peasants, Sir Nigel?" she asked as she finished her account.

"Help the peasants?" he repeated, looking at her incredulously. "Are you not more worried about how Lord Gilbert's wool is to be recovered?"

Joanna frowned. Perhaps she had misread his interest in her concerns. "Surely, looking out for the one would benefit the other," she said, trying to hide her disappointment in the face of yet another rejection. "If the thief were apprehended and forced to return the stolen wool, the peasants would no longer be delinquent in their payment and the lord's coffers would be filled."

"It is hardly that simple," Sir Nigel said. "Have you considered the possibility that the peasants are purposely holding back wool for their own advancement—whether it be for monetary gain or for a future revolt against their lord? In that case, a swift and sure punishment is the only way to send a message that such behavior is destined to fail."

"But do you have any proof that our own peasants are stealing the wool?" Joanna asked. "I heard tell that a band of outlaws from Kent has been stealing from other shearing sheds."

"Which is why Sir Edwyn rode out this morning to investigate," Sir Nigel said. "He will travel as far as Dover to see if there is any truth to those tales."

Relief filled Joanna. If there were any facts behind the rumors, she was confident Sir Edwyn would uncover them.

"And in the meantime," Sir Nigel said, "Lord Gilbert has ordered guards to stand watch at the shearing shed. They will be on the lookout for peasants who appear without just cause."

Sir Nigel's reassurance should have been enough to assuage Joanna's unease, but her sense of disquiet lingered. The guards could do nothing about the wool that was already missing. There was more to this issue, she was sure, but she was equally certain that in Sir Nigel's mind, the subject was now closed. "I am glad to know that you have the matter in hand," she said.

"Of course," he said. "You must not trouble yourself over these things anymore. Instead, set your mind upon other, more pleasant thoughts." He nodded to a passing merchant. "The upcoming archery tournament should be an excellent diversion," he said, offering Joanna a meaningful smile. "After all, I have reason to hope that I will be your escort at the banquet that will follow."

Joanna recognized the deliberate change in the conversation and forced herself to smile. "So you intend to compete?" she said.

He raised one eyebrow. "I intend to win," he said.

✌︎⁓◗Ꮔ⌇◖

That night, Joanna lay awake, reviewing the events of the day: meeting Margery at the market, her disastrous interview with her father, and her awkward exchange with Sir Nigel. Unfortunately, the evening meal later had done little to ease her discomfort. Her father had sat woodenly beside her at the head table, speaking even less than usual, and Sir Nigel had made a point of singling her out, raising his goblet, and winking at her in such a way that she prayed her father would not notice.

She'd left the table with most of her food untouched, and as soon as she'd reached the safety of her bedchamber, she'd dressed in her nightgown and crawled into bed. Convincing Eva that she was simply suffering from an aching head had been easy; preventing her from sending for Beatrice the healer had been considerably harder. She'd escaped a visit from Beatrice only by promising Eva that she'd rest quietly for the remainder of the evening. And even then, Eva had muttered for a good ten minutes about the price Joanna was paying for foolish nighttime trips out of the castle.

Joanna did not tell her lady's maid that her peasant clothing was tucked safely beneath her pillow and that before the first fingers of dawn appeared in the night sky she would be visiting Agnes's cottage again. A slip like that would have certainly brought Beatrice to her room—along with a powerful sleeping potion.

❧❦☙

Lukas awoke early the next morning. Garrick had already left to check his traps, but the wooden crutch he'd been whittling the night before lay beside Lukas's pallet. He reached out and ran his hand across its smooth surface, amazed at the skill the simple-minded man had with a knife and a piece of wood.

"He wanted you to have it when you woke." Slip's voice reached him from the door. "Said you might want to get up first thing."

Lukas struggled to a sitting position. He was wearing one of Garrick's old undershirts and tunics, and the day before, Agnes had covered his ribs with a foul-smelling ointment and wrapped them with long strips of cloth. Although movement was still painful, it was now possible. "That was very good of him," he said. "I will certainly try."

"Do you want help getting to your feet?" Slip asked.

"You wouldn't be wanting to postpone doing the milking by any chance, would you?" Lukas said with a grin.

Slip gave a sly smile. "Never," he said.

Lukas chuckled. "Come along, then. Let's see what you're made of."

Five minutes later, Lukas was left with no doubts as to the strength of Slip's wiry body, but he had serious reservations about his own. He was upright, thanks to Garrick's crutch, but his legs were shaking, and the pain in his thigh was pulsating in time with his racing heartbeat. He wiped his forehead with his clean but worn shirtsleeve and took a steadying breath.

"Here," Slip said, passing him a wooden cup. "Have some water."

Lukas gratefully accepted the cup and took a long drink.

Slip looked at him uncertainly. "Will you be all right on your own? Agnes should be back from gathering eggs anytime now, but I'd best be off doing the milking when she gets here."

"That was harder than I'd imagined," Lukas admitted. "But now that I'm on my feet, I believe I will manage."

Slip still looked unsure.

"Away with you," Lukas said. "I can only imagine what Agnes might do if she learns I'm the reason her goat suffered. Who knows what terrible potion she'd give me."

Slip laughed. "As long as she makes you take it, not me," he said, running for the door.

Lukas watched him go. What he wouldn't give to be that swift of foot right now. With a sigh, he moved his injured leg forward a few inches. He would try walking to the door and back and count his blessings that he could move at all.

He limped his way across the room and had made it halfway back when he heard a light knock and the sound of the door opening. Leaning on his new crutch, he turned around in time to see Lady Joanna walk in. His breath caught in his throat.

"Sir Lukas," she said, her lovely face lighting up as she looked at him. "You're walking!"

Lukas had been the recipient of many flirtatious glances and simpering smiles from attractive noblewomen in the past, but none of them had ever affected him like this. Lady Joanna's joy at his small accomplishments made him want to stand taller, while her unaffected beauty made his weakened legs want to cave altogether.

"Yes, albeit rather slowly," he said with a rueful smile. He steadied himself against the nearby table. "Garrick made me this crutch, and Slip helped me get onto my feet. I couldn't have done it without them."

She moved farther into the room, and he noticed that Grey had followed her in. The dog was still enormous, but he seemed a little less intimidating now that Lukas wasn't lying on the floor.

Lady Joanna stopped in front of him and gazed up at his forehead. "The swelling on your head has gone down too," she said.

Lukas raised his hand to touch the tender area above his right eye. "I'm sure my forehead is turning every color of the rainbow," he said.

This time, Joanna's smile was shyer. "A very regal shade of purple," she said.

He laughed and was gratified to see a slight pink tinge her cheeks. Pulling himself together, he pointed at one of the wooden chairs. "Would you care to sit?"

She nodded, and once she was seated, she waited until he had slowly lowered himself into the other chair before speaking. "Are the others all outside?" she asked as though she'd only just realized they were alone in the cottage.

"Yes," he said. "I didn't see Garrick go, but Slip just left to milk the goat, and Agnes should be back anytime." He glanced at the door, hoping he had a few more uninterrupted minutes with Lady Joanna. "Will you tell me about Agnes, Garrick, and Slip? Their unlikely friendship, along with their kindness to a total stranger, has left me curious about their backgrounds."

Her radiant smile was back. "They are wonderful, aren't they?"

"I don't believe I've ever met their equal," he said, silently adding Joanna's name to the other three.

He had long considered the stable hands at Launceston Castle to be his friends, and he'd always maintained good relationships with the tradesmen and fishermen in the nearby Cornish town, but he'd never met a noblewoman who'd shown such kindness toward those born so far below her own station.

"It's hard to imagine a better person than Agnes," Joanna said. "She shares her gift of healing with anyone in need and opens her heart and home to all—even those who may have been rejected by others." She paused. "I do not know the details of Garrick's story, because he has lived here longer than I've known Agnes, but I was once told that when his parents discovered that he was simpleminded, they refused to acknowledge him as their son, believing he would never be able to earn his keep."

"And Agnes learned of it and took him in," Lukas guessed.

"Yes," Joanna said. "She has raised him as her own."

She looked over at a small battered hat that hung on a hook beside the door. "Slip was orphaned and had been living on the streets in Moreland for several years when Agnes found him and brought him home." She smiled at the memory. "For weeks afterward, things kept going missing from the cottage. Agnes was beside herself until she finally discovered that Slip had been taking them and hiding them in a hollow tree behind the house." She looked at Lukas, her eyes now sad. "It was the way he'd always survived, you see. He took anything he could find in case he could use it later. That was when Agnes announced that he was never to act like or be called Slippery Fingers again."

"So you call him Slip instead."

Joanna nodded. "It took him a little while to get used to his new name, and occasionally a kitchen knife or a piece of fruit will suddenly disappear, but no matter what it is, it always reappears a day or two later."

Lukas understood. "Agnes has gained his trust," he said.

"Yes," she said. "And he has hers."

Lukas waited for a moment, but when it seemed that Lady Joanna would say no more, he asked a new question. "And what of you, Lady Joanna? What brings you to Agnes's cottage in the early hours of the morning dressed in peasant clothing?"

She glanced at her homespun dress. "I suppose you must think my attire very strange," she said.

"No stranger than what I am wearing," he said, wiggling his eyebrows to emphasize his current elegance.

She raised her hand to her mouth to mask a giggle, but her twinkling blue eyes gave her away. "Garrick's tunic is perhaps a little large around the middle," she said.

"Indeed." He pulled on the loose fabric. "But your clothing fits perfectly, my lady," he said. "Perhaps they were made for you?"

Joanna was silent for a moment, and Lukas had the distinct impression that she was weighing her words carefully.

"It is best that no one knows that I leave the castle," she finally said. "That is why I visit Agnes before dawn and why I hide my identity with this clothing." She reached out her hand and ran it down the shaggy neck of the wolfhound at her feet. "Agnes's kindness has touched my life too. Grey was to be my guard dog, but when my father discovered that he was lame, he ordered him killed. I was twelve years old when Agnes rescued my dog and my broken heart." She gave a small smile. "Since that time, I have come to visit as often as I've been able."

Grey raised his head, suddenly alert. Seconds later, the door opened, and Agnes walked in carrying a small basket full of eggs.

❧⬩❧

Joanna smiled as Grey limped toward the door to greet the woman who had cared for him so well.

"Mercy, but those chickens are getting more and more wily," Agnes said, giving the dog an affectionate pat as she moved farther into the room. "It took me an age to find all the eggs this morning."

Lukas struggled to his feet.

"Well, now," Agnes said, stopping in her tracks. "There's a gladsome sight!"

Lukas gave her a crooked grin. "I'm not very sturdy yet but better than yesterday."

"Much improved," Agnes said, looking pleased. She placed her basket of eggs on the table and moved over to the chair where Joanna sat, took her hand, and gave it a gentle squeeze. "I went to market yesterday and heard about the archery tournament."

Joanna's heart sank. For a blissful hour, she'd forgotten all about her father's plan to offer her as a tourney prize. Now her feelings of helplessness and dread came flooding back. "Yes," she said as cheerfully as she could muster. "The stands are already going up in the south pasture."

Agnes seemed to grasp her reluctance to discuss the ramifications of the contest, although she was obviously aware of them. She gave Joanna an understanding look. "Things may yet work out for the best, my lady," she said kindly.

Sir Lukas looked from Joanna to Agnes and back, his expression puzzled. "What is this archery contest?" he asked.

Agnes moved over to the fireplace and stirred the pot simmering there. "Lord Gilbert has announced a grand archery tournament," she said. "There is much excitement in town because it has been many years since anything of the sort has been held at Moreland Castle, and it is anticipated that many visiting noblemen will come to compete."

"And you are not pleased by this announcement, Lady Joanna?" he said, looking at her with bewilderment. "Does it not promise to be an exciting event for all who attend?"

Joanna raised her head to face him. He must not know of her apprehension about the outcome of the archery competition or of her despair over realizing that she was little more than a pawn in her father's grand plan to retain Moreland Castle for his heir.

"I daresay it will be a memorable experience," she said. "And I am glad that the peasants and townspeople have something to look forward to."

"I imagine there is some excitement among Lord Gilbert's knights too," he said. "After all, several of them are probably anxious to compete."

Joanna's stomach churned, and she rose. "I must go," she said.

Looking confused, Sir Lukas took a hesitant step toward her. "Lady Joanna," he said, "if I have said anything that has given offense, I am truly sorry."

To her dismay, Joanna felt the sting of tears. Other than Sir Edwyn, no man had ever worried about her feelings before. "Please do not concern yourself," she said, blinking away the traitorous moisture. "You have done nothing."

Agnes stepped forward, her lips pressed in a firm line. "Is Sir Edwyn at the castle? Can you go to him if you have a need?" she said, taking Joanna's hands in hers.

Joanna shook her head. "He has ridden to Dover," she said. "He's searching for news of a gang of wool thieves from Kent and is not expected back until week's end."

"Wool thieves?" Sir Lukas asked.

Joanna gave an unhappy shrug. "Wool has been disappearing from the Moreland shearing shed. Some of the peasants have heard rumor that a gang of thieves from Kent has been stealing from shearing sheds along the coast. Sir Edwyn has gone to investigate. Without the wool, the peasants cannot pay their taxes."

From the look on his face, it was obvious Sir Lukas recognized the seriousness of unpaid taxes. He took another step toward Joanna. "I am reluctant to ask anything more of you, my lady"—the intensity in his voice drew her eyes to his—"but may I make one more request of you?"

Unsure of what else to do, Joanna gave a small nod.

"The moment Sir Edwyn returns, will you inform him that Sir Lukas, son of Nicholas, is at Agnes's cottage? Tell him that I must speak to him on matters that are vital to the security of Moreland."

Joanna could only stare. "Do you bear news from elsewhere, or do you believe the men who assailed you are a threat to Moreland Castle?" she said.

"I arrived here bearing no news," he said, "but I do believe that the attack I suffered may be a sign of something bigger."

"What exactly?" Joanna asked.

Sir Lukas shook his head. "I do not know enough to be sure, but I believe I have information that may help Sir Edwyn."

"With the wool thieves?"

He raised his hand to his injured forehead as though it was suddenly hurting more intensely. "It is possible," he said.

Joanna felt an unexpected frisson of alarm. "You come here as a stranger, and yet you claim to know more about the troubles facing Moreland than those who live here."

"I know I ask a great deal," he said, "but I beg of you to trust me."

"More than Lord Gilbert's men, whom I've known all my life?"

"More than all but Sir Edwyn," he said. "I know him to be a man of honor."

That was perhaps the only thing Sir Lukas could have said to persuade Joanna. She met his eyes again. The physical strain he was under as he fought to remain standing was reflected there—as was a sense of urgency and pleading. He did not look away.

She glanced at Agnes and sensed her silent support. "I will tell Sir Edwyn as soon as he returns," she said.

"And only him?"

"And only him," Joanna repeated.

Sir Lukas reached for the table as if his relief at her response had replaced his strength. "I am indebted to you once again, my lady," he said. "And I will not forget it."

Voices sounded outside the cottage. The door flew open, and Garrick and Slip came in.

"The tide's rising," Garrick announced as he dropped a small net containing two crabs onto the table.

"Go," Agnes said, giving Joanna a gentle push toward the door. "You must delay no longer."

With one last glance at Sir Lukas, Joanna hurried outside and headed for the beach.

Chapter 8

JOANNA THOUGHT SHE MIGHT GO mad with the waiting. The rain that had started an hour after she'd returned to the castle from Agnes's cottage two days ago had not stopped since. With no word from Sir Edwyn, she found herself pacing her bedchamber still waiting for news on the wool thieves, waiting to pass along Sir Lukas's message, and waiting for an update on Sir Lukas's condition.

There was a general feeling of nervous anticipation in the castle as everyone awaited the pageantry and festivities associated with the upcoming archery tournament, and that added to the tension she felt. In fact, Joanna supposed that the only person who might be almost as worried as she was about the banquet following the tourney was the castle cook, who had been charged with feeding everyone in attendance. Joanna made a point of avoiding the kitchen for the rest of the week, guessing that tempers would be flaring as preparation time grew shorter.

On the third day after she'd visited the cottage, the sun came out, and the castle became a hive of activity again. The laborers headed down to the south pasture and went back to work on the construction of the pavilion. The knights resumed their outdoor target practice with both longbows and crossbows, and the merchants and tradesmen began readying their stalls for the increase in traffic through the town and the outer bailey.

Joanna could not sit or stand or pace inside any longer. She had to learn something new, even if her options for gleaning information were limited.

"Eva," she said, putting away her stitchery for the third time that morning. "Do you know where the shearing shed is located?"

"Yes, my lady," Eva said, raising a questioning eyebrow as she repositioned one of Joanna's dresses that was drying in front of the fire.

"I should like to go and see it," Joanna said.

"See the shearing shed?" Lines appeared across Eva's forehead. "It's a noisy, smelly place, my lady. Not somewhere you'd be wanting to go."

"We don't have to stay long," Joanna said. "But I'd like to see it for myself." She paused. "I've been thinking a lot about Margery and her family," she added.

Eva gave a worried sigh. "I haven't heard that any more wool's gone missing."

"Neither have I," Joanna said. "But I think we both need an outing, and that would be as good a place to go as any."

Eva looked as though she had her doubts on that score, but she dutifully gathered Joanna's cloak, along with her own, and prepared to leave.

"Perhaps it is far enough that we should ride," Joanna said, working to keep a smile from surfacing.

"Indeed," Eva said, suddenly looking far more enthusiastic about the trip. "That's a splendid suggestion, my lady."

"I'm quite sure Timothy will think so too," Joanna said, finally allowing her smile full reign.

Color flooded Eva's cheeks, but her lips hinted at a smile too. "I believe you may be right, my lady," she said.

Less than twenty minutes later, the stable master met the women and Cona at the stable's main doors. "Good day, Lady Joanna," Timothy said, bowing his head respectfully.

"Good day, Timothy," she said. "Eva and I are hoping to ride out to the shearing shed. Would you be good enough to saddle our mounts?"

"Of course, my lady."

Joanna pretended not to notice the wink he gave Eva as he moved farther into the stable, where she knew her mare was stalled. Purposely giving her lady's maid a few moments alone with her betrothed, Joanna turned her attention to the nearest horses. She immediately recognized her father's charger, an enormous dark-brown horse who allowed no one but Lord Gilbert on his back. Next to him stood another charger, almost as tall but black in color and with gentler eyes. Slowly Joanna approached, studying the majestic animal. She did not recognize him, but the carriage of his head and neck and his alert ears left her with no doubts as to his high breeding.

"Has Lord Gilbert acquired a new horse, Timothy?" she asked as the stable master approached with her mare.

"No, my lady," Timothy said. "I wasn't here when this one was brought in, but one of the young stable hands said a nobleman asked that it be stabled here for the time being." He ran his hand down the black horse's neck. "He's a beauty, all right. But I'm guessing he belongs to one of the noblemen here for the tournament, so he won't be here for long."

"I see," Joanna said. As she'd spent most of the last three days in her bedchamber, she'd not yet seen any of the visiting noblemen in the castle, but as she glanced around the stable, she now noted the stalls already prepared with freshly strewn straw. "You will have your hands full as more guests arrive, I daresay."

"Yes, my lady."

Joanna smiled. "I thank you for your efforts. I'm sure they will not go unnoticed this week."

"I'm happy to serve, my lady."

Timothy led Joanna's horse to the mounting block and helped her into the saddle, then turned to do the same for Eva. Joanna noticed that he held Eva's hand a little longer than necessary, and she couldn't help but feel a twinge of envy at the look that passed between them. Would she ever experience being truly loved by another? Her heart yearned to feel such deep emotion, but her head told her it would never be.

She looked straight ahead and urged her mare forward. Cona fell into step beside her. Not for the first time she wondered how different her life would be without her noble birthright.

Eva had been right. The shearing shed was loud and smelly. Shaggy sheep stood huddled in an enclosure on one side of the small stone building. One at a time, they were herded into the building, where they were trapped and pinned down by one of six burley shearers who proceeded to clip the wool off the unsuspecting animals at such incredible speed the whole process was over almost before it began. The sheep were then allowed to escape the shed to join the other shorn members of their flock, and young boys scampered to gather up every last scrap of wool from the shed floor before the next sheep came in.

Upon Joanna's arrival, one wary guard was charged with keeping Cona away from the sheep, and another escorted Joanna and Eva into the building. They stood and watched for only a minute. The odor of wet wool, muddy animals, and sweaty men was almost more than Joanna could bear. But worse than that was the awkwardness that filled the small area the moment she was recognized. The men didn't know how to react to her presence. Some stood, removed their hats, and bowed; some stopped their work but remained seated, holding the bleating ewes uncomfortably by their legs. No one spoke.

Joanna gave a small smile, wished them all a good day, and exited as quickly as she could. As soon as the door closed, the hum of men's voices and the clack of clippers resumed.

"Did you see any of Margery's boys?" Joanna asked Eva as they stepped away from the shed.

"Yes, my lady," Eva said. "Her oldest, John, was gathering wool."

"Could I speak with him, do you think?"

Eva turned to the nearby guard. "Would you call out John Fielding?" she asked. "Lady Joanna would like to speak with him."

A few minutes later, a pale-faced young boy walked out of the shed, wringing his cap in his hand.

"Good day, John," Joanna said.

"Good day, my lady," John said, giving a self-conscious bow before darting nervous glances at Eva and the guard.

"I met your mother at the market," Joanna explained. "Perhaps she told you."

"Yes, my lady. She did tell us." His cheeks reddened. "She didn't talk of anything else for days."

Joanna smiled. "Well, I enjoyed our conversation very much too."

John searched her face and must have recognized her sincerity because the hands that had been torturing his cap relaxed.

"I've been wondering about the bags of wool," Joanna said. "Have you lost any more since market day?"

"No, my lady," John said. "Me and my brothers have been inside the shed every day, and three days ago, his lordship sent guards to watch the outside. They're here day and night. None's gone missin' since then."

"I'm very glad to hear it," Joanna said.

"We'll do our best to pay his lordship's tax with what's left," John said, his eyebrows coming together in a worried frown. "Father says paying it must come ahead of our own needs."

Joanna placed a hand on the boy's shoulder, wishing she could do more to remove the burden he so obviously shared with his parents. "Others at the castle are doing what they can to discover what has happened to the wool," she said. "It may yet be recovered."

John's doubtful look was the image of his mother's, and his reply equally polite. "That would be a fine thing, my lady," he said.

"We will hope for that, then."

"Yes, my lady," he said.

She smiled, hoping to dispel his anxious expression. "Get back to work now," she said. "And when you go home, give my best wishes to your mother."

"Then she'll talk of that for days too," he said, a grin finally piercing the concern on his face.

Eva gave him a playful clip to the ear. "Off with you," she said. "Or your mother will hear of your impudence."

"Yes, my lady," he said again, but as he hurried back to the shearing shed, Joanna could tell his steps were lighter.

Chapter 9

LUKAS STOOD AT THE POINT where the woodland met the ocean and studied the shoreline carefully. To his left, dense trees grew to within a few yards of the pebbly beach. To his right, the loamy soil gave way to limestone rock and the vegetation thinned as the ground rose steeply to form a tall, craggy cliff that ran along the coast to a distant promontory.

On the cliff top, tall trees hid the lower section of Moreland Castle's retaining wall, but the crenellated tops, guard towers, and upper portion of the keep were clearly visible. Colorful flags flew from the towers, a reminder of the tournament Lord Gilbert was hosting in only a few days' time.

After Lady Joanna had left the cottage four days before, Agnes had told Lukas more about the upcoming tourney. At first he'd been puzzled by Lady Joanna's discomfort with the event, especially given his own experience with tournaments held at Launceston Castle. They were colorful, exciting occasions that those of all ages and walks of life enjoyed. But as Agnes had gone on to explain that there had been no such activity at Moreland since Lady Joanna's birth and that her first exposure to such an event would likely be her last as an unmarried woman, Lukas had begun to understand Lady Joanna's apprehension. And the more he thought on it, the more his own disquiet over the situation intensified.

The idea that any man would offer his only daughter as a tournament prize troubled Lukas greatly. He was fully aware that most noblemen and noblewomen entered into marriages arranged for the benefit of their respective families, but picturing Lady Joanna being forced to wed a nobleman whose only recommendation was that he could hit a target with an arrow filled Lukas with an almost irrational dread. He had associated with far too many noblemen who practiced long and well with their bows but whose characters left much to be desired. Despite their titles, such men had no morals and favored selfishness over honor and brutality over kindness.

Lukas flexed his hand, wishing not for his sword this time but for his bow. It was unlikely that he could save Lady Joanna from her father's decree, but he felt confident enough in his abilities as an archer that he could at least remove some of the less suitable contenders from the competition. He groaned. There had to be something he could do for the woman who had saved his life, but without his bow and with no money to acquire another, he was left with few possibilities.

His gaze followed the distant tree line as he tried to estimate where he had been on the path to the castle's north gate when he'd run into his attackers. That was another wrong he must right. He would do everything in his power to bring those men to justice, and if, as he now suspected, they had malicious intentions toward the people of Moreland, he would consider exposing their crimes as another way to repay Lady Joanna.

Viewing the drop from where he now stood was a reaffirmation that his survival was a miracle. He scoured the cliff face, wondering which of the many ledges was the one that had broken his fall. The limestone was pocked with crevices, niches, and sills. He guessed that one of them was the means by which Lady Joanna made her clandestine trips in and out of the castle, but Agnes had remained carefully vague in her description of his rescue and had offered few details of his journey from the cliff face to the cottage.

He shifted his leg, moving his weight from one foot to the other. His injured leg still ached, but thanks to Agnes's ministrations and his regular exercise, he had put aside Garrick's crutch two days before, and his leg was increasing in strength and flexibility every day. Agnes had insisted on keeping Lukas's ribs wrapped. His chest remained sore, but he continued to hope that his ribs were badly bruised rather than broken and that they would heal quickly.

Slip gave Lukas daily updates on the color of his forehead, but Lukas's headaches were lessening in intensity and duration, and even though his rainbow-hued skin had given the boy pleasure, the fact that he could now think more clearly was all that really mattered.

And he'd had plenty of time to think. Limited by his lack of mobility and the rain of the last few days, Lukas had spent hours in the cottage pondering all that had happened to him. As his health had improved, so too had his impatience to act upon the information and theories he had developed regarding his assailants. He sincerely hoped Sir Edwyn would return soon, but it wasn't until the third day had come and gone without an early-morning visitor that he reached the disconcerting realization that even though he *needed* to see Sir Edwyn, he *wanted* to see Lady Joanna even more.

"Sir Lukas!"

Lukas looked up to see Slip running toward him.

"Sir Edwyn is here," the boy cried. "He's waiting for you at the cottage."

Lukas's heartbeat quickened, and he found himself unexpectedly nervous. He had traveled almost three hundred miles to meet this man, but that did not guarantee that his arrival would be well received.

"Come quickly." Slip had now reached him and was pulling on Lukas's borrowed tunic. "He brought stuff."

"Stuff?"

"Yes." Slip's eyes were glittering with excitement. "A wooden chest and the biggest sack you've ever seen."

Despite Slip's urging, Lukas approached the cottage slowly. Garrick was nowhere to be seen. Slip had run ahead and was already standing beside a packhorse, eyeing its load speculatively. Agnes was waiting on the doorstep beside a man with short gray hair. The man was of average height and build, and he wore a crisp white undershirt beneath a dark-blue doublet with matching hose. A sword hanging from his belt appeared to be his only accessory.

When he spotted Lukas coming, he stood silently, his gaze unwavering. Lukas straightened his shoulders, grateful for the additional support of the bandages around his chest. Then, making an even greater effort to minimize his limp, he walked up to the waiting knight and offered a stiff bow. "Sir Edwyn," he said. "Thank you for being willing to meet with me." He raised his head in time to see the expression on the older man's face soften.

"Sir Lukas," Sir Edwyn said. "Your resemblance to your father is remarkable." He waved his hand toward the packhorse. "And as you will see, I have hoped this opportunity would be mine for a long time."

Still puzzled by what the packhorse's load could have to do with him, Lukas focused on the reason for his long journey to Moreland.

"My mother passed from this life less than two months ago," he said. "Only on her deathbed did she tell me of the part you played in ensuring that she and I did not suffer unduly following the death of my father. She told me that you facilitated our removal from Moreland at a time when her life was in jeopardy and that you personally wrote to Richard, the earl of Cornwall, to recommend that I be trained for knighthood at Launceston Castle." He paused. "A debt that great cannot be ignored, my lord."

"You owe me nothing," Sir Edwyn said. "Had your father lived through the battle that took his life, he would have been knighted for his valor. You would likely have followed in his footsteps and been trained for knighthood here at Moreland Castle. As it was, that possibility was stripped from you by an arrow intended for me and by a sword intended for a wolf. I merely did what I could to be sure that you were offered the opportunity you were born to. That is all I can claim. Whether or not you succeeded was out of my hands."

At Sir Edwyn's explanation, myriad emotions swirled through Lukas's heart and mind—gratitude, regret, curiosity, frustration, hope. They were all there, along with a burgeoning desire to learn from the man before him and to meet his expectations. Sir Edwyn could tell him of his father and of the stories from his past that his mother had never shared, but, before all that, he needed to discover what, if anything, Sir Edwyn had found out about the wool thieves and offer the little information he could add to help bring the right men to justice. Perhaps in this small way, he could begin to repay this noble knight.

"Come inside," Agnes said. "It's time Sir Lukas rested his leg."

Sir Edwyn raised an eyebrow. "I confess, after speaking with Lady Joanna this morning, I had not expected to see you walking so well."

"Agnes has taken excellent care of me," Lukas said.

"Of that I have no doubt," Sir Edwyn said.

Slip stayed outside with the horses, but Agnes led the way into the cottage. She took her place at the table and began chopping potatoes. Sir Edwyn claimed a seat and indicated that Lukas do the same. Lukas lowered himself carefully onto the wooden chair, grateful to stretch out his injured leg.

"Now then," Sir Edwyn said, "pray begin your tale. I am anxious to hear your version of what transpired on the cliff."

"It was evening when I arrived at Moreland," Lukas began. "I took the path through the woods from the town to the castle's north gate. Clouds covered the moon, making the woods very dark and still, so I heard the men's voices before I actually came upon them." He grimaced. "My horse alerted them to my presence, and once they had me in their sights, they lost no time in getting rid of me. After receiving a knife wound to the leg, I was knocked unconscious, stripped of my purse and my weapons, then dropped over the side of the cliff to die."

Sir Edwyn leaned forward. "Do you think they were waiting for you in particular or that you simply had the misfortune of being the next unsuspecting traveler to journey that way?"

Lukas met his eyes. "I've had several days to reflect on it, my lord," he said. "And I do not believe the men had planned to attack anyone that night."

Lukas could tell that he had Sir Edwyn's undivided attention. Even Agnes had stilled, her eyes on him, her chopping knife suspended above a small potato.

"Those who intend to waylay others lie silently in wait," Lukas said. "These men were not watching the road. They were talking, albeit quietly, and were removed enough from the path to be hidden from view." He paused. "They were in the woods for a secret meeting, and my unexpected appearance put them and their scheme at risk."

"So you had to be eliminated," Sir Edwyn said.

Lukas nodded.

"Do you have any indication of who they were or what they were meeting about?"

"I do not know their identities," Lukas said, "but I would recognize them if I were to meet them again." He met Sir Edwyn's penetrating look. "And I believe I know why they were met together."

He heard Agnes release a small gasp, and all at once, it felt like the very cottage was listening, waiting for him to say more.

"Are you familiar with the work of smugglers, my lord?" Lukas asked.

Sir Edwyn did little to hide his surprise at Lukas's question. "Enough to know that they keep the king's customs officials busy in Dover," he said.

"Dover is well-known for smugglers," Lukas agreed. "So too is Plymouth."

"An area you know well," Sir Edwyn said.

"Indeed," Lukas said. "And I've learned a few things from the Earl of Cornwall's run-ins with smugglers, and from conversations I've had with customs officials who oversee that portion of the coastline."

"Such as . . ." Sir Edwyn prompted.

"Smugglers work in gangs," Lukas said. "And each member of the gang is vital to its success. They need buyers and sellers—at least one contact man in France and another in England. They need men who are willing to cross the sea and load or unload cargo by night. But most of all, they need a strong leader. His motivation can range from greed to revenge to a desire for adventure, but he is almost always someone who already has enough money to fund the undertaking until illicit sales take over and who has a high enough social standing to believe himself above the law."

Sir Edwyn's eyes widened as understanding dawned. "A nobleman."

"There were four men in the woods outside Moreland Castle," Lukas said. "I heard each of them speak. Two were French, and two were English. The Frenchmen spoke the coarse language of seamen. At least one of the Englishmen was a nobleman."

"You are sure?"

"Completely. The Englishman whose dagger pierced my thigh wore apparel far finer than my own and had a command of the French language that could only be gained through a tutor."

"What of the other Englishman?"

"I believe I would know his voice if I heard it again," Lukas said. "But he remained in the shadows, and I did not see his face or his clothing clearly."

Sir Edwyn frowned. "So based on the fact that two of your attackers were French and one is likely a nobleman, you believe the men are smugglers?"

"I did not come to that conclusion immediately," Lukas said, acknowledging how unlikely it sounded when explained that way. "I arrived upon it only after Lady Joanna spoke of the disappearance of Moreland's wool."

Something flashed in Sir Edwyn's eyes. "What do you know of Moreland's missing wool?"

"When Lady Joanna was here, she expressed her concern that because bags of wool had disappeared from Moreland's shearing shed, the peasants were left with no way to pay the taxes due to Lord Gilbert."

"I spoke with Lady Joanna this morning," Sir Edwyn said. "Her belief in the peasants' innocence in this matter is equal to her father's belief in their guilt."

"She mentioned a band of thieves from Kent," Lukas said.

Sir Edwyn ran his hand across his face, and for the first time, Lukas recognized weariness there. "There had been some talk in the town of Moreland of men from Kent stealing wool from shearing sheds along the coast," he said. "I volunteered to ride as far as Dover to see if I could learn more. Although I stopped at several towns along the way, no one else had heard of these thieves."

"Has any other community lost wool?"

"Friar's Bank, a small village not five miles off Moreland's land, is missing eight bags. But that's the only other place I discovered."

"So it's possible that the whispers of wool thieves from Kent were started by someone wishing to draw people's attention away from the true perpetrators of the crime," Lukas said.

"So it appears," Sir Edwyn said with a sigh. "The question that remains, therefore, is whether it was started by peasants or someone else."

"Like smugglers," Agnes said.

Lukas had almost forgotten she was in the room.

"How likely is it that smugglers would target Moreland's wool?" Sir Edwyn asked.

Agnes shrugged, returning to her peeling. "All I know is that Moreland's sheep produce softer wool than the sheep down Wessex way."

"France has a reputation for fine fabric and clothing," Lukas said. "But they cannot maintain it unless they use the highest quality flax, silk, and wool. The best wool in Europe comes from England. Smugglers know it, and their buyers in France know it.

"According to the customs men in Plymouth, wool is the commodity most often smuggled out of this country."

"But Moreland has no port," Sir Edwyn said. "Not like Dover or Plymouth. That's one of the reasons the castle has never suffered a seaward attack."

"No one follows the cycle of the moon and the tides more faithfully than smugglers," Lukas said. "Their only requirement is a couple of hours on a narrow beach where a small vessel can be loaded or unloaded away from prying eyes."

"Sounds like Moreland to me," Agnes said. "And with all the caves in that limestone cliff, even their hiding places are taken care of."

Both men stared at her.

She raised her eyebrows as though daring them to contradict her. Neither of them did. With a small smile, she resumed her food preparation.

Chapter 10

AT SIR EDWYN'S REQUEST, GARRICK and Slip unloaded the pack-horse and hauled the wooden chest and the large sack into the cottage. They placed both items at the knight's feet before moving back a few paces and eyeing the containers expectantly from a distance.

"What's in that?" Garrick asked, pointing to the chest.

Sir Edwyn unhooked a ring of keys from his belt and flipped through them until he found the smallest one. He placed it in a tiny keyhole in the trunk's lid and turned it. The lock clicked. Sir Edwyn pulled on the lid, and with a protesting screech, the rusty hinges opened. For a moment, everyone was silent.

Sir Edwyn gazed into the trunk, then looked up at Lukas. "When your mother departed Moreland, she had only the clothes on her back and you," he said. "She left behind all her belongings—including things that had once been your father's. When I returned to Moreland Castle on that fateful day, I gathered what I could and locked them away with the hope that one day I would have the opportunity to return them to their rightful owner." He reached into the trunk and pulled out a sword. Laying it flat across his hands, he offered it to Lukas. "I know he would have wanted you to have this."

Lukas reached out and took the sword. Its balance was perfect. The blade was of finely worked steel, and the hilt was decorated with the etchings of a master craftsman.

"This was my father's?" The lump in his throat made it hard to speak.

"It was. He used it in his last battle, coming to my aid when I was outnumbered."

Slip inched closer, his eyes as big as saucers. "You kept his sword all this time?" he said.

"Aye," Sir Edwyn said with a sad smile. "It is good that it finally sees the light of day."

"I cannot thank you enough, my lord," Lukas said, finally finding his voice. "I am even more indebted to you now than I was before."

"You owe me nothing," Sir Edwyn repeated. He reached into the trunk again, this time retrieving a small dagger. He passed it to Lukas, who studied it, turning it slowly in his hands. His father had once held this very knife, had probably used it to cut meat or rope or leather. Had his fingers looked much like Lukas's as they grasped the handle?

"Is that a hauberk?" Slip asked. The boy was now kneeling at the side of the trunk, gazing at its contents. "And a saddle?"

"After all this time, they will likely need to be oiled," Sir Edwyn said, "but I seem to remember there was plenty of wear left in both." He reached into the trunk one more time and withdrew a coin purse. "This was the money your mother saved," he said.

Lukas shook his head. "No, my lord, that belongs to you. She told me how you provided her with coins when we fled, along with giving us your horse."

"That was all I could do at the time to return the debt I owed your father," Sir Edwyn said. "This is a completely separate matter. The money in that purse belonged to your parents. It now belongs to you." He glanced at Lukas's clothing and smothered a smile. "And unless I miss the mark, Garrick will be wanting his clothing returned, and you will need to purchase some of your own."

With a sinking heart, Lukas realized the truth of Sir Edwyn's words. His own purse had been stolen, and without it, he was penniless. Not only did he need clothing, but he also needed a horse. Reluctantly, he accepted the purse, its weight in his hand as heavy as the obligation he felt to the people in the room.

Looking pleased, Sir Edwyn reached for the large sack. "This would not fit in the trunk, but it was your father's prized possession."

"Even more than the sword?" Slip asked in amazement.

"Perhaps you will not see it so," Sir Edwyn said, "but even though Nicholas was a skilled swordsman, his greatest strength was with another weapon."

He untied the string around the neck of the sack and withdrew a longbow.

"It's a bow," Garrick said. But his excitement over recognizing the object quickly turned to disappointment when he noticed the shredded hemp hanging from one end. "It's broken."

"It will need to be restrung," Sir Edwyn said, "but the bow itself cannot be faulted."

Reverently, Lukas ran his fingers along the polished yew. The gentle curvature of the six-foot-long piece of wood was flawless, and despite the years that had gone by since it had last been used, the wood was supple and free of cracks or chips.

"You have treated the wood with beeswax," he said. "More than once, I wager."

Sir Edwyn inclined his head. "I could not let a bow of that caliber be neglected."

"I am most grateful," Lukas said, "for I have never seen its equal."

Sir Edwyn studied him, curiosity shining in his eyes. "Do you favor one weapon over another, Sir Lukas?"

Lukas smiled. "I am honored to own my father's sword, and I aim to wield it well, but I believe you have just uncovered another way my father and I are alike." He raised the longbow. "Using this will give me the greatest pleasure of all."

Sir Edwyn's smile matched Lukas's. "I am glad to hear it," he said.

"Do you shoot well, my lord?" Slip asked.

Lukas gave a modest shrug. "So I've been told."

"You should enter the archery contest," Agnes said.

"Aye," Slip said, jumping up with excitement. "You could use your father's bow."

Sir Edwyn looked at him with raised eyebrows. "The idea has some merit," he said. "I've been pondering the best way to get you into the castle without alerting one of your assailants to the fact that you survived the cliff drop. Perhaps if you arrive under the guise of a competitor at the tournament, your presence will go undetected long enough that we can learn who was behind the attack."

Hope surged through Lukas. After so many days of Lukas feeling helpless, Sir Edwyn was offering him a chance to act. With his father's equipment, his mother's money, and the older knight's support, he could finally start searching for the men who had left him to die. And if, as he suspected, that quest also led to the villains who had stolen Moreland's wool, so much the better.

He thought of the tournament and of what it meant to Lady Joanna, shaken to realize how protective he felt of her and how antagonistic he felt toward the other tourney contenders. He may not have regained his full strength yet, but he could not walk away from this. "I will compete," he said.

A wide smile cut across Garrick's face, and Slip gave a cheer.

With a pleased nod, Sir Edwyn rose to his feet. "I shall send a horse for you later today," he said. "It will be good to have you at the castle. Your insights into the challenges we are currently facing may prove invaluable." The corner of his mouth quirked into a half smile. "And I shall look forward to watching your skills with the longbow."

Lukas stood, carefully placing his weight on his good leg as he stepped forward to grasp Sir Edwyn's hand. Their firm clasp conveyed the trust already forming between them. Lukas felt no allegiance to Lord Gilbert, but he would do all in his power to lessen the burdens that had been placed on Lady Joanna and Sir Edwyn.

❧❦❧

Joanna stood in the shelter of the small copse of trees, looking out at the south pasture, her despondency completely at odds with the excitement emanating from the men within her sight. The town laborers had finished building the stands and were busily staking and embanking the area in front of them to create the lists. She could hear the men's voices as they called out to each other, and the multicolored flags already flying from the top of the stands added further to the construction site's festive air.

On the other side of the pasture, the knights were practicing again, but this time they were armed with longbows and were taking aim at targets set on the circular, turf-covered mounds already prepared for the archery competition. Cheers and jeers accompanied each shot, but Joanna was too far away to observe the archers' success, and she would not move closer.

Her decision to interrupt the knights during their swordplay earlier in the week had been a mistake. Ever since then, she'd been the object of curious looks and barely masked whispers among the knights and ladies in the castle, along with being the recipient of far too much attention from Sir Nigel. As grateful as she was for his friendship, she did not appreciate his assumption that she wished to sit next to him and share his trencher at every meal.

She could not deny that he was handsome. And his attention was flattering. She'd repeatedly caught the envious glances of the other ladies in the great hall when Sir Nigel would single her out. But when he leaned closer to whisper something in her ear, she instinctively backed away, and when he smiled at her across the room, panic welled within her. For the last couple of days, she'd taken her meals in her bedchamber simply to avoid the awkwardness.

Her ineptitude in socializing was obviously something her father had not considered when he'd planned his groom-finding tournament. If her discomfort around Sir Nigel was any indication, the tournament banquet would be torture for her and the archer who was unfortunate enough to win.

Joanna turned her back on the bustling scene below her. "If only noblemen were as easy to talk to as you, Cona," she said, patting her faithful wolfhound's head.

He gazed up at her, and Joanna was reminded of Grey's tired eyes and of the old dog's acceptance of Sir Lukas. She wondered if Sir Edwyn had been to visit him yet. She'd sought him out as soon as she had learned he'd arrived back at the castle. His lack of information about a band of thieves from Kent had been discouraging, but he'd listened intently to her account of Sir Lukas's run-in with the men on the cliff top and had promised to go to Agnes's cottage immediately after his morning meeting with Lord Gilbert.

Joanna wished she could have gone with him. It had been four days since she'd last seen Sir Lukas. Her thoughts had turned to him more often than she cared to admit, but the heavy rain and the increased number of servants preparing food for the tournament meant that escaping through the cellar off the kitchen was too risky. She could do nothing but wait and hope that Sir Edwyn returned to the castle with better news this time.

Chapter 11

THAT AFTERNOON, A CASTLE GROOM arrived at Agnes's cottage. He brought with him a brown horse and a small bundle of clothing. Sir Edwyn had taken the sack and trunk back with him on the packhorse, promising to deliver the longbow to Simon the bowyer to be restrung. He had also offered to find Lukas some clothing suitable for his arrival at the castle. Lukas had insisted that he take some coins for this purchase, and Sir Edwyn had obviously put the money to good use. The bundle contained a white undershirt, a maroon doublet with black and silver edging, black hose, a belt, a fur-lined cape, and soft leather shoes.

As soon as the groom left, Agnes set Garrick and Slip to work filling a tub full of water so Lukas could bathe and shave the beard that had developed over the last six days. When Lukas had finished washing, Agnes returned to the cottage to check his injuries. She carefully replaced the bandages around his bruised rib cage and checked the wound on his thigh. Both areas showed definite signs of improvement, but she pursed her lips at the lingering redness around some of his stitches.

"Come back in a week, and I'll take the stitches out," she said. "In the meantime, you must keep the wound clean and apply this liniment every day." She handed Lukas a jar.

The odor was so strong it reached him through the closed lid. He wrinkled his nose. "Ugh!"

"The worse it smells, the better it works," she said.

He raised his eyebrow skeptically, and she tried to hide her smile. "Well, it helps to think so anyway," she said.

Lukas chuckled. "You have been very good to me, Agnes. I will not forget it."

"I am glad to have been of service, my lord," she said. She paused, her hands stilling as she lowered the cloth bandages she'd been rolling. "But if I may, I would ask one thing of you before you leave."

"Of course."

"While you are at the castle, watch over Lady Joanna."

Lukas felt his muscles tense. "You believe her in danger?"

"Not from this type of attack," she said, pointing to his bruised chest. "But her father has allowed bitterness to chip away at his heart for so long he has forgotten what it is to feel kindness or compassion."

"Can she can get no comfort from her mother?"

The look on Agnes's face immediately told him he'd taken a serious misstep.

"Lady Anabel died at Lady Joanna's birth," she said. "Did your mother not tell you?"

Cursing himself for not making a greater effort to learn more about the residents of Moreland Castle, Lukas shook his head. "I was sent to live at Launceston Castle to train as a page at age seven; I rarely saw my mother afterward. I'd been told that my father had served and died at Moreland, but that was all I knew until I was summoned to my mother's deathbed. Only then did she tell me that it was Sir Edwyn who had helped her return to her family in Cornwall and who had secured my position with the Earl of Cornwall."

Agnes stared at him for a few seconds, then turned to face the fire, her countenance troubled. "Her death changed everything," she said, her voice barely above a whisper.

"Lady Anabel's?" he asked.

She nodded, and he waited, praying she would trust him with the information she held.

"Will you tell me what happened?"

Agnes took a deep breath, as though she were about to face something difficult. "I will," she said. "It is never mentioned in Moreland, but before you enter the castle, you need to know."

She started rolling the bandages again, her fingers not as sure as they had been moments before.

"Lady Anabel was well liked by all at the castle—from the nobility to the lowliest servant. She had a kind word for everyone and stayed cheerful even through the last days of her confinement.

"When her pains started, everything happened fast. Too fast. And even though the baby was delivered safely, Lady Anabel's bleeding would not stop."

Agnes paused, obviously reliving the harrowing scene in Lady Anabel's bedchamber. "I tried everything," she said softly. "But nothing helped, and within an hour, she was gone."

Lukas sat very still. Agnes had been the midwife when Lady Anabel had died. No wonder this memory was so difficult to recount.

"Lord Gilbert was beside himself with grief," she continued. "Those who were with Lady Anabel at the delivery were blamed for her death. Her lady's maids were all dismissed, and those living in the castle were forbidden to mention her name."

"Did he send you away too?" Lukas asked, already having guessed the answer to his question.

"I was told to never set foot in the castle again." There was no bitterness in her voice, only acceptance.

"I am sorry you were treated in such a way."

She shrugged. "I have made a good home for myself here at the cottage. The local people still come to me for remedies, and I do what I can for them. But I have never been back to the castle. Beatrice is the healer there now."

"So even now Lord Gilbert holds on to his grudges?"

"Perhaps he would not have continued to harbor those feelings if another tragedy had not struck so soon after his wife's death." Agnes looked at him pointedly.

"There was a second tragedy?"

"Of course," Agnes said. "The one that involved your mother."

"My mother?" Lukas's voice reflected his shock.

"Did she not tell you of the circumstances surrounding her hasty departure from Moreland?"

With mounting apprehension, Lukas shook his head. "By the time I reached her bedside, she was very weak. Every word she spoke took effort." The image of his mother's pale, pain-filled face filled his mind, and his voice dropped. "She did not have the strength to share any details, but she was determined that I be made aware of Sir Edwyn's hand in our lives. She died moments after telling me his name." He paused. "I wish I'd had more time with her. I know almost nothing of her life in Moreland."

With a look of fresh understanding, Agnes gave a slow nod. "Then I will share what I know."

She began by telling him of his mother's appointment as Lady Joanna's nursemaid soon after his father's death, then she told of the ill-fated hunting party at Langston Forest, of the wolf's attack, and of Gelert's death at the hands of Lord Gilbert just before the baby was found unharmed.

"So Lord Gilbert discovered his mistake immediately," Lukas said.

Agnes sighed. "When his wife died, he lost his faith in God; when Gelert died, he lost his faith in himself. He made a fatal error in judgment and has been haunted by it ever since." She placed the roll of bandages on the table and reached for some bottles on the shelf above. "It is said that Lord Gilbert has not smiled since that day."

"What happened to my mother?" Lukas asked.

"No one knew," Agnes said. "She never returned to the hunting lodge. Some said that her guilt for having left Lady Joanna unattended caused her to flee. Others said that she disappeared out of fear of Lord Gilbert's vengeful punishment. Only today did I learn the truth—that Sir Edwyn helped you and your mother escape Lord Gilbert's retribution." She gave a sad smile. "He kept the secret well."

"He would undoubtedly have been punished if Lord Gilbert had discovered that his own knight had aided her," Lukas said.

"Perhaps," Agnes said. "Although Sir Edwyn has been loyal to Lord Gilbert for many years. He has learned to walk the fine line between his devotion to his lordship and his commitment to upholding what he believes to be right."

"Is that why Lady Joanna turns to him?" Lukas asked.

"Indeed. In many respects, he has been more of a father to her than Lord Gilbert has been. He is one of the few who recognizes her difficult position and shows her kindness." She frowned. "Perhaps Lord Gilbert believed that in saving Lady Joanna's life, Gelert accomplished more than he, the guard, or any other person could have done. Or maybe, since Gelert died at his own hand, he trusted the wolfhound more than he trusted himself. Whatever the reason, he decreed that his daughter was to always be under the watchful care of a wolfhound, and he distanced himself from her.

"As time has gone by, Lady Joanna has become more and more isolated. The only people she can confide in are her lady's maid, Eva, and Sir Edwyn. Eva is loyal but is limited in the support that she can offer by her status as a servant. Sir Edwyn, too, must balance his concern for Lady Joanna with his allegiance to Lord Gilbert."

Agnes turned from her work at the table and faced Lukas again. "And so that is why I ask you to safeguard Lady Joanna," she said. "She is as good and kind as her mother, but she has had little experience outside her restricted world and will have to stand alone as she faces men who may believe her to be nothing more than a decorative trophy in a tournament that could grant them land and wealth."

Frustration that Lady Joanna had been placed in such an untenable situation vied with fury that any nobleman would even consider treating her poorly. Lukas rose to his feet. Ignoring the pain it caused his rib cage, he put on his new doublet and reached for his belt. It was time he left. Up until an hour ago, he'd thought that seeing Lady Joanna again would be a side benefit to his hunt for the men who had wronged him. Now, being with her was a priority.

Chapter 12

Lᴜᴋᴀѕ ʀᴏᴅᴇ ᴛʜᴇ ᴡɪɴᴅɪɴɢ ʀᴏᴀᴅ that cut through the town of Moreland and led to the castle's main gate. Stone buildings with thatched roofs lined the street, and a larger building that looked to be the town hall stood on the other side of a smallish town square. A few people were crossing the square, obviously intent on their business. Others were gathered near the well, perhaps catching up on gossip and the latest town news.

As Lukas approached the gate, a guard stepped out to greet him.

"State your name and business at Moreland Castle," the man said.

"Sir Lukas of Cornwall," Lukas replied. "I'm here to compete in the archery tournament."

The guard eyed Lukas and his borrowed mount warily, but he must not have recognized the horse as one belonging to the castle stable because after a few moments, he waved him through.

"Guests are staying in the west tower," he said. "You can stable your horse over there to the left."

"I thank you," Lukas said, urging his horse through the tall stone archway and into the outer bailey.

Men and women were coming and going from the various businesses lining the castle wall. The pungent smell of the alehouse mingled with the aroma of freshly baked bread coming from the clay ovens nearby. To his right, a woman was arguing with a cobbler over the quality of a pair of shoes. A little farther down, four guardsmen left their barracks and started toward the inner bailey. And in the distance, he heard the faint sound of plainchant coming from the church.

Despite the congestion, Lukas relaxed his hold on the reins. The horse knew exactly where he was headed, and once he was within sight of the stable, he quickened his step until he came to a stop just outside the open wooden doors, where he gave a pleased snort. Within seconds, a man exited the stable and reached for the horse's reins. He was dressed in the coarse clothes of a servant but had the bearing of one who held some authority.

"I hope Teak served you well, my lord," he said, giving the horse an affectionate pat.

Not wanting to make it obvious that his leg was injured, Lukas dismounted carefully. "He was an excellent mount," he said. "I am most obliged."

The man gave a pleased nod. "Never have had any trouble with this one." He moved to lead the horse into the stable. "The name's Timothy, my lord. I'm the stable master here at Moreland. Let me know if I can be of service to you again."

Lukas's frustration over losing his charger, Shadow, surfaced once more. Not only would he be hard-pressed to find Shadow's equal in terms of reliability and training, but he had also lost a faithful companion. "I could use your assistance," he said.

Timothy gave a slight nod. "Of course, my lord."

"I am in need of a horse," Lukas explained. "As stable master at Moreland, you are undoubtedly an excellent judge of horseflesh. Perhaps you'd be good enough to let me know if you hear of something suitable."

"What did you have in mind, my lord?"

"My last horse was a black charger," Lukas said. "Although I daresay it will be difficult to find another mount with his same strength and stature."

"Aye, a good charger is hard to replace." Timothy scratched his head. "Lord Gilbert's charger is a fine animal. And we have a few others stabled here with that same noble bearing. But I have to say, I don't see them as often as I'd like."

"Are any of them for sale?" Lukas asked.

"That I can't tell you, my lord," the stable master said. "Most of them belong to knights who've come in for the tournament."

Lukas was suddenly curious. "May I see them?"

"Of course, my lord," Timothy said. "I'll have one of the stable hands give Teak a brush down, and you can follow me."

Lukas trailed Timothy into the stable's gloomy interior. The sound of shuffling hooves and soft nickering echoed through the spacious building. The stable master handed Teak off to a young boy, then led the way down the narrow aisle that ran between two long rows of stalls.

"This here's Lord Gilbert's horse," Timothy said, stopping at a stall containing a chestnut charger with broad shoulders and intelligent eyes.

"An exceptional animal," Lukas said, studying the horse with appreciation.

"Indeed. And here's another one."

He turned to the next stall, where a black charger stood watching the men. The horse gave a snort and shook its head. Lukas's breath caught, and he took a step closer.

"Shadow?"

The horse leaned over the wooden gate and nuzzled Lukas's outstretched hand.

"Do you know this horse, my lord?"

"I do, indeed," Lukas said, a steely tone entering his voice as he considered his assailants' audacity. "This is my horse. It was stolen from me less than a week ago."

A look of alarm crossed Timothy's face. Horse stealing was a serious matter, often punishable by death.

"Can you prove your claim, my lord?"

"I have not seen more than this horse's head and shoulders," Lukas said, "but I can tell you that there is a white patch above his right front hoof. It's the only marking he has."

Timothy shook his head. "This horse has not been ridden since he arrived, but the stable boys have walked him each morning. I've seen him in the outer bailey. Every one of his legs is black." He looked distinctly uncomfortable. "Is it possible you are mistaken, my lord?"

"No." Lukas knew his horse as well as he knew his fellow knights at Launceston Castle. "Open the stall, if you will."

Timothy unlatched the wooden gate and stood back as Lukas entered the small enclosure. Giving no heed to the dirty straw on the floor, Lukas knelt on one knee, grasped the horse's completely black front leg and ran his hand along its length. When this was done, he raised his arm slightly so he could study his hand in the stable's dim light.

"Join me, Timothy," he said, sliding to one side so the stable master could kneel beside him.

"Take his leg," Lukas said. "Touch the hair above his hoof. Then consider the state of your fingers."

Silently, Timothy reached for the horse's powerful leg and ran a work-worn hand between the knee and the hoof. Moments later, he too raised his hand to look at it. "Charcoal," Timothy said in disgust. "The horse's leg is covered in charcoal."

"Indeed," Lukas said. "And I believe that if one of your stable boys were to take a wet rag to it, he would find that the charcoal hides a white patch."

Timothy rubbed his blackened hand across his tunic, following Lukas as he rose to his feet. "What would you have me do, my lord?"

Lukas patted Shadow's neck, contemplating his options. As much as he wanted to reclaim his horse and ride it freely, he knew his best chance of identifying his assailants and bringing them to justice lay in using Shadow as bait. Could he trust Timothy—a man he barely knew—to be his eyes and ears at the stable? If the stable master didn't keep Lukas's confidence, Lukas ran the risk of losing his charger a second time, along with alerting the men who had attacked him of his survival.

Timothy looked at him, an indignant frown now lining his forehead. "Horse thieves have no place in my stables," he said. "I'm as anxious as you are to have them answer for their crimes, my lord."

Lukas nodded, his decision made. "I would be grateful to have your assistance. But if we are to succeed, it will require complete secrecy. No one must know that I am Shadow's true owner or that I am aware of his presence here."

"I understand," Timothy said. "You can rely on me, my lord."

Lukas offered him his hand to seal their agreement. Surprise lit Timothy's eyes, and Lukas wondered if the knights of Moreland adhered to the rules of social standing more rigidly than he did.

"Sir Lukas of Cornwall," he said. "And I thank you."

Timothy gave a lopsided grin and grasped Lukas's hand to shake it. "You're welcome, my lord."

"Do you know who brought the horse in?"

Timothy shook his head. "He arrived late at night. One of the stable boys took care of him."

"Can you find out?"

"Right away."

Timothy stepped out of the stall and walked a little closer to the main doors. A young boy was sweeping the floor, the broom taller than he was. "Peter," Timothy called. "I'd like a word."

The boy's bowed head popped up, and he quickly set the broom against the wall before hurrying down the aisle toward them. He came to a halt in front of the two men, his hands clenched anxiously at his side. "You wanted to speak to me, Master Timothy?"

"Peter, this is Sir Lukas," Timothy said. "He's taken a liking to this black charger and is interested in talking to its owner. Can you tell me who brought the horse in?"

Mentally applauding Timothy's approach with the anxious stable boy, Lukas awaited Peter's response with bated breath.

"It was Sir William who brought 'im 'ere," Peter said. "But 'e told me someone else asked 'im to take care of it."

Lukas tried to tamp down his frustration. This was not the clear-cut answer he'd hoped for.

"Did he tell you anything more?" Timothy pressed.

"No, sir." Peter's nervousness had returned. "Alls 'e said was that someone had asked 'im to stable the horse and that 'e wasn't sure 'ow long 'e'd be here. There was no special instructions, 'cos I always listen for those."

Lukas reached into the purse hanging from his belt and took out a small coin. He handed it to the startled stable boy, who looked at the gleaming coin in wonder. "That's for taking such good care of the charger," he said. "And when you hear from the owner or receive more instructions from Sir William regarding the horse, there'll be another coin for coming to tell me about it."

"Yes, my lord," Peter said, his face shining as brightly as the coin he clutched in his fist.

Timothy placed an encouraging hand on the boy's shoulder. "Good lad. Now off to work with you."

Peter ran back to the broom and was sweeping with a newfound vigor in a matter of seconds.

"Sir William is a knight at Moreland, I assume?" Lukas said.

Timothy's expression was troubled. "Aye. He's been in Lord Gilbert's service for many years."

"You will need to be on your guard when someone comes to the stable for Shadow," Lukas said. "No matter how familiar he may be, I expect you to get word to me immediately."

"Yes, my lord," Timothy said.

Lukas gave a crisp nod. "We shall discover who is behind this, Timothy. And ensure that it never happens again."

Chapter 13

LUKAS ARRIVED AT THE GREAT hall early so he could choose his seat carefully. He wanted a good view of the head table, but he was also eager for his first look at the noblemen who'd come to Moreland for the tournament. He'd not yet seen anyone he recognized, but that didn't surprise him. He was a long way from Cornwall.

He spotted the brown-haired young man standing beside one of the far tables as soon as he entered the great hall. The man's relaxed stance suggested that he was in a familiar environment, and when he called out a greeting to another nobleman, Lukas felt fairly sure he'd identified one of Moreland's knights. He stepped forward to introduce himself. "Sir Lukas of Cornwall," he said with a small bow.

"Welcome," the man said with an answering bow. "Sir Ivan of Moreland. You are a long way from home. Have you come so far to compete in the archery tournament?"

"Aye," Lukas said. "I arrived at the castle only today."

"Ah," Sir Ivan said, a knowing look crossing his face. "And you are anxious to speak with someone who has lived here somewhat longer."

Lukas chuckled. "You are most astute, Sir Ivan."

With a grin, Sir Ivan pointed to the bench. "Shall we sit? I may not have answers for all your questions, but I am willing to entertain them."

Grateful to be off his aching leg, Lukas eased himself onto the bench. Already the great hall was filling up, and spaces on the benches were disappearing quickly.

"How many noblemen have come for the tournament?" Lukas asked.

"Alas, it seems that I am to fail you immediately," Sir Ivan said ruefully. He looked around the room. "I cannot give you a number, but I can tell you that I recognize only half the people currently in the great hall."

Lukas did a rough head count and guessed that there were between twenty and thirty people who were strangers to Moreland. That constituted a significant gathering of knights, and any number of them could be excellent archers. He flexed his fingers. It had been a couple of weeks since he'd practiced target shooting—and the next time would be with an unfamiliar longbow.

Not wanting to dwell on his disadvantages, Lukas turned his attention to the head table. Sir Edwyn was already seated next to a silver-haired man whose commanding presence identified him at once.

"That is Lord Gilbert, I assume," he said.

Sir Ivan nodded. "Aye. And Sir Edwyn beside him."

Lukas studied the man Agnes had told him about. Despite his age, his broad shoulders still spoke of strength, and his blue eyes—so like his daughter's—were alert as he watched eight men take their places at the head table.

"Who are the men he has with him?"

"His most trusted knights," Sir Ivan said. "Sir Edwyn has been with him the longest, and Sir Thomas, Sir William, Sir Guy, and Sir Robert have been at Moreland almost as long. Sir Nigel is the youngest one up there. He took over his father's position as Lord Gilbert's advisor. Then there's the steward, Gerard Bartholomew, and the priest, Father Jerome."

Lukas focused on Sir William. His brown hair was streaked with gray, and although he had undoubtedly been a strong young knight, the weight that had once resided across his shoulders and chest had sagged to his girth. His ruddy complexion seemed to suggest that he spent considerable time outdoors or in his cups. Since he was already holding his empty goblet, Lukas supposed the latter was the best guess.

"Who will sit to Lord Gilbert's right?" Lukas asked after all the men had taken their seats and an empty spot remained between Lord Gilbert and Sir Nigel.

"That is Lady Joanna's place," Sir Ivan said.

Lukas's heart rate quickened. "Is she expected tonight?"

Sir Ivan shrugged. "She eats with us on occasion, but I have not seen her for several days."

"Do you know her well?"

Sir Ivan snorted. "No one knows her well." He inclined his head, as if about to impart a secret. "Lady Joanna is the jewel of Moreland Castle—stunningly beautiful but completely out of reach."

"Out of reach?"

Sir Ivan leaned back. "As soon as you see her wolfhound, you'll understand," he said. "Her lady's maid, Eva, and Sir Edwyn are the only ones allowed anywhere near her." He looked thoughtful. "Although, recently, she seems to have added Sir Nigel to that short list."

"That may make things difficult for the winner of the archery competition," Lukas said.

"Indeed." Sir Ivan raised one eyebrow as he fought back a smile. "And now you know why I am not entering the tournament. I value my limbs too much to offer them up as dog food."

Lukas chuckled again. He found himself liking Sir Ivan. It would be good to have a friend in this castle full of strangers.

❦

Joanna stood, leaning against her bedchamber wall, the sounds of men's voices and laughter from the great hall reaching her through the heavy wooden door. She felt nauseated. Everyone was gathering for the evening meal, and she was expected to sit at the head table beside Lord Gilbert. She'd avoided the increasingly large crowd in the great hall for the last few meals, but her father had noticed her absence and had not been pleased. This afternoon, he had sent word insisting upon her presence.

"It's time, my lady." Eva's voice was quiet but firm.

"No," Joanna said miserably. "It's *past* time. And I'm dreading opening that door as much now as I was half an hour ago."

Eva gave her a sympathetic smile. "Be brave, my lady. It may not be as bad as you think."

Bravery. What did she know of bravery? She was no knight trained to battle fierce opponents. But if she was honest with herself, neither were some of the bravest people she knew. Margery's young sons were guarding the shearing shed from thieves who were likely armed. Garrick had stumbled down the steep mountainside with Sir Lukas on his shoulder without complaint. Agnes had made a new, worthwhile life for herself after being banished from the castle. And Slip had overcome enormous challenges every day while living on the streets of Moreland.

Each one had experienced fear, but they'd challenged it with courage. Surely she was being asked to do no more than they'd already done.

"The moment I enter," Joanna said, "I'll likely trip and fall on my rear or forget the names of all the knights I've known since birth or be unable to speak a coherent sentence or . . ."

"Or have every nobleman in the room fall in love with you before you take your seat," Eva finished for her.

"Eva, you are ridiculous."

Her lady's maid laughed. "My suggestion is far more likely than any of yours, my lady."

Joanna rolled her eyes. Eva's words did nothing to calm her nerves. She was quite sure the men on the other side of the door expected far more of her than she could give. Meeting one suitor at a time would have been bad enough; facing them en masse was terrifying. She knew of nothing she could say that would be of interest to any of them. She had no hidden talent to share. Not even a talent for bravery. Perhaps pretending to have the courage she lacked would be enough. She thought of Margery and her family, of Agnes, Garrick, and Slip, and she squared her shoulders. She would face her fears as they had. "Come, Cona."

The wolfhound moved to stand at her side, and Eva gave her an encouraging nod.

"All will be well," Eva said, but the words sounded more hopeful than sure.

Joanna took a deep breath, and before she could talk herself out of it again, she took hold of the brass ring and pulled the door open.

As she entered the great hall, the men's voices dropped, and a hush fell upon the room. Joanna sensed the stares but kept her own eyes focused on the head table, where her father sat watching her approach. He rose to his feet, and everyone in the room did the same.

"You are late," he said.

"I apologize," Joanna replied. "I did not realize you were waiting for me."

Lord Gilbert clapped his hands, and immediately a small army of servants ran in carrying platters of roast pheasant, duck, and venison, bowls of crusty bread, and flagons of ale. He and Joanna took their seats, followed by everyone else in the room, and as trenchers and goblets were filled, the sounds of talking and laughter gradually resumed.

Joanna found herself positioned between her father and Sir Nigel, and she wasn't sure which made her more uncomfortable. Her father had not said a word to her after his reprimand over her late arrival; Sir Nigel had not stopped talking since she'd sat down. She reached for some bread, tore a small portion off, put it in her mouth, and forced herself to chew. It was as tasteless as wood shavings, but at least a mouthful of food excused her from responding to Sir Nigel's flood of conversation. And when she realized that a smile or a nod following each of his monologues seemed to be all that was required of her, she took the opportunity to surreptitiously survey the crowded room.

Lord Gilbert's senior knights and advisors occupied the head table. She recognized them all. Sir Edwyn sat at her father's left, and beyond him, Sir William, Sir Thomas, and Father Jerome. On the other side of Sir Nigel were Sir Robert, Sir Guy, and Gerard Bartholomew.

Perpendicular to the head table, more long tables had been positioned end to end, creating a large U shape around the central fireplace. She glanced at the occupants of these tables. There were a few token noblewomen among the guests. Their fine dresses and elaborate headpieces stood out, even among the richly colored tunics and doublets of the many noblemen in the room. Some of Moreland's younger knights also occupied these tables, along with a number of castle clerics, but the majority of the men in front of her were strangers.

With difficulty, Joanna swallowed the bread in her mouth and reached for her goblet. Over the rim of her cup, she studied the newcomers. The men ranged in age from those who appeared as old as Lord Gilbert to those who looked too young to have been knighted. Most of them were talking animatedly with their neighbors, a few had eyes only for their food, and others were silently watching those around them as though still assessing the castle's occupants and sizing up their competition.

"Quite a sight, isn't it?"

With a start, Joanna realized Sir Nigel had finished his speech on the virtues of using goose feathers over turkey feathers for arrow fletchings and had asked her a question. She lowered her goblet. "I have never seen the great hall so full," she said.

"By the guards' latest tally, twenty-two noblemen have arrived to participate in the archery tournament. More may come tomorrow, but with the competition beginning the day after that, they would be left with little time to practice."

"Have you watched any of them at the training butts?"

"A few." He raised his goblet, took a big gulp of ale, then lowered his cup to the table again. He leaned closer, and Joanna tried not to squirm. "That knight over there with the red hair"—he pointed at a tall, gangly young man in the corner—"couldn't steady his bow long enough to take aim." With a jerk of his head, he indicated another man at the same table, this one portly and balding. "And I'm quite certain that one can't see the target. Not a single one of his arrows hit the butt." He gave a satisfied smile. "I believe Moreland's knights will make a good showing in two days' time."

It seemed to Joanna that she should feel some measure of relief at hearing that the tournament winner would likely be a knight she knew well rather than a stranger, but the pit in her stomach remained. "That will please Lord Gilbert," Joanna said.

Sir Nigel gave her a winning smile. "I hope it pleases you too, my lady."

"Of course," she said, looking away to hide her growing discomfort.

On the far side of the great hall, a dark-haired knight in a maroon tunic was talking to Sir Ivan, one of Moreland's most recently dubbed knights. As though sensing her gaze, he paused his conversation and turned to face her. Joanna's breath caught in her throat. He was clean-shaven and dressed as a nobleman. His dark hair was brushed forward to cover the fading bruise on his forehead, and he was sitting in the castle's great hall rather than lying in Agnes's tiny cottage. But she knew him. Even from this distance, his brown eyes were unmistakable.

How had he come to be in the castle? Were his wounds truly so well healed that he had made the journey from the cottage unaided? She glanced at Sir Edwyn. Had it only been earlier this morning that she'd approached him about Sir Lukas? Could he have orchestrated his relocation so fast?

Sir Edwyn was listening to Lord Gilbert's update from the guards at the shearing shed. His brow was furrowed in concentration, and as much as she wanted to interrupt, he would not wish to answer her questions now. She looked back at Sir Lukas. His eyes met hers, and he gave a subtle nod. Warmth filled her. Without a word being said, he had understood. And in one small gesture, he'd told her what she wanted to know: Sir Lukas had Sir Edwyn's support.

Chapter 14

LUKAS WASN'T SURE WHAT WAS wrong with him. He couldn't focus on anything Sir Ivan was telling him, even though it was information that could be vital to the search for his assailants. And at a time when he should be scouring the room for anyone who might remotely resemble one of his attackers, his eyes kept wandering back to Lady Joanna.

When she'd first walked into the great hall, her natural beauty and elegance had quite simply taken his breath away. She was wearing a dark-blue silk dress with silver trim at the ends of the long sleeves, neckline, and hem. A narrow silver girdle emphasized her tiny waist, and her golden hair was loose, falling halfway down her back in gentle waves.

He'd tried telling himself that he was reacting this way because he'd only ever seen her in peasant clothing with her hair pulled back in a single braid. But deep down he knew he was responding to far more than that. He may have spoken to her for only a few minutes at Agnes's cottage, but during that short time, she'd been completely herself—unfettered by protocol or expectation—and he'd been given a glimpse of her kindness and her vulnerability.

The unhappiness in her face as she'd approached the head table had made his chest ache. Knowing that her quiet reserve and innate goodness were going unrecognized and unappreciated only increased his frustration over Lord Gilbert's coldness toward his daughter. And watching Sir Nigel inch closer and closer to her made him want the wolfhound at her feet to rise to its full height and position itself squarely between the two of them, preferably with its teeth bared.

The moment she'd spotted him across the room had been the highlight of his evening. He'd seen her eyes widen with recognition, and when he'd nodded in affirmation of her unspoken question about Sir Edwyn, she'd given her first genuine smile of the night. Was it wrong that he'd been happy that her smile had been directed toward him, not Sir Nigel? Lukas stifled a groan at his own fatuity.

"Is something wrong?" Sir Ivan asked.

"I apologize," Lukas said. His groan had obviously not been stifled well enough. "Tiredness is getting the better of me."

Sir Ivan nodded. "A long journey will do that."

Lukas didn't bother to clarify that his exhaustion was due more to physical injury and emotional turmoil than to an extended horse ride. He glanced at the two musicians who'd been entertaining the guests for the last hour. They were putting away their viol and lute. "Perhaps others are ready to retire also," he said.

"So it appears," Sir Ivan said, rising to his feet. "Lord Gilbert and his party are leaving."

Lukas stood, grateful that the pain in his leg was continuing to improve. Mobility would be vital in the next few days.

As Lord Gilbert exited the great hall, followed by most of his knights, Lukas kept his eyes trained on Sir William. The knight exchanged a few words with Sir Thomas and Father Jerome, then stopped beside a young squire, who handed him a sword and belt. Sir William quickly exchanged them for the more decorative belt he'd been wearing over his green tunic.

"Is Sir William planning to practice his swordplay this late at night?" Lukas said, inclining his head in the direction of the knight and his squire.

Sir Ivan looked that way and frowned. "That's hard to believe. He's more than happy to skip his turn with the pells during our scheduled practice time. And it's dark outside."

Lukas glanced at Sir Ivan, one eyebrow raised. "Are you curious?"

Sir Ivan grinned. "Exceedingly."

With his sword in place, Sir William started toward the door, and the two men cut across the room to follow him outside. Just before he reached the exit, Lukas turned back, his eyes seeking and finding Lady Joanna. She was leaving the head table, her hand on Sir Nigel's arm and her wolfhound at her side. He wished that he could stay to exchange a few words with her, but for now, discovering what Sir William was about had to take precedence.

Sir William took the stairs out of the keep and walked briskly through the inner bailey until he reached the arched entrance to the outer bailey. Here he paused, looking left and right before continuing toward the stables. Sir Ivan and Lukas stayed several yards behind, the moonlight allowing them to keep him in sight.

When Sir William reached the main stable doors, his steps slowed, and Lukas experienced a moment of panic. If Sir William took a horse, they would lose him. Even if Sir Ivan had a mount, it would take too much time to convince a stable boy to hand over one of the castle's horses to a stranger. He was frantically thinking through his options when, instead of entering the stable, Sir William stopped beside the mounting block, bent over, and pulled something out from behind the wooden structure.

"What do you think that is?" Lukas whispered.

From their position at the outer bailey's entrance, Sir Ivan peered at the dark shadow in Sir William's hand. "It looks like a rag or a sack."

They watched as Sir William rolled the fabric into a tight wad and tucked it under his arm.

"Well, whatever it is," Lukas said, "there doesn't appear to be anything in it."

Sir William set off again, this time heading away from the castle's main gate. He walked past the castle garden, the brewhouse, the garrison, and the west tower before veering left toward the castle's outer wall.

"He's making for the north gate," Sir Ivan said quietly.

Lukas nodded. It made sense. When he'd arrived in Moreland, he'd been told that the north gate was the only possible entry to the castle at night. It would be Sir William's way in and out too.

"We must move closer," Lukas said. "He will be harder to follow once we're outside the castle."

Both men quickened their pace. Up ahead, Sir William kept walking. He gave a token wave to the guard and passed through the gate unimpeded.

"It appears the guard is familiar with Sir William's comings and goings," Sir Ivan said.

"Aye. But he may not take kindly to us passing through without good cause."

Sir Ivan's teeth gleamed in the moonlight. "I believe I can take care of that."

He stepped up to the guard with Lukas right behind him. "We need to reach Sir William," he told the startled man. "Did he pass this way?"

"Why, yes, my lord. Only minutes ago."

"Excellent," Sir Ivan said. He turned to Lukas. "Come. If we are fast, we may yet catch him."

"He took the woodland path," the guard said, pointing into the darkness.

"I thank you," Sir Ivan said. "Your help has been invaluable."

Then both men hurried away.

"That was masterfully done," Lukas said softly. "Have you tried this before, by any chance?"

"Ah, the stories I could tell of trailing my older brothers," Sir Ivan said with a quiet laugh. "By age thirteen, I had perfected hiding in shadows and getting in and out of anywhere. And as suspicious as they were of my antics, neither one of them ever caught me. Not once."

Lukas grinned. "I chose the right man as my companion tonight, then."

"I haven't enjoyed an evening this much since I followed my oldest brother to the castle garden and caught him kissing his intended in the moonlight." He stopped abruptly and pointed to a narrow path that cut through the trees. "Sir William must have gone that way, but it will be much darker once we're in the trees, and it will be harder to travel silently."

"We shall have to hope that the noise he makes covers our own," Lukas said, remembering too well what the sound of a cracking stick had cost him a week ago.

Once their eyes had adjusted to the filtered moonlight, it ended up being fairly easy to follow Sir William's trail because he seemed to be making no effort to hide his presence. His heavy, regular footsteps told them he was still moving forward, and his muttered oaths warned them of obstacles up ahead. Only when those noises suddenly stopped did Lukas and Sir Ivan slow their own steps and proceed more cautiously.

"Look. There," Sir Ivan whispered, pointing to a spot where the path forked.

They moved into the undergrowth and crouched behind a wide oak tree. Sir William was bent over, brushing leaves off a flat rock. With a loud grunt, he pushed the rock aside and lowered his hand into a hollow beneath. Something clinked, and he uttered a curse. With an impatient shove, he slid the rock back into place and got to his feet.

"Blasted Frenchies!" he growled. "Full moon, they said." He jerked his head toward the silver light shining above. "It doesn't get more full than that!" With a grunt of disgust, he brushed his hands off on his hose and picked up the fabric he'd set on the ground. It looked to be a smallish sack. And it was still empty. He wadded it up in his hand, then marched back the way he'd come, unknowingly passing Lukas and Sir Ivan with only inches to spare.

"Well," Sir Ivan said when the sound of Sir William's footsteps faded into the night. "That was disappointing."

"Disappointing?" Lukas was still trying to put together the disjointed pieces of this confusing puzzle. Sir William was expecting to find something here. Something important enough to bring him here at night with his sword at the ready. Something delivered by Frenchmen. Surely it must be the same Frenchmen he'd encountered in the woods on the night of his attack.

"Why, yes," Sir Ivan said, bringing Lukas back to his complaint. "I was hoping for a duel at least."

"This way is less messy," Lukas said, already hastening down the path toward the rock. Ignoring his throbbing leg, he knelt and pushed the smooth stone aside. A good-sized hole had been dug into the ground beneath.

"What's inside?" Sir Ivan said, kneeling beside him.

Lukas put his hand into the hole and pulled out four empty bottles, followed by a small purse. Judging by the jingling sound and the weight of the purse, it was full of coins.

Sir Ivan reached for a bottle and put its neck up to his nose. "French wine," he said, reaching for another bottle and doing the same thing. "Of the highest quality."

Lukas sat back on his heels and studied the items on the ground. "It seems your fellow knight is receiving his very own regular shipment of wine direct from France."

"But how?" Sir Ivan asked.

Lukas still did not know much, but one thing was certain: from now on, Sir William would need to be carefully watched. "Smugglers," he said.

Chapter 15

LADY JOANNA WAS UP EARLY the next morning. There was only so much lying in bed staring at the ceiling that she could take. She'd retired soon after the banquet in the great hall was over, but that didn't mean she'd slept. For what seemed like hours, she'd lain awake thinking of Sir Lukas, wondering how he'd come to be at the banquet dressed so elegantly, wondering about her unsettling response to his presence, and wondering what Sir Edwyn had decided to do about the attack Sir Lukas had endured.

By the time the cock crowed, she'd determined that the only way she could get answers to her questions was to make a personal visit to Sir Edwyn before he began his duties for the day. She was dressed and washed before Eva entered her bedchamber, and she sat just long enough to have Eva fashion her long hair into a braided coronet around her head before announcing that she was leaving.

"But you haven't eaten yet," Eva said with a frown.

"Cook has enough to do without sending up anything this early in the morning," Joanna said. "If I'm not back before the meal is served in the great hall, set aside some bread and cheese for me, and I'll eat it when I return."

At the mention of food, her stomach growled, and she remembered that she'd barely eaten anything at the banquet the night before.

Eva placed her hands on her hips and looked at her pointedly. "It's not proper to go visiting at this hour of the morning. What will you do if Sir Edwyn is still in his nightshirt?"

"I will give him time to dress," Joanna said.

"Merciful heavens, you'll be the death of me," Eva muttered as she dropped her hands.

Joanna leaned forward and placed a kiss on her cheek. "After this, I will behave properly all day," she said.

"Perhaps," Eva said.

Joanna laughed and reached for her cape hanging near the door. "Come, Cona," she called. Immediately, the dog materialized at her side and silently followed her out.

The castle was quiet. Joanna could hear a few distant voices and some clanging coming from the kitchen below, but the great hall was empty except for a single servant girl who was cleaning out the enormous fireplace. The servant was so intent on her work that Joanna and Cona slipped by without her noticing. At the main door, Joanna turned right and made her way up the outer staircase to the keep's upper floor.

The morning was brisk, with a hint of rain in the air, and Joanna was grateful for her fur-lined hood. The staircase ended at a small ledge, where a watchman stood guard beside the door. Joanna saw his eyes widen when he spotted Cona and realized who was approaching.

"Good morning," she said as though visiting the knights' quarters at this hour of the day was a normal occurrence.

"And to you, my lady," he said, bowing low.

"I'm here to see Sir Edwyn," she said. "Would you be so good as to see if he's available?"

"At once, my lady." He disappeared through the door, and Joanna and Cona took his place on the ledge.

From this position, she could see most of the castle, along with the town of Moreland, with its outlying farms, and beyond that, the woods and the sea. It was a spectacular view, and in that moment, Joanna could understand why her father was willing to do almost anything to retain this land.

The door creaked open, and the guard reappeared. "If you'll follow me, my lady," he said. "Sir Edwyn will see you now."

Joanna stepped into a narrow antechamber. Through an archway on her right, she could see a small portion of the large room that served as the knights' quarters. Pallets were lined up along the walls, most of them occupied. Averting her eyes from the sleeping men, she turned to watch the guard give a light knock on a door to her left. At the sound of Sir Edwyn's voice, the guard pushed the door open and stepped aside so Joanna could enter.

As Lord Gilbert's senior knight, Sir Edwyn claimed a room of his own. But it was a modest one. A single bed, two large trunks, a small table and chair, and a washbowl sitting on a wooden stool were the only furnishings. Weapons of various kinds lined one wall, and a few coals smoldered in the fireplace. Joanna wrapped her cape around herself more tightly.

"I apologize for coming to see you so early, my lord," she said. "I did not know what time your other duties would begin."

Sir Edwyn moved toward her, and as he did, she realized he was not alone. She gasped and took an instinctive step back.

"Lady Joanna," Sir Lukas said, rising from where he'd been sitting on the edge of the bed.

"As you can see," Sir Edwyn said with a gentle smile, "there is no need for an apology. I had another visitor arrive even earlier than you."

Joanna's heart was racing so fast it was hard to think. She took another step back. "I am interrupting," she said.

"No. It is good that you are here."

"Good?" Based on how her heart was reacting, Joanna failed to see anything good about this situation.

"We have much to discuss," Sir Edwyn said. "And some of it involves you."

"Me?" Merciful heavens, what was wrong with her? If she couldn't come up with more than a one-word response to everything Sir Edwyn said, he would soon revise his welcome.

Sir Lukas gestured toward the single chair, inviting her to sit. "Please stay," he said.

Joanna took a hesitant step toward the chair. She should say something to him. But what? "I am glad to see that your wounds have healed so well."

He smiled. "Thanks to Agnes's care, they are much improved."

"So much so, he is to compete in the archery tournament tomorrow," Sir Edwyn said, moving to sit on the edge of his bed.

Joanna's gaze shot back to Sir Lukas. A slight flush seemed to be creeping up his neck.

"Sir Edwyn thought that the tournament would be the best way to explain my presence at the castle," he said.

Her momentary spark of hope was instantly dowsed. Sir Lukas's decision to compete had nothing to do with her and everything to do with exposing the men who had assaulted him. She would do well to remember that. "It was a wise suggestion," she said. "I've never seen so many strangers at the castle. Your true motive for being here will be well hidden."

"I have more than one reason for being here, my lady," he said. His brown eyes held hers for a moment, then he looked over at Sir Edwyn. "With your permission, I should like Lady Joanna to know of our connection."

Sir Edwyn nodded. "It is time," he said.

Joanna looked from one knight to the other. "What connection?"

Sir Lukas lifted the washbasin off the stool and placed it on the table. Then he pulled the stool a little closer to the fireplace and sat down. She watched as he slowly stretched out his injured leg. It was obviously still giving him some discomfort. "The connection the three of us share," he said.

Joanna was sure that her confusion was evident on her face. "Would you explain?"

"It appears that you and I were acquainted as infants," he said.

Joanna's heart was pounding again. If this kept up, she might not live through the day. "Sir Edwyn?"

"It's true," Sir Edwyn said. "Sir Lukas is the son of my former squire, Nicholas. When Nicholas died in battle, his wife, Katherine, became your nursemaid. She was tending you the day Gelert died."

Snippets of the tales she'd heard about the faithful wolfhound, the servants' hushed gossip about her nursemaid, and their whispers of tragedy striking her father came swirling back. Many times during her youth, she'd asked to know more, but Lord Gilbert had forbidden it. One servant after another had denied her request, and after a while, those who knew died or left, and all talking on the subject ceased. She'd never known the truth.

"Will you tell me what happened?" she asked.

Sir Edwyn nodded slowly. He looked into the fireplace, his eyes focusing on the few coals still burning, but his thoughts were clearly far away. He began by describing the hunting expedition, the ferocious wolf, and the tragedy of Gelert's death. With anguish in his voice, he explained his need to defend his squire's wife and child from Lord Gilbert's wrath and shared what he had done to facilitate their escape.

When he finished speaking, there was complete silence in the room. Then Joanna rose, walked over to Sir Edwyn, knelt in front of him, and took his worn hands in hers. "You made the right choice," she said.

Sir Edwyn gave a sad smile. "I do not believe Lord Gilbert would share your opinion, my lady, but it was many years ago, and I have long since come to terms with my decision."

She turned to face Sir Lukas. "How long have you known of this?"

"I heard a full account only yesterday," he said. "But my mother told me of Sir Edwyn's benevolence on her deathbed."

"And so you came to Moreland in search of him."

He nodded. "That was my initial reason for coming. And now I find that I have other compelling reasons to stay."

"To discover your attackers," she said.

"And to expose smugglers," he added.

Joanna looked at Sir Edwyn in bewilderment. He squeezed her hands and released them. "You should take your seat again, my lady. This will be an even longer tale."

Half an hour later, Lukas was afraid he and Sir Edwyn had shared too much. They'd told Lady Joanna what Lukas knew of smugglers and how they functioned and had presented his theory that smugglers were at work in Moreland. As he'd recounted what he'd learned from the cliff-side attack, the castle stable, and Sir William's visit to the woods, Lukas had seen her expression flit from subdued to shocked, from indignant to despairing.

He'd felt strongly that she should be informed of what was underfoot, partly because of her position at Moreland and partly for her own protection. Although he'd asked Sir Ivan to keep a close eye on Sir William, he'd hoped Lady Joanna would share her views on the matter with him—an insight borne of her longtime residence at Moreland or a suggestion for how to proceed from here—but she did neither of those. Without a word, she rose to her feet and walked over to the tiny window. Then she stood, her cheek against the stone, looking out at the gray skies and stone walls.

With mounting concern, Lukas glanced at Sir Edwyn.

The older knight raised his hand as though signaling him to wait. "Give her time," he said softly.

Next to the chair, the wolfhound yawned and rested its long nose against its front paws. The dog didn't seem the least bit anxious about his mistress. Neither did Sir Edwyn. But Lukas understood the shock of having an unknown past suddenly revealed. And that was quite apart from learning that some of her father's knights could be smugglers or horse thieves or murderers. He ached to offer her comfort and to tell her she wasn't alone, but all he could do was wait.

Eventually, Sir Edwyn cleared his throat. "I have one more thing to add to all that we have discussed."

Lukas raised his head, and Lady Joanna turned from the window.

"Last night at the banquet, Lord Gilbert informed me that more wool has been stolen."

Lukas was on his feet in an instant. "I thought guards had been placed at the shearing sheds?"

"There were two guards. One was knocked unconscious; the other is missing."

Only Lady Joanna's presence in the room prevented Lukas from expressing exactly what he was feeling. "How much was taken?"

"Five full bags," Sir Edwyn said.

Lady Joanna moved to stand beside Lukas. "What of the boys who were standing watch inside the shed?"

Regret etched Sir Edwyn's face. "Young John was knocked unconscious too."

"I must go to Margery," Lady Joanna said, already walking to the door. Cona rose from his resting spot in the corner of the room and padded over to join her.

"Let me come with you," Lukas said.

She froze, then slowly turned to face him. "You would visit a peasant family rather than search for a missing guard or investigate Sir William or practice for the archery competition?"

"If you will allow it."

She smiled then, and Lukas wondered if he'd ever seen anything so beautiful.

"Eva and I will meet you at the stables within the hour," she said.

Chapter 16

WHEN JOANNA, EVA, AND CONA arrived at the stables, Sir Lukas was already there talking to Timothy. The men were standing by the doors next to three saddled horses, but as the women approached, they both turned to greet them.

"Good morning, my lady," Timothy said, bowing slightly. "Sir Lukas told me of your intended trip, so I took the liberty of readying your horses."

"I am grateful to you, Timothy," Joanna said, moving to stand beside her chestnut mare and giving its neck an affectionate pat. "I am anxious that we be on our way."

Sir Lukas stepped forward. "May I assist you?" he asked.

Joanna had never had anyone but a groomsman help her onto a horse before, and she'd promised Eva that she'd behave circumspectly for the rest of the day. Was it appropriate to allow Sir Lukas to lift her up? How she wished she were more experienced in these matters.

She glanced at Eva, but her lady's maid had eyes only for Timothy, who was already helping her to mount. "Yes," she said. "I . . . I thank you." She raised her hands, hesitantly placing them on his broad shoulders. He placed his hands around her waist and lifted. One moment later, she was sitting in her saddle, but his hands were still around her, and the look in his brown eyes was setting a hundred butterflies loose in her stomach.

"You are lovely," he said softly. Then, before she could gather her wits enough to respond, he released his hold, turned, and swung himself onto the saddle of the brown horse standing beside her own.

With her thoughts in a whirl, Joanna watched Cona take his place to the right of her horse. The dog raised his head, looking at her with languid eyes. And despite her befuddled state, Joanna made a startling realization: Cona was calm. Not once had her protective wolfhound objected to Sir Lukas's proximity—not even when the knight had held her. It was something she'd never seen before. She wound her trembling fingers through the reins. Actually, if she were being completely honest with herself, nothing she'd experienced in the last two minutes had ever occurred before.

Sir Lukas inched his horse closer. "Would you lead the way?"

She nodded, still not sure if words would come. Then she urged her horse forward, and Sir Lukas took his place at her left, with Eva right behind.

They made their way out of the castle's main gate and took the road that led away from the town toward the outlying farms. The skies were still overcast, but the muted light deepened the greens of the rolling hillsides, and even from this distance, it was possible to see the white dots of sheep grazing in the meadows.

Birds sang in the trees. A stray dog ran out from beneath the hedgerow to greet them, but upon spotting Cona, it quickly ran off in the other direction. Sir Lukas chuckled at the poor little dog's understandable intimidation, and Joanna glanced his way and exchanged a smile. Escaping the castle with its tension and intrigue had been the best thing she could have done.

What she'd learned in Sir Edwyn's room had been overwhelming. The fact that the archery tournament would begin the next morning only added to her disquiet. But this familiar pastoral scene touched her soul in a different way. It helped calm her confused feelings and enabled her to look outward again.

They reached a series of long, narrow bridges that spanned the confluence of two rivers. Joanna's horse crossed first. The wood was damp and slippery, so she traveled slowly, stopping once she was across to wait for Sir Lukas to reach her.

"Was Timothy able to give you any news from the stable?" she asked as he joined her.

Sir Lukas shook his head. "No one has checked on Shadow. One of the stable boys has given him a good wash down, and the white patch on his leg is now clearly visible."

Joanna sighed. "It's all so unbelievable."

"It was wrong of me to trouble you with what has been happening over the last few days," Sir Lukas said. "What Sir Edwyn shared with you this morning was sufficient for anyone. I regret burdening you with too much at once. Forgive me."

Joanna gazed down at the frothing river gurgling its way toward the sea. How could she explain her feelings to him when they were still so raw and new? She had not yet had a chance to put them into words. "No one has ever shown such confidence in me," she said. She looked up at him, hoping he would understand. "I have been sheltered my whole life. And I've never known why. My father has kept himself as aloof from me as he has from the lowliest of servants. Certain conversations were forbidden in my presence; secrets were kept from my ears."

Joanna paused. She'd never shared these things before, and she wasn't quite sure why she felt compelled to do it now. "It's hard to know yourself when you've never been tested," she said. "I've always hoped that somewhere deep inside I would find valiancy and honor, goodness and strength, but I've never been given the opportunity to discover it.

"Today, Sir Edwyn gave me back a portion of my past, and you gave me a chance to alter my future. You trusted me, not knowing ahead of time how I would react to the information you shared. I was taken aback, but I was grateful." She met his gaze. "And even though the circumstances are unpleasant, I am still grateful that you confided in me." She stretched out her arm to encompass the land around them. "These are my people. If evil men are doing them harm, I want to know about it. I want to help."

In the distance, she could hear the trip-trap of Eva's horse crossing the last bridge. Sir Lukas moved his horse closer, the emotion in his dark-brown eyes deepening.

"You have remarkable insight, Lady Joanna," he said. "But you are wrong about one thing—you manifest your valiance and honor, goodness and strength in all that you do. If you had not already developed those virtues, I would not be alive today."

Warmth flooded Joanna's cheeks, and she dropped her gaze. Cona gave an impatient whine, caring nothing about Sir Lukas's proximity to his mistress, only wanting to be moving again.

"I think you've bewitched my dog," she whispered.

He shrugged. "Well, that's only fair." He swung his horse around, and seconds later, Eva arrived muttering under her breath about horses that were afraid to cross a little water.

Joanna tried offering her a few words of sympathy but found it a struggle to put a coherent sentence together.

"Are we getting close to our destination?" Sir Lukas asked.

"Yes, my lord," Eva said. She pointed to the right. "Margery's family lives in the cottage just up the hill from here."

"Excellent," he said, taking his place beside Joanna again.

She tried to put their conversation behind her, but it was impossible. Once or twice, she glanced over at him, but his focus stayed on the road, and he said nothing more. Finally, she could stand it no longer. "Why is bewitching my dog 'only fair'?" she said. She thought she saw the corners of his lips quirk upward, and she had the distinct impression that he'd been anticipating this question.

"Because," he said quietly enough that Eva would not hear, "I'm beginning to think you've bewitched me too."

⚜

As they approached the small cottage, a young girl ran outside and stood at the side of the road, watching them with wide eyes.

Lady Joanna waved. "Hello, Cecily," she called.

The little girl immediately ran back into the house, but within seconds she was back, dragging a woman behind her. The woman wore a worn gray dress and wimple, with a coarse brown tunic and long woolen shawl. When she saw who had arrived, her eyes grew almost as wide as her daughter's, and she hurriedly bobbed a curtsy.

The three riders came to a stop, and Lukas dismounted, moving to stand beside Lady Joanna's horse. His sore ribs were already protesting his earlier lift, but at that moment, it was of no matter. Lady Joanna gave him a tentative smile, and without a word, he placed his hands on her waist, grateful that despite his recent admission, she reached for his shoulders without reservation. When she was on her feet, he released her, sorry when she dropped her hands and stepped away.

By the time he'd helped Eva off her horse, Lady Joanna was bending down beside the little girl, the hem of her lavender silk dress becoming more and more mud spattered as she guided the child's small hand into Cona's shaggy fur. Charmed by the look of wonder on the little girl's face and the kindness on Lady Joanna's, Lukas watched silently until Lady Joanna rose to her feet.

"Margery," she said. "This is Sir Lukas of Cornwall. He was good enough to accompany Eva and me today. We heard that John was injured and wanted to be sure he is recovering well."

Margery bobbed another curtsy, this time to Lukas. "It's very good of you to come, my lady," she said. "John did have a nasty bang on the head, but Agnes has been to see him. She gave him a couple of stitches, and apart from the dizziness, he's much improved." She hesitated for a moment. "He's inside. Would you care to see him yourself?"

"I would love to," Lady Joanna said.

"Cona and I will wait out here," Eva said. "So we don't overwhelm the boy."

"Thank you, Eva," Lady Joanna said.

Cecily hovered at the doorway, watching Cona, while Lukas and Lady Joanna followed Margery into the humble home.

The cottage was a tiny, one-room building built of stone with a thatched roof. Other than the front door, the only light came from one small window and the hole in the roof where the smoke from the fire in the center of the room escaped. Despite the damp conditions outside, there was no fire burning, and the room was dank and dark.

Lukas stood still, blinking as his eyes adjusted to the dim light. A young boy lay on a pallet on the far side of the room, his head swathed in a cloth strip.

"Hello, John," Lady Joanna said, stepping closer to the pallet. "Do you remember me?"

"Yes, my lady," the boy said. "I . . . I'm sorry I can't stand to greet you. My head makes it so I can't stay upright as I should."

"I understand," she said gently. "And so does Sir Lukas." Lukas moved to stand beside her, and he watched the boy gingerly move his head so he could see him. "He had a head injury not too long ago too."

"Did it hurt like the dickens, my lord?"

"It did indeed, John," Lukas said. "But I would wager that mine was not near as bad as yours. I had no stitches."

The boy gave a faint smile.

Lukas crouched down beside him on the dirt floor. "Would you tell me what happened?"

John ran his tongue across his lip. "I will tell you what I can, my lord, but there's parts I don't recall."

"Whatever you remember, then," he said.

"It hadn't been dark long when I heard a horse coming along the lane," John said. "I was in the shed, but I heard the guards talking outside, so I knew they'd heard it too, and I didn't worry too much about it. Then the sound of hooves stopped, and I heard a big thump. A man's voice said, 'I need you to load up all the wool in the shed. Lord Gilbert is sending men to take it to the castle tomorrow morning so it has to be done now.'

"Another man said, 'There's a boy inside,' and the first one said, 'Well, take care of him, then. Just like you did with Ralf. You'd best not forget that we assigned you here to do a job.'"

John paused, and Lukas noticed that the hand that held his thin blanket was trembling.

"I got scared then, my lord. I knew Ralf was the name of one of the guards. He'd shared his lunch with me that day and told me I reminded him of his little brother."

"You had every right to be afraid," Lukas said. "I would have felt the same way."

John stared at him. "But you're a knight."

Lukas gave a soft chuckle. "Just because you own a sword doesn't mean you feel no fear."

John seemed to ponder that idea for a moment. "I suppose so," he said. "But all I had was a pitchfork."

"Did you use it?"

A look of chagrin crossed the boy's face. "I would have, but the other guard opened the door so fast I didn't have a chance. He whacked me on the head with a big stick, and I went down like an apple off a tree."

"So you never saw the man who came on the horse?" Lukas said.

"No, my lord."

"Did he speak English like a commoner or a nobleman?"

John's face scrunched up in concentration. "He sounded like a nobleman, but . . ." He hesitated.

Lukas waited, sensing that he was searching for the right words. "What else?"

"His voice was a bit strange." John frowned. "I can't explain it. It was just different."

Lukas's pulse quicken. One of the Englishmen at his attack had stayed out of view, but his voice had been unusual. Distinctive even. Could John have encountered the same man? If so, it would support his theory that the noblemen were from Moreland. And that at least one of them had enough authority to know Lord Gilbert's plans and to adjust the castle guards' duties. Perhaps Sir Edwyn could help him narrow down the suspects based on who had access to the guards' rosters.

He opened the purse at his belt and took out a few coins. Taking John's hand in his, he pressed four coins into his palm. "Every brave guard deserves his pay," he said.

John swallowed hard and gazed at the coins in his hand. Then he stretched out his arm and offered the money back. "I don't deserve this, my lord," he said. "For I am not brave."

"Yes, young John, you—"

"I could have done more." Behind him Margery gasped to hear her son interrupt a nobleman, but Lukas was far more concerned about the agony in the boy's voice. "I could have saved the wool."

"What do you mean?" Lukas asked.

"The blow to the head knocked me out," John said. "But I woke up before they had taken all the wool out of the shed." He looked at

Lukas with tortured eyes. "I should have done something, but I just lay there, too scared to move or say a word."

"You did the right thing, John," Lukas said. "If they'd known you were awake, they would likely have killed you."

"But the wool . . ."

Lukas curled John's fingers around the coins and pressed them into a fist. "I will do everything in my power to return the wool to its rightful owners. And others at the castle will do the same."

"You have only two days," John said.

Lukas stiffened. "Why do you say that?"

"I didn't understand everything I heard." He touched his fingers to the bandage on his forehead. "When I woke, my thinking was muddled. But they were talking about Frenchies and a cave and a storm coming. And needing to be ready in two nights' time."

Lukas could barely believe what he was hearing. "Do you recall anything more?" he pressed.

"No, my lord. They were angry at someone, but I heard no names."

Lukas shook his head in amazement. "John, you deserve ten times the payment I offered for the information you've given me. I thank you." He rose to his feet. "I must return to the castle immediately, but if you think of anything else, no matter how small, send word to me there."

John's fingers tightened around the coins, and a light of hope shone in eyes that had previously been dull. "I will, my lord."

Lukas turned to Lady Joanna. "I must speak with Sir Edwyn," he said.

She nodded, her face pale in the poor light. He offered her his arm, and she placed her hand on it.

"Thank you for letting us speak with John," she said to Margery.

"He's a fine young man," Lukas added.

Margery dabbed at her cheek with the corner of her shawl and curtsied. "My lord, my lady," she said, her voice breaking slightly. "I thank you. My family is most grateful."

Chapter 17

THE RAIN THAT HAD THREATENED all day was finally falling. Joanna stood at the window in her bedchamber and watched the droplets bounce off the flagstones below. Every once in a while a servant or guard would hurry across the courtyard, but for the most part, the castle's inner bailey was empty of everything but large puddles.

She wondered how the south pasture was faring in this late-spring deluge. The workmen had finished erecting the stands, and the flags were flying. The lists were ready for the many spectators anticipated at the tournament the next day. All that was needed to make the event a success were sunshine and archers. Joanna's stomach twisted. In one short day, she'd gone from dreading interacting with any of the competitors to desperately wanting one of them to win. She knew nothing of Sir Lukas's skill with the bow, but she prayed he was up to the challenge. He was the only man she wanted at her side following the competition.

As soon as they'd arrived back at the castle, Sir Lukas had gone in search of Sir Edwyn. She'd not seen or heard from either of them since, and she could only hope the two knights were making progress in discovering who was behind the smuggling operation. For her part, Eva had insisted that Joanna return to her chamber, bathe, change out of her soiled dress, and make proper preparations for dining with her father and his guests. Joanna sighed and moved away from the window. It had been a long and torturous few hours.

People were already gathering in the great hall. The shuddering of benches being dragged across the wooden floor punctuated the steady stream of voices. Through the thick wooden door, Joanna heard Sir Thomas's hearty laugh. If the senior knights had arrived, it was time for her to join them. She must not be late again.

"Come, Cona."

Obediently, the wolfhound joined Joanna at the door.

"You look lovely, my lady," Eva said. "You'll draw every nobleman's eye in that dress—Sir Lukas's especially."

Joanna felt color warm her cheeks. Would her appearance please Sir Lukas? She was wearing her new forest-green gown, and as she walked, the tiny gold bells on her belt tinkled softly. Her long hair was pulled up into a gold net hair caul, and a string of pearls ran across her forehead. It was a far cry from the peasant clothing she'd worn when he'd first met her.

"Aha," Eva said, grinning impishly when Joanna blushed. "It's as I thought. You're starting to develop feelings for that handsome knight."

"Eva!"

Her lady's maid's smile was unrepentant, and Joanna had a sinking feeling that things might become even more uncomfortable if she didn't act quickly. "I must go," she said, and before Eva could say another word, she opened the door and stepped into the great hall.

The castle priest, steward, and senior knights were already gathering at the head table. Sir William and Sir Thomas broke off their conversation to bow as Joanna approached. Gerard Bartholomew gave her an acknowledging nod. Sir Nigel offered her a smile, Sir Edwyn's expression was worried, and Lord Gilbert was conspicuously absent. Sir Nigel pulled out the chair next to his, but before she sat down, Sir Edwyn stepped closer.

"My lady," he said softly. "Lord Gilbert is not feeling well enough to join us this evening. He has asked that I welcome everyone on his behalf."

Joanna stared at him in shock. Lord Gilbert was never ill. And for him to miss a banquet that had been specifically designed to impress his many guests seemed inconceivable.

"Is he very poorly?" she asked.

"I believe so, my lady."

Joanna hesitated. "Should I go to him?"

"I believe he would want you here for the banquet," Sir Edwyn said. "But you could certainly check on his condition when the meal is over."

"Very well." Joanna knew Sir Edwyn's suggestion was wise, but it didn't make sitting down between Sir Nigel and her father's empty chair any easier.

"My lords, ladies, and gentlemen." Sir Edwyn spoke loudly enough that his voice carried across the great hall, and immediately a hush fell upon the guests. "My name is Sir Edwyn, and on behalf of Sir Gilbert, I welcome you to Moreland and to the archery tournament that will, weather permitting, begin tomorrow morning." There was a low murmur as several people muttered about the rain to those sitting beside them. "Sir Gilbert regrets that he cannot be in attendance this evening but hopes that you will enjoy the meal that has been prepared for you." He turned to the priest sitting at the end of the head table. "Father Jerome will now offer grace."

As soon as the short prayer was over, servants poured into the room carrying platters of food. Joanna watched four servants transport an enormous wooden board holding a whole roast pig with a bright red apple in its mouth to the center of the room. She wondered vaguely if she'd be able to eat any more than she'd managed the night before. She thought it unlikely.

"What ails Sir Gilbert?" Sir Nigel asked, filling his trencher with roast duck.

"I do not know," Joanna said. "I've only just learned he is unwell."

Sir Nigel began eating. "He's a strong man. I'm sure Beatrice will have him feeling better in no time."

Joanna picked at the food in front of her, her feeling of unease growing. "I hope you are right," she said.

Sir Nigel washed the roast duck down with a large swig of ale. "You mark my words, he'll be on the stands to view Moreland's excellent showing at the archery contest tomorrow."

"Were the archers practicing all day today?"

Joanna could not have asked a better question. Sir Nigel launched into another one of his monologues about the varying levels of skill found in the visiting noblemen, the quality of the longbows, the wind's influence on arrows, the steadiness of his arm, and the excellence of his eyesight. Joanna let him speak while her mind wandered.

She looked over at Sir Edwyn. The older knight's face was drawn; his shoulders slumped as though a new and heavy burden had been placed upon them. Very little of the food in his trencher had been touched. Was concern about Lord Gilbert affecting him?

A movement in the far corner of the room caught her eye. Sir Lukas and Sir Ivan entered the great hall together. Even from this distance, Joanna could tell that their boots were muddy and their hair wet. They took two seats on the bench farthest from the head table, but once they were seated, Sir Lukas turned to study those sitting at the head table. His gaze slid from Sir Edwyn to the empty seat next to him, and she saw a frown appear on his face. When his eyes turned to her, the lines on his forehead softened, but no smile touched his lips or eyes. He acknowledged her with a slight nod, then his gaze moved to Sir Nigel, and his expression hardened again.

The knot in Joanna's stomach tightened. She pushed her trencher away and leaned across the unoccupied chair toward Sir Edwyn. "I wish to excuse myself, my lord," she said.

Sir Edwyn gave an understanding nod. "Very well."

She turned to Sir Nigel. "I'm sorry to interrupt," she said, breaking into his description of a short, stout archer from Canterbury. "But I am needed in my father's chamber."

Sir Nigel stared at her in astonishment. "You are leaving?"

"I feel I must." She was already on her feet. He tried to rise, but she had started walking away. "Good evening, Sir Nigel," she said. Keeping her eyes forward and trying to ignore the uncomfortable sensation that she was being watched, Joanna walked halfway around the perimeter of the great hall until she reached the entrance to the grand chamber. She gave a single rap on the door, then lifted the latch and entered.

The usually imposing room felt empty and cold. Even her father's large table was devoid of its usual pile of papers. She cut across the room, stopping at the door that led to her father's bedchamber. Here again she knocked. This time, her knock was followed almost immediately by the sound of footsteps. She waited. Seconds later, Beatrice stood in the open doorway, a steaming kettle in her hand.

"Lady Joanna," she said, raising her eyebrows in surprise.

"Good evening, Beatrice," Joanna said. "I'm here to see my father."

The older woman pursed her thin lips. "Now's not a good time, my lady."

"Is he so severely ill?" Joanna asked, taken aback that the healer would so summarily dismiss her.

"He's very weak," she said. "The hallucinating and vomiting have taken a heavy toll."

Joanna could hardly imagine her powerful father in such a debilitated state. And she was surprisingly shaken by the realization that he might not always be as strong as he had been. "Can you heal him?"

From somewhere behind Beatrice came an agonized moan, and Joanna saw a flicker of fear in the healer's eyes.

"Father?" Alarm prickled up Joanna's spine.

"Good night, Lady Joanna," Beatrice said. "I must attend to Lord Gilbert." Then she swung the door closed.

❧

When Sir Edwyn rose to leave the head table at the end of the meal, Lukas and Sir Ivan slipped out ahead of him. They paused in the entryway. Rain was still falling, rattling against the wooden door.

"You understand what needs to be done?" Lukas asked.

Sir Ivan nodded. "At first light, I'll ride directly to the port authorities in Dover."

"If the king has organized them as he has the men in Plymouth, there will be a collector of customs and a controller of customs. Either of those officers can call upon tidesmen, searchers, land waiters, or tidewaiters to assist us. They are well used to boarding ships to tally and weigh goods going in and out of port.

"Tell them that we believe the smugglers are using caves in the cliffs below Moreland Castle, and if John's information is correct, their best chance of catching them moving the goods will be tomorrow night."

"If I ride hard, I can be back by then."

Lukas had decided to share John's story with Sir Ivan in the hope that the adventuresome knight would be willing to help him search the cliff for the smugglers' hiding place. They'd ridden out to the beach together only to discover that the tide was too high to allow them access to the rock face. Despite the fact that they'd not been able to find tangible proof of illegal activity, however, Sir Ivan had volunteered to ride to Dover to inform the authorities of their suspicions.

"I pray they take you seriously," Lukas said. "If it weren't for the tournament, I would ride with you. Perhaps with two of us . . ."

"You have a fair maiden to save; I have a customs official to collect. God willing, we will accomplish both."

Lukas ran his fingers through his hair. Sir Ivan was right. Given what Lukas now suspected about the black-hearted nature of at least one of Moreland's archers, he had to be at the tournament tomorrow. He'd had no opportunity to test his father's bow, which would put him at a huge disadvantage in the competition, but at some point during the last couple of days, Lady Joanna's future happiness had become more important to him than bringing brigands and smugglers to justice. He wanted to win. He could no longer deny it. But if he could not, he would do everything in his power to ensure that a nobleman worthy of Lady Joanna took the prize.

Sir Ivan put on the cape he'd left hanging in the entryway. It was still wet, but he raised the hood to cover his head. "I will not return without the men we need," he said.

Lukas extended his hand to him. "Then I wish you Godspeed."

Sir Ivan's grasp was firm. "Until tomorrow eve," he said, then he slipped out the door.

Lukas did not have to wait long after Sir Ivan left for Sir Edwyn to arrive at the great hall door.

"Walk with me," Sir Edwyn said by way of greeting.

Both men donned their capes and walked out into the rain. It was dark. Clouds hid the moon, and the castle's torches burned low, struggling to stay lit in the damp air.

"There's less chance of us being overheard here," Sir Edwyn said as they walked across the empty courtyard.

"Were you able to discover who changed the guard's roster?" Sir Lukas asked.

"Yes."

Lukas waited, but Sir Edwyn offered nothing more.

"I talked with Sir William," Lukas said. "I told him I was interested in the black charger and I'd been told he was the man to talk to."

"What did he say?"

"He told me he'd been doing some business outside the castle and was returning late at night when he met Sir Nigel, who was astride his own horse and leading the charger through the woods toward the castle. The horse had no saddle, and Sir Nigel told him he'd just purchased the charger from a knight who'd come to Moreland for the archery competition and had been forced to sell it to pay off his gambling debts."

"A significant debt to accrue in so short a time," Sir Edwyn said dryly.

"As the person who knows exactly how much that charger is worth, I agree," Lukas said.

Sir Edwyn gazed into the blackness. "And the French smugglers had conveniently taken care of your saddle and belongings for him."

"I assume so," Lukas said.

"Did Sir William give a reason for the fact that he, not Sir Nigel, took the horse to the stables?"

"He admitted some surprise that Sir Nigel did not want to take care of the animal himself, but he said Sir Nigel had received an urgent message that he was needed at the shearing shed."

"I daresay he was," Sir Edwyn said, a hint of anger in his voice now. "But not by the peasants of Moreland."

Lukas considered Sir Edwyn's response. From the time he'd heard Sir Nigel's name, Sir Edwyn had seemed troubled, irritated, perhaps even infuriated. But he'd not once acted surprised.

"If I may say so, my lord, you do not seem unduly shocked to learn of Sir Nigel's involvement in this affair."

Sir Edwyn sighed. "I have learned that time has a significant impact on our views," he said. "Yesterday, to suspect Sir Nigel of such treachery would have been inconceivable. Two hours ago, when I saw his name on the guard roster, it became possible. Now, with Sir William's report, it seems sure."

They were both silent for a moment. From the keep, the sound of a door closing and footsteps on the staircase echoed through the night. Another door banged, and it was quiet again.

"We have no proof," Sir Edwyn said. "We cannot act without it."

"Then we must find the cave the smugglers are using before all evidence is removed."

"Even that may not be enough to convict him. We must catch him there."

"Then that's what we will do," Lukas said firmly.

Chapter 18

JOANNA LAY AWAKE STARING AT the odd shadows cast by the beams on the ceiling of her bedchamber. Sleep had eluded her for hours. She'd heard the rain stop. She'd heard the changing of the guard. She'd heard Cona snuffle and whine as he dozed. And all the while, her thoughts had continued to spin.

How could everything feel so wrong? Sir Lukas had stolen her heart, but by the end of the day, she would likely be promised to another. The people of Moreland had tried so hard to save their wool, yet it had been taken again. And her father, obdurate and unyielding though he was, was lying in his bedchamber as close to death as he'd ever been.

In the dimness of her bedchamber, Joanna had never felt so help-less. "Please, Father God," she whispered. "Surely something can be done. If not for me, then for the peasants of Moreland and for my father."

At some point in the early hours of morning, exhaustion finally caught up with her, and she fell into a fitful sleep. She woke to the sound of a cock crowing, and even though her bleary eyes protested the first rays of daylight shining through her window, her mind was clear. The heavy weight of hopelessness felt lighter, and as she slid out of bed to face the challenges ahead, she knew what she must do first.

"Eva!" she called.

Cona raised his head, his ears twitching at the urgency in Joanna's voice.

"Eva!"

"My lady." Joanna's lady's maid staggered off her pallet in the corner of the room. "What's wrong?"

"I need to get a message to Agnes," Joanna said.

Eva's forehead creased. "Very well. I'm sure someone can be sent to her cottage."

"It's too late for that." Joanna started fumbling with the ties on her nightgown. "I have to catch her now. She rises so early, she's probably already on her way to the south pasture so that Garrick and Slip have a good place to view the tournament."

Eva reached out and placed her hand over Joanna's, forcing her fingers to still. "My lady, you cannot go out looking for Agnes. You must prepare yourself for the tournament."

"Eva." Joanna met her eyes, willing her to understand the seriousness of the situation. "Lord Gilbert is so ill I fear for his life. All night I have fretted over what can be done. This morning, I know. Agnes must return to the castle to care for him."

Eva's eyes widened. "Agnes? But you know that Lord Gilbert himself banned her from ever entering the castle again."

"Be that as it may," Joanna said. "With Lord Gilbert indisposed, I am taking responsibility for who may or may not enter the castle. And I wish Agnes here immediately."

Something that looked remarkably like pride flashed across Eva's face. She reached for her dress. "Seeing as the servants aren't about yet, I'll go to the stables," she said. "Timothy can send one of the stable boys to fetch her."

"Tell him to have Agnes go directly to Lord Gilbert's chamber," Joanna said. "I will meet her there."

"Only if you're dressed and ready first," Eva said sternly.

Joanna hid a smile. She was quite sure that Eva sometimes forgot that she was a maid and not an older sister. But there had been too many times that she'd been grateful for Eva's blunt honesty and loyal camaraderie to chastise her for forgetting her position. "Then you'd best hurry," Joanna said.

"Cona, do not let her out of this room," Eva said, wagging her finger at the dog.

A smile tugged at Joanna's lips, and she felt her spirits rise. Something was going to change—and the change would be good.

Joanna had washed and put on her light-blue dress by the time Eva returned pink cheeked and out of breath.

"The stable boy left right away," Eva reported. "He's going to check the pasture first, then he'll take the path to the cottage."

Relief washed over Joanna. "Thank you, Eva."

"You're welcome." She took a deep breath. "Now sit down, and let's see what we can do with your hair."

Eva brushed Joanna's hair until it shone like gold. Then, taking a few strands from each side of her face, she wove Joanna's hair into an elaborate braid and tied off the end with one of the ribbons she'd bought at the market.

"There now," she said. "It's just as I thought. This ribbon matches your dress perfectly." She placed her hands on Joanna's shoulders and turned her so they were facing each other. "But you remember"—the twinkle was back in her eye—"if you've a mind to bestow a favor on any particular knight today, the ribbon would be just right for that too."

Joanna's heart beat a little harder. Did she have the courage to show preference in a tournament where every competitor was vying for her hand? Oh, how she wished that the tourney prize were something else—something wholly unconnected to her. What a difference that would make in the way she was feeling today.

"I must go to my father," she said, rising to her feet.

"Aye," Eva agreed. "You must get there before Agnes."

The great hall was still quiet, although sounds were starting to drift upward from the kitchen below. She reached the grand chamber and entered without knocking. The room was dark and cold, and a frisson of fear shot through her. What if she was too late? What if the bleak atmosphere of this outer room was merely a reflection of what she would find in the bedchamber?

There was no sign of Agnes, so Joanna left the door open and crossed the room. At Lord Gilbert's chamber, she knocked. There was no response, and Joanna's anxiety rose. She knocked again. After a few moments, she heard footsteps, and the door swung open. Beatrice stood before her, a large stain on her dress and her wimple even more askew than before.

"How is—?"

Beatrice did not let her finish. "Lord Gilbert is no better, my lady. He's certainly not in any condition for visitors."

Joanna released the breath she hadn't realized she'd been holding. He was still alive. That was all that mattered at present. She stepped forward, and Beatrice's eyes widened. "I will see my father," Joanna said.

Beatrice straightened her shoulders. "Lord Gilbert is under my care; I will not allow anyone to enter his bedchamber."

"I see," Joanna said calmly. She turned slightly and indicated the outer door. "Then you are dismissed."

Beatrice's mouth dropped open, and she stared at Joanna like a fish gasping for air.

"My lady, Lord Gilbert is gravely ill. You cannot—"

"I will ensure that my father is in the best possible hands," she said, taking her turn to interrupt.

Beatrice stiffened, her voice accusing. "You have no experience with healing remedies, and without them, he will surely die."

"Lady Joanna may not, but I do." The voice from the grand chamber startled them both. Agnes stood in the center of the room, her eyes trained on Beatrice.

Beatrice gasped. "What are you doing in here? You're not permitted inside the castle."

"Agnes is here by my invitation," Joanna said. "She will take over the care of Lord Gilbert."

Anger contorted Beatrice's features. "You know not what you do, Lady Joanna. This woman killed your mother. She will use her evil potions on your father, and when he dies, you will be as accountable as she is."

Beatrice's spiteful words hit Joanna like arrows. And as though he could see the barbs aimed at his mistress, Cona's hackles rose. He gave a low, throaty growl. Beatrice took an instinctive step back, her eyes darting from the dog to Joanna.

Joanna reached down and placed her hand on Cona's leather collar. "If you leave now, I will restrain my dog."

Beatrice edged her way out of the bedchamber, keeping as much distance as she could between herself and the wolfhound. Cona strained forward, his lips curled back. When she reached the safety of the great hall, Beatrice swung around. "The castle steward will have something to say about this," she said. Then, with an indignant sniff, she stalked away.

Agnes moved to Joanna's side and took her shaking hand in hers. "Come," she said and led her into Lord Gilbert's chamber.

The stench hit them immediately. Joanna raised her arm so that her elbow covered her nose and mouth, but that only slightly lessened the impact of the disagreeable odor.

"What is it?" she asked, muffling a cough.

Agnes hurried to the corner of the room, lifted a large pile of soiled bed linens into her arms, and deposited them outside the bedchamber. "That foolish woman," she said, indignation sparking in her eyes. "She was so concerned with preventing anyone from seeing Lord Gilbert in this state, she must have barred the servants from doing their jobs." She made another trip out of the room, this time with the chamber pot. "No healing can take place in these conditions."

Joanna moved closer to the bed. Her father was lying on his side, his face gray and drawn, his eyes closed. Without warning, he swung his arm back and mumbled something, his breathing suddenly rapid and ragged. Joanna jumped, but Agnes stepped up behind her and placed a hand on her father's forehead. At her touch, Lord Gilbert calmed, and Agnes bent down, placing her ear against his chest. She frowned. "No fever, but his heart is racing."

"What does that mean?"

Agnes stood up, her expression pensive. "That is what I must discover."

A tentative knock sounded on the door. "Lady Joanna?" Eva was standing in the doorway.

With a last long look at her father, Joanna crossed the room. "Is it time?"

"Yes, my lady. Sir Edwyn is waiting in the great hall to escort you to the stands." Agnes joined them, and Eva reached out and gave the healer a warm embrace. "It's good to see you back where you belong, Agnes."

"You are kind," Agnes said. "Others will feel differently, I have no doubt, but I will do all I can to help Lord Gilbert recover." She pointed to the discarded items on the floor. "Would you be willing to send for a servant to collect these things? And have someone bring me some clean bed linens and a nightgown for Lord Gilbert, along with a bucket of water, some soap, and a scrubbing brush."

Joanna frowned. "Agnes, you're a healer, not a chambermaid."

Agnes gave a small smile. "I've done far worse things than scrubbing the floor, my lady." She glanced back at the bed. "Beatrice was right to prevent the servants from coming and going. Lord Gilbert deserves more respect than that. But his room must be clean.

"I sent Slip back to the cottage for my remedies. Until he returns, I will clean and use the time to observe Lord Gilbert's condition."

Joanna leaned closer and kissed Agnes's soft cheek. "You are a gift to us all. There's no one who could care for my father better than you, and yet I wish I did not have to go."

"Your father would want you at the tournament," Agnes said.

Eva nodded. "Quite apart from all those noblemen who are hoping to win your hand, most of the people of Moreland have waited their whole lives to attend a tourney like this. It wouldn't be the same without the lady of the castle in attendance." She gave Joanna an encouraging smile. "I'll make sure Agnes gets all the help she needs. No one else need know she is here."

Joanna swallowed past the lump in her throat. She'd done all she could for her father; she wasn't needed here. And whether she liked it or not, she *was* needed at the tournament. "Very well," she said. "But please send someone to inform me if Lord Gilbert takes a turn for the worse."

"I will," Agnes said. She paused. "Have courage, my lady. You are stronger than you think."

Joanna mustered a weak smile. "I hope you are right," she said. Then she walked out of Lord Gilbert's bedchamber with Cona at her side.

Chapter 19

LUKAS WALKED AROUND THE BUTTS, studying the targets affixed to the top of the three circular, turf-covered mounds. They stood about four feet off the ground and were perhaps fifteen feet apart. The targets' central two bands were painted yellow, the next two were red, then two were blue, two were white, and the outer ring was black. Everything about the setting was familiar. He had practiced on similar butts too many times to count. And yet this time he felt an unaccustomed nervousness.

He licked his finger and raised it, monitoring the cold air as it came in contact with his wet skin. The blustery wind had blown away the rain clouds—at least temporarily—but was going to make the archery competition all the more difficult. He frowned. An unfamiliar longbow and capricious gusts of wind would not help his chances today.

Behind him, townspeople and peasants were rapidly filling in the spaces along the lists, and members of the nobility were already taking their seats on the stands. Lukas glanced at the front center seats reserved for Lord Gilbert and Lady Joanna. They were still empty. He hadn't had a chance to talk to Lady Joanna since they'd returned from Margery's cottage, but he'd thought of her often. Too often. He flexed his fingers around the smooth wood of his father's bow. Winning this tourney was becoming more and more important.

With a last glance at the targets, Lukas started back to join the other competitors waiting in the open area in front of the stands. Out of the corner of his eye, he saw someone wave.

"Hullo, Sir Lukas!"

Lukas turned to see Garrick leaning against the fence to the left of the stands. He was grinning broadly and waving with abandon. Lukas veered that way.

"Good morning, Garrick," Lukas said when he reached him. "It's good to see you again."

"Slip said you'd be here," Garrick said. He gave a proud smile. "I'll tell him I saw you first."

Lukas chuckled. "You do that." He looked around. "Where are Agnes and Slip?"

"Agnes went to the castle to help Lady Joanna," Garrick said. "And Slip had to go get her remedies from the cottage."

The pleasure Lukas had felt moments before evaporated. "Is Lady Joanna unwell?"

"I dunno. Slip just told me to save his spot."

Lukas ran his fingers through his hair. Only something extremely serious would persuade Agnes to return to the castle. He scoured the nearby stands again, looking for Sir Edwyn. There was no sign of him.

"Look!" Garrick said, with childlike excitement. "There's a dog just like Grey."

Lukas followed his pointed finger. Cona was walking toward them, his head high, his eyes alert. Beside him was Lady Joanna with her hand on Sir Edwyn's sleeve. Lukas thought his heart might pound out of his chest—and he couldn't tell if it was out of relief that Lady Joanna appeared healthy and well or because of the vision she made with the morning sun glinting off her golden hair and light-blue dress.

"Hullo, Lady!" Garrick called as soon as he recognized her.

Around him, several people tutted their disapproval at his casual address, and an older woman muttered loudly about his shameful disrespect. Garrick, however, was blissfully unaware of their censure and waved enthusiastically.

And when Lady Joanna saw him, her solemn expression dissolved into a warm smile. "Garrick!" she said. "I'm so glad you're here."

A ripple of whispers passed through the curious onlookers.

"I'm glad you're here too," Garrick said.

The simple exchange seemed to touch her. "Thank you."

Garrick beamed. "I found Sir Lukas as well."

Lady Joanna turned to Lukas. They both bowed their heads in greeting.

"Good day, Lady Joanna."

Her somber countenance returned. "I hope it will be," she said softly.

"Let's walk a little farther," Sir Edwyn said, shifting his head slightly to indicate that he'd like Lukas to accompany them.

Lukas recognized the cue and fell into step beside them. He waited until they were out of earshot of anyone in the crowd before speaking again. "Garrick told me Agnes is in the castle."

Lady Joanna nodded. "I sent for her. My father is gravely ill."

Lukas was quite sure that it was wrong to feel relief that Lord Gilbert was suffering, but when he considered the alternative—that Lady Joanna could have been Agnes's patient—he felt nothing but gratitude. "Agnes will give him the best possible care," he said.

"I believe so."

Her eyes were exactly the same shade of blue as her dress. Why did noticing that detail make it impossible to think of anything else? He cleared his throat, but before he could formulate a fluent sentence, she spoke again.

"Will you be competing today, Sir Lukas?"

He raised the longbow in his hand. "Sir Edwyn offered me my father's bow. My greatest wish is that I use it as skillfully as he did."

"That is also my wish," she said, a light blush rising on her soft skin. She reached for the braid that lay across her shoulder and untied the ribbon at its end. With the gentle shyness he was coming to find endearing, she held it out to him.

Ignoring his injured leg's protestation, Lukas dropped to one knee. "I am honored to accept your favor, my lady," he said.

She stepped closer and tied the ribbon around his upper arm. Each brush of her trembling fingers sent a frisson of awareness all the way down to his fingertips, and he wondered fleetingly if his arm would ever be the same again. She moved back, and Lukas realized the crowd's excited voices had silenced. Slowly, he rose to his feet, and as he did, the spectators erupted into loud applause and cheering. Lukas raised his bow in salute, and Lady Joanna's blush deepened.

"A perfect way to begin the tournament," Sir Edwyn said with a gratified smile. He extended his arm to Lady Joanna once more. "We should take our seats, my lady."

She placed her hand on the senior knight's sleeve.

"May your arrows fly true, Sir Lukas," she said. Then Sir Edwyn led her away.

Lukas watched them until they reached the stairs leading to their cushioned seats, then turned and walked to the other end of the stands, where his competitors were gathering. Most of the men had obviously witnessed Lady Joanna's gesture. Some offered him a wry smile; others ignored him and the ribbon on his sleeve. Sir Nigel was the only one to approach him.

"I did not realize that you and Lady Joanna were so well acquainted," he said, his mouth twisting into a smile that did not reach his eyes.

"Indeed," Lukas said, forcing himself to be civil even though he longed to wipe the smirk off the other knight's face. "We met many years ago."

Sir Nigel's expression was a combination of disbelief and suspicion. "Lady Joanna knows no one outside Moreland."

"So you say," Lukas said.

Anger sparked in Sir Nigel's eyes. "Everyone knows that."

"Well, I would dare say that everyone is mistaken, then," Lukas said, fixing him with a level gaze. "Because she clearly knows me."

Lukas was vaguely aware of Sir Edwyn's voice welcoming everyone to the tournament, along with a general shift of the knights from their current position to one at the front of the stands. But he did not move. He held Sir Nigel's glare without wavering, and finally, with a snort of derision, the furious knight spun on his heel and stormed off to join the others. Lukas took a deep, calming breath and slowly followed.

❦

Joanna sat in her chair on the stands, politely acknowledging each knight with a nod as Sir Edwyn introduced the competitors. There were so many. Twenty-four to be exact. And she knew only five of them: Sir Nigel, Sir Guy, Sir Thomas, Sir Henry, and Sir Lukas. Sir Guy and Sir Thomas were two of the older knights in the group, but there were half a dozen others whose hair was as gray and sparse as theirs. Sir Henry and Sir Nigel were younger, but in Joanna's opinion, neither they nor the assortment of other knights of various ages, heights, and build were anywhere near as handsome as Sir Lukas.

Like the other knights, Sir Lukas stood with his quiver full of arrows over one shoulder and his longbow in his hand. Today he was dressed in a dark-blue doublet with gold trim over a white undershirt and brown hose and boots. The light-blue ribbon she'd placed on his arm fluttered wildly in the breeze, and Joanna pushed back the memory of her response to touching his muscular arm. She still couldn't quite believe she'd plucked up the courage to give him her favor.

Sir Edwyn introduced Sir Nigel, and the crowd cheered loudly for one of Moreland's own. Sir Nigel raised his eyebrow and gave her an enigmatic smile. Joanna wasn't sure what he meant by it, but she smiled in return. Then Sir Lukas was introduced, and the spectators roared their approval of the unknown knight who'd won their lady's favor. Sir Nigel's face darkened at the crowd's positive response to his opponent, and Joanna experienced a twinge of unease. Perhaps singling out one knight had been a mistake.

In front of the stands, Sir Lukas dropped to one knee once more and, with his fist clenched and his arm bent so that her ribbon lay directly over his heart, he bowed. The cheers from both sides of the lists crescendoed, and joy swelled within her. Even if her happiness was destined to be short-lived, she would always have this moment to remember. Foolish or not, she was glad Sir Lukas wore her ribbon.

Two tournament officials approached the knights, organizing them into three groups. Then they marched each group down the field and lined them up behind a marked spot directly in front of the three targets.

"The archers will begin shooting two hundred yards from the target," Sir Edwyn explained. "Each knight will have three arrows. Points are given based on where the arrow hits the target. The two knights with the highest score in each group advance to the next round, where they will have to shoot from a three-hundred-yard distance."

Joanna watched as the first three archers took their positions.

"Ready your bows," the official called.

In unison, the knights raised their longbows. Then, one by one, he shouted the familiar commands. "Nock! Mark! Draw!"

Each archer pulled back on the string, holding it taut, his arrow ready.

"Loose!"

Three arrows flew through the air simultaneously. Sir Guy, who was closest to the stands, hit his target within the blue ring. The archer next to him hit the red section. The one on the far side of the field hit the bull's-eye. Cheers erupted from the spectators. The officials made note of the scores, and the knights prepared themselves for their second attempt.

Joanna's gaze moved from the men readying their bows to Sir Lukas. From his position in the group closest to the stands, it appeared that he would be one of the last competitors to shoot, but he was not idly awaiting his turn. Even from this distance, she could see the concentration on his face as he studied the flight of his opponents' arrows.

Movement among the men in the next group over caught her attention. Joanna looked that way and instantly spotted Sir Nigel. His focus was as complete as Sir Lukas's, but he was not watching the archers' performances. He was staring at Sir Lukas. And at the expression on his face, a large ball of dread formed in Joanna's stomach. Never before had she seen such a look of unadulterated hatred.

Chapter 20

THE WIND WAS CAUSING THE archers problems. Lukas glanced upward. Fluffy clouds were scudding across the sky, and to the west, a large bank of gray rain clouds was moving ominously closer. He shook his arms, trying to work out the tension that had been building as he'd waited for his turn. His leg was aching from standing too long, and his torso was stiffer than he'd like, but he would make no excuses. Today, he needed to shoot well no matter his injuries.

He looked to his right. The number of men on the field had dwindled to five: the two officials and the last three knights awaiting their turn. Across from the farthest butt, a tall, thin knight with long, wheat-colored hair was anxiously pacing back and forth, his feet wearing a muddy track in the grass. Next to him was Sir Nigel. He stood perfectly still, his face a closed mask.

"Take your positions."

The officials moved away from the targets as the knights lined up across from each other.

"Ready your bows."

Lukas tried to clear his mind of everything but the longbow, the arrow, and the target. He listened as the official called out his instructions.

"Nock! Mark! Draw! Loose!"

The moment he released the arrow, Lukas felt the extra gust of wind. The fletching quivered as its course altered, and seconds later, the tip entered the target three inches below the bull's-eye. In frustration, he looked to see how his opponents had fared. The tall knight's shoulders were slumped, and Lukas understood why. His arrow had barely hit the outer edge of the target. Sir Nigel, however, wore a smug smile. His arrow had landed in the very center of the target.

"You'll have to do better than that to win Lady Joanna's hand," Sir Nigel said with a condescending sneer.

Lukas remained silent.

"What are you going to blame?" Sir Nigel goaded. "The weather? The wait? Or your inferior bow?" He slid his hand up the shaft of his longbow as though wanting to emphasize its superiority.

Biting back a scathing retort, Lukas was about to turn away when he noticed Sir Nigel's arm against his bow. It was raised high enough that his sleeve was pulled up. And on his forearm, clearly visible from fifteen feet away, was an ugly scar in the shape of a *C*.

It was as if all the air suddenly left Lukas's lungs. There it was. The proof he'd been searching for since he'd awoken in Agnes's cottage. Not only had Sir Nigel stolen his horse, but he'd been the one who'd thrown the dagger into his leg and tossed him over a cliff to die.

"Ready your bows!"

Without ceremony, the official's voice brought Lukas back to his present, pressing task. He swung around and faced the target, banking down the fury that was clamoring for release. He would have his moment with Sir Nigel. But this was not it. Taking a deep, cleansing breath, he lifted his father's bow, positioned the arrow, and pulled back the string. "For Lady Joanna," he said, and he let his arrow fly.

It hit the bull's-eye. He heard the crowd roar their approval, but he ignored their accolade. He slid another arrow out of his quiver and took his position again. Minutes later, another perfect shot landed in the center of the target. Without a word to anyone, he turned and started walking toward the stands.

"Sir Lukas!"

Lukas looked back. One of the officials was hurrying to catch up with him.

"You and Sir Nigel are through to the next round, my lord," the man said, panting as he spoke. "We will reconvene at the three-hundred-yard mark after the midday meal."

"I thank you." Lukas managed a nod of appreciation. He had no doubt that Sir Nigel was happy to continue their rivalry into the afternoon. What the villainous knight didn't realize, however, was that no matter how he fared in the archery tournament, to have any chance of marrying Lady Joanna, he'd have to make a second, more successful attempt at killing Lukas first.

❦

Joanna made straight for Lord Gilbert's bedchamber, cutting through the great hall without stopping to talk to anyone. She was grateful to have a reason to excuse herself from eating a meal with the rest of the nobility. Watching Sir Lukas battle back from his first errant shot in the archery tournament had twisted her stomach into knots. She did not want food. She did not want to make polite conversation. And she definitely did not want to sit beside Sir Nigel at the head table.

When she reached her father's door, she knocked. Agnes responded immediately and stepped aside to invite her in.

"How is he?" Joanna asked.

"He's resting at the moment," Agnes said. "During his wakeful times, he's still hallucinating, but he's not as fretful as he was."

Joanna could understand the change in her father's demeanor. The filth, foul odor, and disarray he'd been subjected to earlier were gone. The wooden floor was scrubbed clean, and fresh linens covered his bed. The clutter on the table and floor had been removed, and the pleasant smell of lavender filled the bedchamber.

"You've worked wonders in here," Joanna said, glancing at the tidy row of medicinal potions lined up on the table. "It's no wonder that Lord Gilbert is more peaceful."

"But still gravely ill, I fear."

"Do you have any ideas as to what ails him?"

The healer's eyes met hers, her expression troubled. "Yes, my lady."

Like the wisps of early-morning fog, an eerie sense of foreboding swirled into the room. "What is it, Agnes?"

"Lord Gilbert was poisoned."

Joanna caught her breath. "Are you sure?"

"As sure as I can be," she said. "This morning, his noticeable symptoms pointed to foxglove poisoning—the vomiting, hallucinating, tremors, and irregular heart rate. And when he woke up, his pupils were dilated and he talked of lights and his vision yellowing." She walked over to the corner of the room and picked up a small pestle and mortar. "Then I found this next to the kettle at the fireplace." She offered the bowl to Joanna. "It's ground foxglove leaves."

Joanna stared at her in shock. "You believe Beatrice was administering this to Lord Gilbert?"

Agnes laid a worn hand on her forehead. "As hard as I've tried, I can't think of any other reason for it being in his bedchamber."

"But why? Why would she do such a thing?"

Agnes shook her head sadly. "I cannot tell, my lady."

From his bed, Lord Gilbert gave a low moan. Joanna looked over at him, anger, confusion, and hurt vying for dominance as she considered what Beatrice had done.

"Will he recover?" she asked.

"God willing," Agnes said. "Most of the symptoms will improve as the poison leaves him, but his heart . . ." She shook her head. "It must have a regular beat if he is to fully recuperate."

"Do you have a remedy?" Joanna could hear the desperation in her voice. Her relationship with her father had never been good, but the thought of losing him was terrifying. He was the one constant in her shifting world and her only family.

Agnes gave a worried sigh. "There is one plant known to influence the heart rate," she said. "But the treatment has its own risks."

"What kind of risks?"

"The antidote comes from the belladonna."

Joanna looked at Agnes in horror. "But belladonna is even more poisonous than foxglove."

"Aye. Unless the dose is small enough that the heart is regulated rather than stopped."

Joanna covered her face with her hands. Why did Beatrice—or someone with great influence over her—want Lord Gilbert dead? Was the damage to her father's health already irreversible? Did his only hope of recovery come from a dose of poison that could just as easily cause him to take his last breath? As one overwhelming question tumbled over another, a sob escaped her.

"There now, child." Agnes wrapped her arms around Joanna. "Your father is a strong man. Mayhap the strongest man I know. He will fight back."

Joanna could not remember the last time she'd been held by someone who cared, and Agnes's compassion was her undoing. Her load was too heavy, her anxiety too great. Resting her head on the kindly woman's shoulder, she allowed herself to cry.

"What must be done for him?" she asked when her tears finally slowed. She raised her head and wiped her cheeks with her fingers.

"I've been giving the matter some thought," Agnes said, her unruffled manner doing much to calm Joanna's tumultuous emotions. "It may be a few days before Lord Gilbert is able to take anything more than tea, but if you are willing to talk to the cook, I think it wise that I be the only one to prepare his food or drink."

Joanna had not even considered the possibility of another poisoning attempt. "I will speak with her today."

"Slip brought me some belladonna leaves and berries," Agnes continued. "They're not as potent as the plant's root. If Lord Gilbert's heart worsens, I will make him a belladonna infusion." She gave Joanna's hand an encouraging pat. "But you and I both know he's quite stubborn enough to overcome this poison on his own."

"Yes," Joanna said, giving her a watery smile. "He is that."

She took a steadying breath and moved to stand at her father's bedside. He was lying on his back, his eyes closed, his breathing even. She lowered herself onto the edge of his bed and took one of his hands in hers. Immediately, his eyes flickered open. Joanna held completely still as he looked at her. He was clearly struggling to keep her in focus.

"Anabel," he whispered.

"No, father, I'm—"

Agnes placed a warning hand on her shoulder. "He believes you are your mother," she said softly. "Let him speak."

"You've been gone for so long," her father said. "And I've missed you every day." He reached out his free hand and ran his fingers down her cheek. "You are so beautiful. And Joanna . . . she is just the same." A single tear ran down the side of his nose. "I have failed her, Anabel. I failed her as an infant when I left her unprotected. Only Gelert knew the danger. A dog. Not me. And I killed him." Another tear joined the first. "And I've failed her now that she's grown. She is like you in every way—her hair, her stature, her courage, her kindness. And every time I am with her, the pain of losing you returns." He tightened his grip on her hand. "I cannot . . . I cannot bear it."

Joanna could hardly believe what she was hearing. Was this truly why her father treated her the way he did? After all these years, was his grief over losing her mother still so raw?

"But now you are back." He smiled. "All will be well now that you're here."

With a start, Joanna realized that this was the first time she'd ever seen her father smile. His stern, unfriendly countenance transformed into something kind and tender.

"Show her that you love her," she whispered brokenly. "That's all Joanna needs."

"No!" The familiar and forbidding Lord Gilbert returned in an instant. "She must have protection. The wolfhound cannot do it alone. She shall have a husband who can defend her better than I did."

The tournament. At last, Joanna understood. Viewed through her father's distorted perspective, the physical battle for her hand in marriage made sense. If her future husband was a skilled archer, he would also be a competent guardian.

"She must be safeguarded, Anabel," he said, his voice starting to fade as his eyes closed. "She's all I have left."

Numbly, Joanna watched her father's breathing deepen. A dull ache filled her chest. After years of yearning for her father's love, of wishing that he felt something more for her than dutiful tolerance, she finally understood why he'd pushed her away.

"We all get hurt in this life, my lady," Agnes said quietly. "Some people carry their wounds on the inside and think their injuries will be hidden from the world, but they don't understand that if they never allow those wounds to heal, they fester and the toxin spreads."

Agnes was right. Her father's guilt and loss, with their attendant bitterness, had colored his life, but there was no reason for his misery to become hers. The pain his actions had inflicted belonged to her past. Only by insisting that she marry the tourney winner could he hurt her now. She gasped. She had no idea how much time had passed; the tournament may have already resumed. "I must go." She rose to her feet and hurried across the room.

"Lady Joanna." Agnes's voice stopped her at the door. "Your father is mistaken about a great many things, but he is correct about one: you are as brave and true as your mother. She would be proud of you."

Joanna swallowed the lump in her throat. There would be no more tears. "Thank you, Agnes," she said. "For everything."

Then, with her wolfhound at her side, she walked out of Lord Gilbert's bedchamber and did not look back.

Chapter 21

GIVING A PERFUNCTORY NOD TO the guard standing at the castle gate, Lukas entered the outer bailey. The area was largely deserted. Members of the nobility were presumably lingering over their meal in the great hall, and the peasants, farmers, and townspeople had remained in the south pasture to enjoy time away from their everyday duties. A few enterprising merchants had chosen to benefit from the large gathering by selling warm buns, nuts roasted in honey, apples, and pears near the lists, but the businesses in the courtyard were closed for the day.

Lukas walked past the quiet garrison, glad to be away from the noisy throng and alone with his thoughts. Now that he knew the identity of his attacker, he had to decide on his best course of action—especially as Sir Nigel was undoubtedly involved in the smuggling operation too. A couple of stray dogs watched him pass from their resting places beneath the eves of the brewhouse, and a wild chicken made a dash for freedom while the canines' attention was diverted. A few yards distant, a horse neighed, and Lukas turned toward the stables.

The stable boy, Peter, was outside the main doors emptying a bucket of horse manure into a wheelbarrow. He looked up as Lukas approached, and smiled with recognition.

"Good day, Peter," Lukas said. "I'm surprised to see you here. I thought you'd be at the tournament."

The young boy's face fell. "Master Timothy and the other lads went, but someone 'ad to stay with the horses."

"You lost the draw," Lukas guessed.

"Aye." Peter looked down. He kicked a small rock, and it bounced away.

Lukas reached over and ruffled the boy's hair. "Not to worry," he said. "There'll be more tournaments."

"Will there though?"

Lukas realized he'd spoken without thinking. This was the first tournament Moreland had seen in almost two decades. Who knew if Lord Gilbert would organize another one once Lady Joanna was betrothed. "I certainly hope so," he said.

Peter sighed. "Me too."

Lukas pointed at the stable doors. "I thought I'd go in and take another look at the black charger."

The stable boy perked up. "'E's a beauty, that one." Then he lowered his voice. "No one's come t' check on him, my lord. I've been keeping me eye out."

"I thank you, Peter. I knew I could count on you."

The young boy stood a little taller. "Of course, my lord."

Lukas hid a smile and entered the dimly lit stable. A few of the horses studied him curiously as he walked past their stalls, but the black horse in the stall on the right gave a welcoming nicker.

"Hello, Shadow," Lukas said, lifting the latch and letting himself into the stall. He patted the horse's strong shoulders. "I've missed you."

Shadow lowered his head and rubbed his nose against Lukas's other hand. Lukas chuckled. "Alas, I don't have anything for you today. I didn't even stop to buy myself an apple."

The horse snorted as if expressing his disapproval, then he raised his head and faced the door, his ears twitching nervously.

"Saddle my horse, boy! And be quick about it."

Lukas froze. He knew that voice. The nasal speech was unmistakable.

"Right away, my lord." There was a hint of fear in Peter's voice, and Lukas heard the boy's hurried footsteps cross the cobblestones and enter the stable.

Quietly, Lukas slipped into the far corner of Shadow's stall. He could just make out Peter's silhouette as the boy went into a stall on the other side of the stable. Seconds later, Peter led out a tall stallion and walked him to the main doors. There was a jingle of metal and the creak of leather as he retrieved the bridle and saddle and readied the horse.

Lukas's thoughts whirled. In less than two hours, he'd seen the scar of the man who'd assaulted him, and now he was listening to the voice of the man who'd watched his attack from the trees. Who was he? Peter obviously knew him and knew his horse, which suggested that he was from Moreland. Where was he going on the day of the castle's much-anticipated tournament? And more to the point, why was he in such a hurry?

Other than marching outside and confronting the man, there was only one way to find out. Moving to the front of the stall once more, Lukas retrieved the tack hanging beside the door.

"It looks like we're going for a ride, Shadow," he whispered as he slid the bridle over his horse's head.

Outside the stable doors, the nobleman was still barking demands at Peter, chastising him for taking so long to prepare his horse.

"Take your time, Peter," Lukas muttered, working to secure Shadow's borrowed saddle. "I'm almost ready." He reached over the stable door, released the latch, and led Shadow out. Upturning a nearby bucket and using it as a mounting block, he was in the saddle in seconds. A confidence born of familiarity flooded him. This was his horse; they knew each other well enough to work as one.

"Nice and easy, boy," he said, patting Shadow's neck. "This will be a hunt."

Shadow tossed his head and gave a snort, anticipation rippling through him.

Lukas waited until he heard the clatter of hooves leaving the stable, then he urged Shadow forward. Peter was standing at the doors, watching the rider disappear toward the north gate, but at the sound of a horse approaching from behind, he swung around, his eyes widening as he saw Lukas astride the black charger.

"My lord," he began. "That horse—"

"Who was the man who just left?"

A look of confusion crossed Peter's face at Lukas's brusque tone. "It was the castle steward, Gerard Bartholomew, my lord."

The steward! No wonder he hadn't had any luck discovering a man with a distinctive manner of speech among the knights. And no wonder the peasants were suffering so badly. The man charged with administering the affairs of the castle and its lands was the very person cheating them of their hard-earned yields.

"Did he tell you where he was going?" Lukas pressed.

"No, my lord." Panic was beginning to manifest itself in Peter's eyes. "He was angry 'cos of how long I took to saddle 'is horse. Said the tide would be up before I finished."

The tide. That was it. He hadn't taken the time to think through the ocean's cycle. Lady Joanna visited Agnes in the early hours of the morning because the tide was low. That meant it would also be low in the early hours of the afternoon. He and Sir Ivan had gone to check the caves too late in the day, and the rising seawater had made their quest impossible. The steward obviously had reason to access the caves while he still could. And Lukas needed to do the same.

He wheeled Shadow around. "I will return shortly," he told the stunned stable boy. "And do not concern yourself over the charger. The horse's owner has granted me permission to ride him."

Before Peter could sputter any kind of response, Lukas took off, following the path the castle steward had taken. He rode through the quiet outer bailey and out the castle's north gate. Pausing momentarily to listen for another horse up ahead, he entered the woods, knowing he had to reach the beach before Gerard disappeared.

When the path's downward slope finally leveled off, it joined another trail Lukas recognized as the one he'd taken from Agnes's cottage. Urging Shadow forward, he followed this path until he saw her humble home set back among the trees. He took the narrow track that led to the cottage and rode around to the other side of the small structure. Dismounting quickly, he led Shadow over to the makeshift pen where Agnes's goat watched their approach with a suspicious stare. He heard Grey barking from the cottage.

"I'm keeping you out of sight this time," Lukas said. He tied Shadow's reins to one of the posts and pointed a warning finger at the goat. "He won't be here long, so I'll thank you not to aggravate my horse."

The goat gave a slow blink, then turned her back on him and went back to grazing tuffs of grass in the far corner of the pen. Lukas shook his head at the obstinate creature, then set off on foot for the nearby beach.

When he reached the edge of the woods, Lukas slowed his steps, stopping behind a large but gnarly scrub oak. He pushed a few branches aside and looked across the small cove. Already the tide was rising. Gerard was walking his horse through two inches of seawater toward the cliff below Moreland Castle. Lukas watched as the steward reached a rocky outcrop, climbed off his mount, and tucked the reins in between the large boulders. Then, with surprising agility, the older man started up a barely discernible trail along the cliff face.

Lukas followed his climb until the steward was about twenty feet above the beach, and then, in the blink of an eye, the man disappeared. Stepping out from behind the trees, Lukas focused on the spot where he'd last seen Gerard. Beside a few scraggly bushes, a slight shadow darkened the chalky rock, and he realized he was looking at a long fissure that ran several feet up the cliff. If this was where the smugglers' goods were stored, the narrow entrance must widen into a larger cave. His heart rate quickened. One look inside would confirm all his suspicions. He simply needed the steward to leave before the sea level was too high for him to cross.

Waiting was torture. Especially as it was accompanied by the steady lapping of the ever-rising tide. But at last, Lukas spotted movement near the bushes. Gerard was on his way down the cliff side. Making sure he was well concealed by the oaks, Lukas watched as the steward clambered onto the boulders and mounted his horse. The well-trained animal did not balk as it walked through the swirling waves, and when it reached the path that led back to the castle, Gerard gave a swift kick of his heels, and the horse immediately picked up speed, cantering into the woods and out of sight.

Lukas didn't hesitate. Leaving the safety of the trees for the rocky shore, he waded through the six-inch-deep water, heading straight for the cliff. His progress was painfully slow, and his boots became heavier with each step he took, but he pushed on until he reached the boulders where Gerard had left his horse. Here, he left the water and followed the track the steward had taken up the cliff.

If it hadn't been for the scraggly bushes marking the spot, he would have missed the cave's opening completely. The crevice was hidden behind a large rock spur, and only by turning sideways was it possible to see that the crack was far more than a shallow cleft. It was, in fact, wide enough to accommodate a man carrying a moderate load.

He stepped inside and stopped, waiting for his eyes to adjust to the dimness. Above his head, holes had formed in the limestone, allowing pinpricks of sunlight through and enabling him to see a few feet ahead. Rain had obviously gained entry the same way, because the rocky floor was strewn with puddles and the air was cold and damp. Lukas's feet were already soaking wet, so he paid no heed to the water but forged ahead until the narrow tunnel bent sharply to the right.

Suddenly there was light again. A torch blazed brightly from a sconce in the rock wall, illuminating a large, round cave. Filling one side of the cave, almost to the rock ceiling, were bulging bags of wool. About a dozen small wooden barrels were stacked next to the wool, and a blanket and a small sack sat alone on the other side of the rock chamber.

Lukas had just enough time to absorb the scene and realize a burning torch and a blanket likely meant someone else was already in the cave when a crack sounded right above his left ear. A searing pain exploded through his head, and the next moment, his world turned black.

Chapter 22

By the time Joanna reached the stands in the south pasture, most of the nobility were already seated. The spectators standing along the lists on either side of the large pavilion had swelled to even greater numbers than had been there that morning. Despite the fact that the sky was darkening and the breeze had become a brisk wind, no one wanted to miss seeing the best archers compete in the final rounds of the tournament.

Joanna took her place beside Sir Edwyn. "I apologize for arriving so late," she whispered.

"It is no matter," he replied. "I would have escorted you had I known you were still at the castle, as I too was delayed." He looked at her expectantly. "How does Lord Gilbert fare?"

"In health, he is much the same, but he's more comfortable and is resting more peacefully."

"Good." He studied her face, a worried crease appearing on his forehead. "But something else is amiss."

"You are very perceptive, Sir Edwyn," Joanna said. She glanced around, hoping they were speaking softly enough that no one could hear them over the noise of the crowd, the drums, the pipes, and the horns. "I had a unique interaction with my father, which, I confess, has left me somewhat bewildered, but the matter of greatest concern at the moment is that Agnes believes Beatrice has been poisoning Lord Gilbert."

Sir Edwyn tensed. "Does Agnes have proof?"

"She says that Lord Gilbert's symptoms are all indicative of fox-glove poisoning," Joanna said. "And when she cleaned his bedchamber, she discovered a mortar and pestle full of crushed foxglove leaves be-side the kettle."

Sir Edwyn uttered an oath and rose to his feet. "How long ago did you dismiss Beatrice?"

"It was right before the tournament began this morning," Joanna said, alarm setting in as the look on Sir Edwyn's face became even more grim. "Did I do something wrong?"

"No. You were right to act as you did. It may be the only thing that saved your father's life." He scanned the area until he spotted a guard standing at the bottom of the stairs. "Unfortunately, she knows that Ag-nes will realize what she was about, and she will not want to risk being accused of attempted murder. We must place a trusted guard outside Lord Gilbert's chamber to protect both him and Agnes." He started moving toward the top of the stairs. "If Beatrice has not already quit the castle, the guards will find her."

With a sinking feeling, Joanna watched from her chair as Sir Ed-wyn consulted with the guard below. Minutes later, she saw three more guardsmen join the first in a hurried march across the field toward the castle.

Sir Edwyn reclaimed his seat. "The guards will return and report as soon as they've conducted a thorough search," he said quietly. "If fortune is on our side, they will find Beatrice in her chamber."

Neither she nor Sir Edwyn seemed willing to explore the pos-sible ramifications if Beatrice were not found right away. Outside the castle, the desperate woman could hide anywhere.

A gust of wind sent the flags flapping loudly, and a farmer's hat sailed past the seated guests. Sir Edwyn used the distraction to redi-rect the conversation. "These are difficult weather conditions for the archers."

Joanna nodded. She was already searching for Sir Lukas among the small group of men gathered around the officials near the butts.

He had compensated well for the gusty conditions after his first arrow had fallen prey to the wind's capricious nature in the first round. She prayed he could do it again.

There appeared to be five knights waiting with bows in hand and two officials in deep consultation with one another. Sir Nigel stood slightly apart from the others, a smug expression on his face. The other men, all strangers to her, wore varying looks of concern, nervousness, or relief. Sir Lukas, however, was nowhere in sight. She scanned the men again, noting the officials' concern this time.

"Sir Lukas is missing," she said.

Sir Edwyn studied the men on the field. One of the officials was now walking toward the stand, making straight for Sir Edwyn and Lady Joanna. Sir Edwyn rose to meet him, and a dread like spiraling noxious smoke filtered into Joanna's chest. It was suddenly hard to breathe.

"My apologies, Sir Edwyn," the official said, leaning over the railing so he could talk to the senior knight. "In Lord Gilbert's absence, I've come to ask your permission to begin the last round of the tournament. We are missing one of our finalists, but with the worsening weather, we feel it best that the competition recommence as soon as possible."

At that moment, a roll of thunder sounded, and an anxious murmur rippled through the audience.

"By all means," Sir Edwyn said. "Let the tournament continue." He glanced up at the billowing storm clouds. "But if the weather worsens, I believe a suspension is in order."

"Yes, my lord." The official gave an accepting nod and hurried back across the field.

"Something has happened to Sir Lukas," Joanna said. "You and I both know he would not miss this competition unless . . ." She swallowed hard, unable to finish the sentence. The five knights were taking their positions in front of the targets. "Why did you allow the tournament to go on?" she asked, her voice breaking. "We should be sending guards out to look for him too."

"The rules clearly state that to participate in each round, the competitors must be ready when the officials call their names. If I were to modify the rules to benefit one knight, the others would be up in arms."

Joanna turned and held his gaze. "By 'others,' you mean Sir Nigel. He's undoubtedly the only knight who would object."

How she knew that, she could not fathom, unless she was finally coming to recognize the self-centered nature of her father's advisor. Over the last few days, his flattering smiles had turned smarmy, and his previously attentive conversation had become boastful monologues. Perhaps those traits had always been there and her lack of experience with men had blinded her to them. Or maybe time had opened her eyes to characteristics he'd initially hidden from her. Either way, the thought of being married to him made her physically ill.

"Please, Sir Edwyn," she begged. "Do not enable Sir Nigel to win simply because Sir Lukas is absent. I . . . I do not think I can . . ."

"No matter what Sir Nigel believes," Sir Edwyn said grimly. "He will *never* win your hand or be master of Moreland."

"But if he is victorious today, the prize has already been determined."

"That is true," Sir Edwyn said. He scanned the menacing sky again, and a new level of assurance filled his voice. "But I have appealed to a higher power, and I believe He is going to help us."

At that moment, lightning tore through the clouds in a brilliant burst of white. Women screamed, and near the lists, children ran to find their parents. An acrid smell of burning filled the air. Thunder rolled, and the first heavy drops of rain began to fall.

Sir Edwyn rose to his feet. "I declare the archery tournament suspended," he called in a voice loud enough to be heard by the officials and archers across the field. "Weather willing, we will resume the competition tomorrow morning."

There was a general groan of disappointment from the spectators, but no one protested Sir Edwyn's decision. And within seconds, people were hurrying away from the danger of the open pasture for the protection of their homes.

"Come, my lady." Sir Edwyn held out his arm to Joanna.

She rose and rested her hand on his arm.

At the bottom of the stairs, they ran into Garrick and Slip.

"Where's Sir Lukas?" Slip asked. "He's s'pposed to be here."

"We are wondering the same thing," Sir Edwyn said.

"I fear he's in some kind of trouble," Joanna said, wiping away the telltale moisture from her cheek. "I intend to start searching for him immediately."

Slip's expression brightened. "We can help." He turned to Garrick. "Want to play hide-and-seek in the castle?"

"Yes," Garrick said. "I like that game."

"We're going to look for Sir Lukas."

Garrick smiled broadly. "I'm good at seeking. I find you every time." He patted Joanna's shoulder with a clumsy hand. "Don't cry, Lady. We'll find him, and then you can have a turn."

Joanna's heart swelled with gratitude for his simple, unconditional friendship.

"Garrick, would you be willing to hunt for Sir Lukas with me, and Slip can help Lady Joanna?" Sir Edwyn asked.

Garrick looked worried. "Do you go as fast as Slip?"

"I fear not," Sir Edwyn said.

Garrick's expression cleared. "That's good. I don't either."

Sir Edwyn gave him a good-natured slap on the back. "Then we shall be excellent partners," he said.

Thunder rumbled again, and the rain started falling in earnest. Within seconds, water was running off the pavilion's awning.

"Come," Joanna said. "We must be on our way."

When they reached the castle, they divided. Sir Edwyn and Garrick headed for the west tower. The visiting noblemen were all being housed there, and Sir Edwyn wanted to be sure Sir Lukas hadn't simply gone to take a rest after the morning competition and inadvertently slept too long.

Joanna and Slip were still searching the outer bailey when Sir Edwyn and Garrick reappeared carrying a shirt.

"He's not there," Sir Edwyn said, "but this was lying on his pallet, and I wondered if Cona could help us. The chances are good that Sir

Lukas passed through the outer bailey, but the rain may have already washed away any trace of him."

Joanna took the shirt and placed it against Cona's nose. "Sir Lukas, Cona," she said, lowering the piece of fabric and pointing across the courtyard. "Find Sir Lukas."

Cona put his nose to the ground and started sniffing. He wandered around in ever-growing circles, and as the rain continued to fall, Joanna's discouragement increased. She was just about to suggest that they move their hunt to the inner bailey and the keep when Cona raised his head and gave a short bark.

"What is it, Cona?" she cried, running to join the wolfhound. But the large dog did not wait for her. With his tail flapping wildly, he loped across the courtyard toward the stable. At the main doors, he dropped his head again, sniffing the area and giving a few more excited barks. Moments later, Timothy appeared.

"Can I help you, my lady?" he asked, eyeing Cona warily.

"That is my hope," she said. "Has Sir Lukas come by the stable today?"

"Not as far as I know," he said, scratching his head. "But I was at the tournament until the storm hit." He opened the a little wider. "Peter!"

A stable boy hurried out to join them, his anxious eyes flitting from Timothy to Joanna to Sir Edwyn and back. "Yes, Master Timothy," he said.

"Did Sir Lukas stop by earlier?"

The young boy's look of anxiety catapulted to full-blown panic, and Joanna wondered if the leather strap in his hand would withstand the twisting.

"You have nothing to fear, Peter," she said. "We're simply trying to find him."

"'E . . . 'e came to see the charger," Peter said.

"When was that?" Sir Edwyn asked.

"About midday, my lord."

"And you haven't seen him since then?"

Peter lowered his head. "'E said 'e'd return shortly and that 'e 'ad permission to take it fer a ride. 'E . . . 'e was too fast fer me to stop 'im."

"Just a minute." Timothy's voice was stern. "Are you telling us Sir Lukas left on the charger?"

"Yes, Master Timothy." Peter's voice was barely above a whisper.

"Did he tell you where he was going?" Sir Edwyn asked.

"No, my lord. 'E jus' took off after Gerard Bartholomew. But the steward didn't say where 'e was goin' neither."

"Has the steward returned?"

"Yes, my lord. 'E got back some time ago. 'Is horse's legs were covered in sea salt, so 'e 'ad me wash them off, but the stallion's been in 'is stall since then."

The stable boy looked at Timothy as though hoping his care of the steward's stallion might reduce his punishment for the loss of the charger.

"Thank you, Peter," Sir Edwyn said. "You've been most helpful."

"Welcome, my lord," he mumbled.

The knight's praise was obviously not as important as reassurance from the stable master. Sir Edwyn exchanged a look with Timothy.

"Don't fret, lad," Sir Edwyn said. "I have it on good authority that Sir Lukas was well within his rights to ride off on the charger." He drew a coin out of his purse and tossed it at the surprised boy. "For your honesty and hard work."

Joanna saw appreciation for Sir Edwyn's gesture on Timothy's face, and her concern for the stable boy diminished. As long as Timothy recognized Peter's integrity, all would be well with the boy. She only wished she felt the same sense of calm about Sir Lukas's welfare.

Chapter 23

"I WAGER SIR LUKAS WENT to check on the caves," Slip said when they were far enough away from the stables to speak freely.

"Undoubtedly," Sir Edwyn said, his expression puzzled. "But why? What triggered his need to go in the middle of the tournament?"

"That's when the tide's low," Garrick said matter-of-factly.

"Of course," Sir Edwyn said.

"And something prompted him to follow Gerard Bartholomew," Joanna added.

"Indeed." Sir Edwyn looked thoughtful. "It must have been something very compelling if he was willing to risk revealing his identity by riding Shadow."

"Maybe those men ambushed him again," Slip suggested.

"That's highly unlikely during daylight hours," Sir Edwyn said. He glanced at Joanna worriedly. "Highly unlikely."

Joanna felt as though she were going to be sick. She did not wish to be reminded of Sir Lukas's condition when she'd first found him. Neither did she want to stand in the courtyard considering possibilities or probabilities. There were too many. All she knew was that her sense of urgency to find Sir Lukas was increasing at an alarming rate.

"See if you can discover what the steward was doing at the beach," she said. "I'm going there myself."

"The tide will be in by now," Sir Edwyn said. "There is nothing you can do."

Joanna shook her head. "No, my lord. It is *all* I can do."

"I will go with you," Slip said.

She gave him a grateful smile. "I would be glad of your company."

"Are we going seeking again?" Garrick asked.

The concerned frown had not left Sir Edwyn's face, but he managed a weak nod. "Aye, lad. But this time we are looking for Gerard Bartholomew."

"All right," Garrick said happily.

"Will you not reconsider, my lady?" Sir Edwyn said. "You may be placing yourself in grave danger."

Joanna's mind was made up. "I must do this," she said. "And it should be done right away."

"I will watch out for her, my lord," Slip said, moving to stand beside her.

Sir Edwyn gave a heavy sigh. "I shall count on it."

❦

As consciousness slowly returned, Lukas wondered why he was lying on the cliff ledge again. The pain in his head and the hard, unyielding rock beneath his bruised body was all too familiar. But he felt sure he'd recovered from this fall once before.

"Joanna." His voice was barely above a whisper. Was she there?

"The name's Audric, and you'll get no help from me, mate." The gruff voice was accompanied by a cruel kick to his side.

The air escaped Lukas's lungs in a swift hiss, and he rolled forward only to find that his hands and ankles were bound. Forcing his eyes open, he blinked against the flickering light, struggling to bring his eyesight into focus. He was lying on his right side on a stone floor. Immediately in front of him stood a man wearing worn leather boots and a dirty, tattered guard's uniform. Behind him, large sacks overflowing with fluffy wool swirled in slowly moving circles across his blurred vision until they finally settled into orderly rows stacked against the rock wall.

Memory came flooding back. He'd found the cave and the stolen wool, but he'd been unprepared for the guard. As far as he could tell, his head had borne the brunt of his error in judgment. He slowly rotated his neck, studying his left shoulder. His doublet and white shirt were stained brown. He had no idea how long he'd been unconscious, but there had been enough time for his blood to dry and discolor.

He licked his lips, trying to sort through his muddled thoughts. He'd been an idiot to enter the cave unarmed. He'd been so anxious to uncover evidence against the smugglers he'd failed to recognize the obvious. Gerard had arrived and left empty-handed. With no goods to deliver, the reason for his hasty trip was undoubtedly to convey a message to someone waiting inside the cave.

"It must have been important news to bring Gerard Bartholomew out here during daylight hours," he said.

Audric's dark eyes narrowed at Lukas's mention of the steward's name. "What do you know of him?"

"Very little," Lukas said. "Except that he's clearly a dishonest louse of a man who cares nothing for the people he's supposed to be serving."

Audric grinned, revealing a row of broken and blackened teeth. "Offends your knightly sensibilities, does it, my lord?"

Lukas remained silent, studying the man. His long, greasy hair hung lank around his shoulders, and the smell that attended him suggested that personal hygiene had not been a priority for some time. But his clothing, filthy though it was, included a tabard emblazoned with the Moreland crest, and that gave Lukas a pretty good idea of his captor's identity.

"It seems you've had significant practice in knocking people unconscious this week," he said. The grin on Audric's face evaporated, and Lukas knew he'd guessed correctly. "Your fellow guardsman and a young peasant boy." He let that sink in for a moment. "Gerard Bartholomew doesn't stoop to doing his own dirty work, I assume."

Audric scowled and turned away. "Enough," he said. "No more talking."

Lukas rolled onto his back, and biting his lip against the agony the movement produced, he heaved himself upright. The room swam, and he fought back the nausea that came with it. Taking a few deep breaths, he lowered his head until the dizziness subsided. It would be so much easier to lie down and close his eyes against the throbbing in his head, but he had to stay alert. "So after all you've done for him, has the good steward remembered to bring you food and water while you've been holed up in here?"

"I've had sufficient," Audric said, a malicious glint in his eye. "But it's all gone now, which makes leaving you here to starve to death even easier."

Lukas guessed that a more accurate description of the guard's food supply would be *meager*, and it was likely that hunger could drive him to even greater violence. He was reluctant to goad the man too far, but he needed to know what the smugglers' plans were.

"I didn't realize you were going anywhere," he said.

"By tomorrow morning, I shall be in France," Audric said, his look daring Lukas to defy him. "And all this wool is going with me. I shall have more money in my purse than you can dream of, and you will be left to die in an empty cave."

Lukas raised one eyebrow. "It seems that you've put a lot of faith in the word of two rogues," he said. "I wonder how their purses will compare to yours."

Audric's face reddened, and he unleashed a string of oaths. He reached for the closest bag of wool and tore a long strip of fabric off the top. Advancing on his captive, he knelt and stuffed the fabric into Lukas's mouth, pulling it back so tightly that Lukas started choking.

"Knocking you senseless again would give me great pleasure," he said, his mouth inches from Lukas's ear. "But I think I'd rather let you watch everything and everyone disappear before your eyes." He yanked the fabric again and tied it in a knot behind Lukas's pounding head. "You are about to experience a new level of helplessness, my lord." He surveyed his handiwork with a self-satisfied smirk. "But I don't want to hear one word about it."

Lukas sat still as Audric moved to the other side of the cave and lowered himself to a sitting position on the blanket there. He'd paid a price for provoking the guard. His mouth and tongue were already completely dry, and breathing was difficult. The gag's coarse fabric was cutting into his cheeks and had reopened his head wound. He could feel blood running down his neck, but he tried not to dwell on his discomfort. He was still conscious, and he'd been able to confirm young John's information. The goods were to be moved tonight.

His thoughts flew to Sir Ivan. Had he reached the customs officials in Dover? Did they believe his tale? And would he bring help in time? Lukas pulled on the cords binding his arms. They were tight. So tight they were biting into the flesh at his wrists. But he had to try to loosen them. Freeing his hands was the only hope he had for escape.

❦

Joanna led Slip through the large castle kitchen. They had stopped at Joanna's bedchamber to drop Cona off with Eva. Her dog had moped about being left behind, and her lady's maid had been frantic about the decision. But it was worth it. Even without her home-spun-clothes disguise, Joanna had passed by the busy scullery maids without a single one raising her head long enough to recognize her. Cona's presence would have made that impossible.

She opened the door that led to the cellar and reached for the torch on the wall. Using the flint she'd taken from her peasant dress, Joanna lit the torch and held it up until she and Slip arrived at the bottom of the stairs.

"You must swear that you will tell no one about this tunnel," Joanna said. "No one at all."

"You have my word," Slip said. He was fairly twitching with excitement.

"Very well," Joanna said. "Turn around."

"What?"

"I need your back to me," she said. "You may know about the tunnel, but you may not know how to access it."

Slip folded his arms. "What if I need to go for help?"

"Then I might tell you," Joanna said.

"What if you are unable to speak?"

Joanna chuckled. "Turn around, Slip."

With a pout, the boy spun around and faced the other way. "Ready?" he said when the sound of stone grinding on stone ended.

"Yes." Joanna stood beside the hole, holding the torch.

"Good. The rats are crawling all over my feet," he said, stepping closer. "Whoa!" He gazed into the darkness below. "Are we going all the way down?"

"I shall go first," she said. She descended the ladder quickly. Then she elevated the torch above her head to guide Slip down. When he reached the ground, he looked around in wonder. "Who made this?"

"I do not know," Joanna said. "But it's likely been here as long as the castle itself." She pushed the rock lever that closed the trap door while Slip's attention was elsewhere. "Come."

Joanna guided Slip through the dark, damp tunnel until she saw the first glimpse of sunlight filtering through the gloom. "We are close," she said. "Remember, the ledge is narrow, and the sea level is high."

Slip nodded, and when they reached the entrance, he dropped to his hands and knees and crawled across the ledge until he was able to look over the precipice at the scene below. "The ocean's troubled today," he said.

Joanna inched her way forward. The rain had slowed to a light drizzle, but the ledge was wet and slippery, and puddles had formed among the rocky pockmarks and depressions. Wishing she'd taken the time to change into her serviceable peasants clothing, she hiked up the muddy hem of her new silk dress and knelt beside Slip.

He was right. The sea was rushing the land in angry gray swells, each wave battering the coast with indomitable strength. A lone seagull flew by, coasting on the buffeting wind, but every other creature must have taken cover from the storm. From the woods to the rocks, from the water to the sky, the scene before her was disconcertingly empty of any animal life.

"What are we looking for, exactly?" Slip asked.

"I don't know," Joanna said helplessly. "Anything out of the ordinary. Anything that might indicate that a person passed by."

Slip gave her a skeptical look. "A person. All the way up here. We'll be lucky to find traces of a bird or a rabbit. Especially in this kind of weather."

"What else can we do?"

"I dunno," he said. He lay flat on his stomach and rested his chin on his arms, studying the cliff below. "Does a gorse bush ever have white flowers?" he asked.

"No," Joanna said. "The blossoms are bright yellow."

"That's what I thought." He raised his head and gave her his characteristic crooked grin. "There's a gorse bush down there with big, white blobs on its branches. If I didn't know better, I'd say it was wool stuck to the thorns. There's no sheep foolish enough to climb this cliff, but Sir Lukas seemed to think wool smugglers might be."

Joanna bent down next to him. "Show me."

Slip pointed to a spot about halfway between the ledge they were lying on and the ocean. "See that outcropping of rock?" he said. "Just to the left of it are two or three bushes. They look like gorse to me. Not much else grows here."

Joanna's heart started to thump uncomfortably. The rain had caused the white appendages to the bush to hang in uneven strings. And from this distance, the strings looked remarkably like spun wool.

"Do you see anything else down there? A path or a cave?"

Slip leaned forward a little more, and Joanna reached out and grabbed his tunic. "Not too far," she warned.

"There might be a path," he said, scooting back a few inches. "It's difficult to say from here, but it doesn't look like much more than a rabbit trail."

"We must go down," Joanna said, crawling back to the safety of the tunnel before rising to her feet. "If the smugglers are using a cave near those bushes, there's a good chance Sir Lukas is there."

Slip blanched and scuttled backward like a crazed beetle. "Did you not see how steep and slippery it is?" he cried, standing to bar her way. "If you fall, there's nothing between you and the angry sea." He ran his hands down the sides of his tunic. "Sir Edwyn will put me in the stocks if anything happens to you, and . . . and after that, Lord Gilbert will leave me to rot in the dungeon."

Joanna understood his fear. Truth be told, she felt it too. But an emotion far greater than fear was at work in her heart. "I cannot allow Sir Lukas to die due to my lack of courage," she said.

"But we don't know if he's truly down there."

"I'm willing to take the risk."

"He would not want you to. Sir Edwyn and your father and Eva would not want you to." Slip's voice was increasing an octave with every sentence. "I do not want you—" He stopped abruptly. Cocking his head to one side, he studied her with a furrowed brow. "You have feelings for him," he said accusingly. "You're in love with Sir Lukas."

Joanna ignored his comment and the traitorous tear running down her cheek. "I have to do this, Slip."

He groaned. "Why didn't I stay with Garrick?"

"You can wait here or go back to the castle," she said.

He gave her a reproachful look. "It would be better for me to take my chances on a watery grave than to face Sir Edwyn were I to let you climb down alone."

"I am sorry," she said.

"Not nearly as sorry as me," Slip muttered. He looked down at the forbidding water churning below. "Do you think it's as cold as it looks?"

"I have no intention of finding out," Joanna said. "And you won't either. We've done this climb before, Slip. We can do it again."

He turned to face her once more. He did not look happy, but he now wore an air of reluctant acceptance. "I daresay," he said. "And this time I will take comfort in knowing that I won't have to worry about Garrick landing on me."

Chapter 24

SLIP INSISTED ON GOING FIRST. Joanna held her breath as he took his initial step off the ledge and onto the narrow trail. He clung to a nearby boulder as grit shifted beneath his feet.

"I already told you that this is a very bad plan, correct?" His face was the same color white as his knuckles.

"Yes," she said. "But there is no other option."

"So you say." He reached for the next boulder and slid his feet over. "Waiting for the tide to go out would be far too simple, I suppose."

"I do not especially wish to locate Sir Lukas at the same time as the smugglers."

"Good point." He took another tentative step. "Every time my legs seize up, I will imagine a Frenchie with a knife in my back. That will get me moving again."

With relief, Joanna recognized Slip's sense of adventure resurfacing. Praying that it would overcome his trepidation, she followed him onto the trail. She had hoped that making the journey in daylight would be easier than doing it in the faint light of dawn, but that benefit was offset by the wet conditions, which made the track significantly more treacherous. Their feet dislodged small rocks that bounced down the side of the cliff. The branches of the scrubby bushes clinging to the cliff face were slippery, and the waterlogged tufts of grass were too mushy to be secure.

They had been moving slowly but steadily for some time when Slip halted beside a large jagged rock.

"I can see the woolly bushes," he said. "We should join the track I saw from the ledge soon."

Joanna shifted slightly, straining to see what Slip had spotted. Suddenly the earth gave way beneath her foot. With a cry of terror, she grasped for the closest tuft of grass, but it pulled way in her hand.

"Jump!" Slip yelled.

Her survival instinct took over. Without considering the consequences, Joanna leaped over the gaping hole, landing on her knees on a craggy sliver of ground right beside Slip. He seized her arm in an iron grip.

"Are you all right?" he asked.

Joanna's breath was coming out in shallow gasps, but she managed a shaky nod. Her knees were stinging so badly they were making her eyes water. But she was alive.

"Can you stand?"

She eyed the boulder behind Slip. Perhaps if she held on to that, her legs would hold her weight. She reached out one hand, placing it securely around the edge of the large rock. Her limbs were shaking. She closed her eyes. "Please, Father God," she whispered. "Help me. Help Slip. Help Sir Lukas."

Gingerly, Joanna raised one knee and placed her foot firmly on the ground. Using her hold on the rock as leverage, she carefully pulled herself upright. She heard Slip gasp, and she glanced at him.

"Your . . . your dress," he said.

She looked down. The light-blue fabric was torn, and dark bloodstains marked the positions of both her knees. She ran her free hand over the dirty material, brushing at the grit embedded in her palm. "I fear that Eva will not be happy with me," she said.

Slip gave her an incredulous look. "Are you able to walk?"

Joanna took a wobbly step toward him. "Yes." She lowered her head to hide her grimace as pain pulsed through her legs. "We must go on."

"It looks like the trail might be a little easier from this point," he said.

It was probable that Slip was stretching the truth, but it didn't matter. His bravery was enough. "I'm glad you came," she said.

He gave her an unsteady smile. "You forgot why I'm in the lead. If you'd jumped a little farther, you would have landed on me. It would have saved your knees."

By the time they reached the gorse bushes they'd seen from the ledge, Joanna's legs were shaking so badly she feared they would collapse beneath her. She leaned up against the cliff, wishing there were enough room on the narrow trail for her to sit and rest.

Slip pulled a white mass off the thorns on the nearest branch. "It's wool," he said. "Wet and stringy, but definitely wool."

He handed it to Joanna and looked around. On the other side of the bushes, a narrow outcropping of rock blocked his view, so he stepped around it and immediately disappeared from sight. Joanna wrapped her fingers around the small woolly wad. She held their only clue to Lukas's whereabouts, and she had no idea what to do next.

"Lady Joanna!" Slip appeared as if by magic. "I think I've found something." He reached out and took her hand, pulling her behind him. "Behind this rock, there's a big crevice. I didn't go in very far, but it looks like it's a tunnel."

Joanna stumbled after him, renewed hope keeping her limbs from giving way. "Wait, Slip," she said. "Not too fast."

⁓⦿⁓

Lukas lowered his chin to his chest and tried to relax his arms. Ever since Audric had started snoring, he'd been rubbing the rope around his wrists against the wall behind him, hoping to find a rock fragment abrasive enough to cut through the threads that bound him. His upper arms were on fire, and his skin beneath the rope felt raw, but he couldn't give up. Somehow he had to escape—if not for himself or the capture of the smugglers, then for Joanna.

The image of her face as she'd handed him her ribbon before the tournament had been haunting him since he'd regained consciousness. She'd offered him her favor, had put her trust in him, and he'd let her down. His chest hurt at the thought of her sitting in the stands waiting for him to show up for the next competition only to have those expectations crushed. Would she ever forgive him for failing her so completely? Could he ever forgive himself?

He raised his hands and started the sawing motion against the wall again. It would be too hard to stay on at Moreland with Joanna betrothed to another, but before he left, he would make sure Sir Nigel and Gerard Bartholomew were exposed for the knaves they really were. Surely once Lord Gilbert knew of his advisor's treachery, he would not allow the man to marry his daughter, no matter how well he performed in the archery tournament.

Audric grunted in his sleep, and Lukas held perfectly still, waiting for the deep, even breathing to begin again. And then he heard a voice. At least, he thought he did. Lukas tilted his head slightly, straining his ears. It sounded like a boy talking quickly and excitedly. Had the bang to his head affected his hearing? He listened again. Now the voice sounded like a woman's.

Joanna. His heart started to pound. How could that be? Surely the tide had not yet dropped enough to make the cliff accessible from the beach. But the voices were getting louder and more distinct. They must be in the tunnel. He glanced at Audric. The guard was stirring again.

"Go back," he whispered helplessly behind his gag. "Go back."

Slip and Joanna appeared at the cave entrance within seconds of each other. Joanna's face was pale, her hair wet and tangled. There was mud smeared across her cheek, and large stains marked the lower portion of her damaged dress. She blinked several times as her eyes adjusted to the bright torchlight, then her eyes settled on him.

"Lukas!" she cried. Then she was stumbling toward him.

From the other side of the cave, Audric leapt to his feet. Slip saw the guard and ran at him, wrapping his skinny arms around the man's legs and toppling him to the ground. But Slip was too small to keep the battle-hardened guard down. Within moments of his fall, Audric was back on his feet, holding the boy by the scruff of the neck with one hand and clasping a wicked-looking knife in the other.

Joanna crumpled to the floor. "Let him go." The agony in her voice was the worse form of torture, and Lukas pulled even harder at his restraints.

"Why would I want to do that?" Audric said. He dragged Slip over to one of the woolsacks and cut the rope off the top. "Now then," he said, pointing the knife at Joanna. "If you sit perfectly still, I'll tie this boy up without any injury. One move, mark you, and he'll feel my blade." As if needing to prove his point, he placed the tip of his knife on Slip's arm and pushed just enough to draw a drop of blood.

"Stop!" Joanna said. "Don't hurt him. I will not move from here."

Lukas had never wanted the use of his arms more than he did at that moment. But if they'd been free, he didn't know what he wanted to do most—wrap one protectively around Joanna's shaking shoulders or hook one threateningly around Audric's worthless neck. Instead, he watched helplessly as the woman he loved sobbed silently and Slip was bound hand and foot.

"I'm so sorry, Slip," she said.

"It's all right, my lady." The young boy was as stoic as the bravest knight. "I was wanting a sit down anyway."

"Well, you'll get that," Audric said, tossing the boy unceremoniously onto the floor a few feet from Lukas. "You can stay right there until your bones rot."

Slip slowly rolled over and squirmed himself into a sitting position, but Audric's attention was already elsewhere. And the evil glint in the guard's eyes made Lukas's blood run cold. He tugged at the rope on his ankles and wrists, the friction burning even more deeply than before. *Oh, Father God*, he desperately prayed in silence, *I can do nothing. Please protect her.*

"It seems that it's your turn, Lady Joanna," Audric said. Without taking his eyes off her, he cut another piece of rope off a third sack. "And I believe this will be a far more pleasurable trussing."

Joanna sat up tall. "You do not have permission to touch me," she said.

Audric gave a vile sneer. "You're not in your fancy castle anymore, my lady. I'm in charge here, and we play by my rules."

"That's not what Lord Gilbert's men will say when they walk in," Slip said. "They were right behind us."

"Shut yer mouth, boy. Or you'll end up with a gag in it."

Slip shrugged. "It's your neck."

Audric glared at him. "No one can get here till the tide goes down."

"That's a well-known fact hereabouts," Slip said. "'Course, Lady Joanna and I didn't get here by swimming or flying—but that's neither here nor there."

The guard looked as though he were going to grind what few teeth he had left into dust. "Low tide's at midnight," he growled.

"And what exactly is your timepiece in here? Do you know how long you were asleep before we came in?"

"Enough," Audric roared. He hurriedly wrapped a rope around Joanna's wrists and cinched it with one pull. "I have not finished with you yet," he said. Then he pointed his knife at Slip and started backing across the cave. "The moment I return, I'm putting a gag on you."

"Hurry, Lady Joanna," Slip said as soon as the guard disappeared into the tunnel. "There's a knife in my left boot. Take it out and cut Sir Lukas free."

Joanna hastened over to the boy, and Lukas was grateful that even though her hands were tied, they were not behind her back. Within seconds, she had the knife. Lukas swiveled around so his back was to her, and moments later, he felt the pull of the blade against the rope as she severed the strands.

"Your wrists are covered in blood," she said brokenly.

Lukas shook his head, trying to tell her it was no matter.

"Quickly," Slip urged. "As soon as his hands are free, give him the knife."

"Here," she said, and he felt the cool metal handle against the palm of his hand.

He grasped it and pulled his arms forward. His fingers were swollen and discolored, but the knife was sharp and needed very little help to cut through the ropes around his ankles. The moment his legs were free, he reached for Joanna's hands and sliced through the rope at her wrists. He placed the knife back in her hand and pointed to Slip. Staggering to his feet, he tugged at the gag, tossing it to the floor as he scoured the cave for anything he could use as a weapon.

"Cut Slip free," he croaked.

Near the entrance to the tunnel, a large rock lay on the ground. Lukas forced his legs forward, hoping his numb feet would support him. He reached the opposite wall and bent down to pick up the rock. A dark-brown stain marked one side of it, and Lukas grimaced. It was undoubtedly his blood.

"He's coming back." Slip spoke softly, and Lukas focused on the sound of footsteps echoing off the rocks.

Lukas waited until the tip of Audric's shadow touched the cave floor, then he raised the rock and brought it down in a glancing blow across the guard's head. The man reeled, a look of shock crossing his face, and then he crumpled in a heap.

"Help me, Slip," Lukas called.

He placed his swollen hands beneath Audric's arms and waited until Slip had his feet. Then they dragged the unconscious man to the far corner of the cave.

"It was not a hard blow," Lukas said. "He could awaken at any time, so we must tie him securely."

Joanna pulled a piece of rope off a woolsack and handed it to him. His fingers were still not functioning well, but between him and Slip, they cinched the ropes tightly around Audric's hands and feet. He removed the knife from the scabbard at the guard's waist and patted him down to make sure he wasn't hiding any other weapons.

"What about a gag?" Slip asked.

Even though Lukas's mouth still felt like sawdust and his cheeks were chafed raw, he shook his head. "It may be necessary later, but not yet." He placed his hand on the boy's shoulder. "You were magnificent, Slip. I cannot thank you enough for saving Lady Joanna from this man's foul intentions."

Joanna moved to Slip's side and dropped a soft kiss on the boy's forehead. "I am in your debt once again."

Color flooded Slip's face, and Lukas experienced an unexpected flash of envy. He looked away, pulling on Audric's bindings once more, even though he knew they were secure. Seconds later, however, Joanna's hand reached out and pulled his back.

"Leave it now," she said. "Your fingers need time to heal."

Next to his, her hand was small and soft and white. It was covered in scratches and smeared with blood and dirt, but he didn't want to ever let it go. Slowly, he bent his inflamed fingers around hers, his breath catching as she gently reciprocated. It was wrong of him, he was sure, but for that fleeing moment, he could believe that she was his.

Chapter 25

FROM THE TIME JOANNA HAD first spotted Lukas tied up on the far side of the cave to the moment he'd knocked out the guard, she'd been surviving on energy drawn from profound desperation. Now that the crisis was at least temporarily behind them, exhaustion was setting in.

With Audric safely bound, Slip volunteered to walk to the entrance of the tunnel to check on the position of the sun and the level of the tide.

Lukas guided Joanna over to the guard's blanket. Her legs throbbed. Walking was becoming more and more difficult as her knees stiffened, so she was grateful to finally lower herself onto the woolen fabric and ease her legs out in front of her.

"You're in pain," Lukas said with a frown.

"As are you," she said.

He sat beside her. "Yes," he said. "But my discomfort almost feels normal."

"I am sorry," she said softly.

"Don't be," he said. "Had I not suffered any injuries in Moreland, I may not have met you." He looked at her. "After that first day on the cliff, it was not long before winning both your heart and your hand became my greatest desire." The regret in his eyes brought tears to hers. "I am aware of your father's determination that you wed the winner of the archery tourney. Nothing Audric could inflict upon me hurt as much as knowing that I was missing the final rounds of that competition."

Joanna's heart was pounding. "You have already won the first, my lord," she said. "And I still dare hope that you will win the second."

His brow furrowed in confusion. "How can that be?"

"Sir Edwyn suspended the remaining portion of the competition due to the storm," she said. "Not one of the competitors took a shot. The final rounds will be held tomorrow if the weather clears."

Shock. Disbelief. Elation. Myriad emotions crossed Lukas's face in a matter of seconds. "Are you saying the tournament did not continue without me? That you're not yet betrothed to another?"

She nodded, and the movement released a tear. He raised his hand and cupped it around her cheek, tenderly wiping away the moisture with his thumb.

"When you entered the cave, you called me by my given name." He spoke quietly. "You called me Lukas."

"I . . . I . . ." Beneath his hand, Joanna's cheeks flamed. When had she begun thinking of Sir Lukas as simply Lukas? However could she explain such a breach of etiquette? "I apologize, my lord," she stammered. "The strain of the moment must have—"

"I wish you would continue," he interrupted gently.

The intense gaze of his deep-brown eyes captured hers, and she wondered if her heart would ever find its normal rhythm again.

"Then, will . . . will you call me Joanna?" she whispered.

His answering smile eclipsed the blood, dirt, and wounds on his face. And for a brief moment, their injuries and dire circumstances faded into insignificance.

"I pray you win the tourney, Lukas," she said.

From the tunnel came the sound of Slip's footsteps drawing nearer.

"Then your prayers will be added to mine," he said, and like the touch of a gentle butterfly, his lips brushed hers.

Seconds later, when Slip entered the cave, Lukas was facing forward and Joanna was trying to remember how to breathe.

"The tide has turned, and dusk is approaching," Slip announced. "The rain clouds have moved on, and there's a full moon, so even though our feet may get wet, I daresay we could cross the beach within two or three hours."

Lukas looked thoughtful. "I think it best if we are out of the cave before midnight. One rock and two knives will not be sufficient to defend ourselves against seasoned smugglers. We need reinforcements—both men and weapons."

"I'm grateful you brought a knife, Slip," Joanna said.

"Actually," Slip said, with a grin. "That was Audric's spare."

"But it was in your boot."

She heard Lukas chuckle and turned to see him exchanging a knowing look with the boy. "You took it when you wrestled."

Slip wiggled his fingers, his smile widening. "It's good to know they still work, isn't it? The hilt wasn't too far into his boot, so it wasn't hard to transfer it to mine."

"You . . . you snitched it!" Joanna put her hand to her mouth as her giggle surfaced, and the next minute, all three were laughing. "Oh, Slip, what will Agnes say?"

Slip gave a sheepish shrug. "Mayhap we should not tell her."

"That would be an excellent idea, unless you ever want to boast about how you single-handedly saved us," Lukas said, but at the boy's crestfallen look, he offered another suggestion. "Perhaps you could tell how you both arrived at the cave during high tide instead."

Slip looked at Joanna expectantly, but his shoulders slumped when she gave a slight shake of her head.

"I fear that will have to remain a secret too," Slip said.

Lukas raised his eyebrows in surprise. "Can you tell me?"

Again Slip turned to Joanna. Touched by his deference and loyalty, she gave him a small smile. "I believe we should share how we came to be here," she said. "Much of importance has happened at the castle during the last few hours, and some of those things are unknown to Sir Lukas." She glanced him. "I daresay he has much to tell us also."

"I would like that very much," Lukas said. He looked at her expectantly. "Would you be willing to start us off?"

She glanced down at her bloodstained, torn, and dirty dress. Had it really been only this morning that she'd donned the gown for the first time? She felt as though she'd lived an age since she'd risen for the day. So much had changed in that relatively short time.

"Today, I learned that Beatrice, the castle healer, has been poisoning my father," she said.

Lukas stared at her in shock. "How did you discover this?"

"With the help of Agnes," Joanna said. She went on to describe all that had happened from the time she'd knocked on Lord Gilbert's bedchamber door and confronted Beatrice to when Agnes had handed her the mortar and pestle full of dried foxglove leaves.

"What is being done about it?"

"As soon as Sir Edwyn learned of her treachery, he sent guards to locate her. But I do not know if they were successful."

"Because then we had to start looking for you," Slip said.

He picked up their account, telling Lukas that when he'd not appeared for the final portion of the tournament, they'd searched for him at the castle. And that Cona had led them to the stable, where Peter had told them of his contact with Lukas and Gerard Bartholomew.

"We could not fathom why you followed the castle steward," Joanna said, "so Sir Edwyn and Garrick went to speak with Gerard Bartholomew while Slip and I continued our hunt for you."

"Lady Joanna was sure you were at the caves." Slip's eyes were alight with excitement. "So we went through a secret tunnel under the castle and came out high above this cave. From there, we saw wool on the bushes and climbed down to see if we could find you."

"You climbed down the cliff face?" Lukas's expression was a blend of admiration and horror.

"In the rain," Slip said. Now that he was safely in the cave, he seemed quite proud of their lunacy.

Lukas glanced at the blood on Joanna's dress. "Then your fall must have put your life in danger."

"It was bad," Slip admitted. "The earth gave way beneath her feet."

Lukas's hand reached for hers, and he held it tightly. "It's best that I did not witness it."

Joanna gave his hand a gentle squeeze, as anxious to move on from that part of the account as he seemed to be. "Tell us how you came to be following Gerard Bartholomew."

He gave a slow nod. "I will, but first you should know that I have learned the identities of the two Englishmen who attacked me."

Slip gasped. "Who are they?"

"Sir Nigel and Gerard Bartholomew."

For a few moments, all Joanna could do was stare at him, astounded. He was charging her father's advisor and the castle steward as accomplices in an attempted murder. Was there to be no end to the betrayal at Moreland?

Lukas studied her, his expression concerned, but when she said nothing, he continued. "Sir Edwyn and I suspected Sir Nigel's involvement last night," he said. "That was when we learned that it was Sir Nigel who had charged Sir William with the task of delivering my saddleless horse to Moreland's stables the night I was attacked. And it was he who rewrote the guard schedule to ensure Audric's assignment at the shearing shed when the last of the wool was stolen." He sighed. "I did not know for certain, however, until Sir Nigel made his forearm bare during the archery competition and I recognized the distinctive scar of the man who had plunged a dagger into my leg."

Joanna's grip on Lukas's hand tightened. He gave her a grateful smile. "I left the field quickly, needing to gather my thoughts, and found myself at the stable, visiting my faithful charger. That's where I heard the voice of the man who had remained in the shadows during my assault."

"The steward always sounds as though he has a peg on his nose," Slip said.

Lukas's lips twitched. "His voice is distinctive," he said. "And when I learned who he was and that he was headed to the beach, I followed. He led me to this cave. I waited until he left before entering, not thinking beforehand that a guard would be stationed inside." He grimaced. "I should never have entered unarmed."

Joanna glanced over at Audric's insensible form. How long would it be before he awoke? Or before his accomplices arrived? Sir Lukas had managed to gather most of the threads necessary to unravel the web of deceit that had been spun within Moreland, but there were still things they did not know. "Have you learned anything of the smugglers' plans?" she asked.

"Audric admitted that the Frenchmen are scheduled to pick up the wool at midnight tonight. I assume Sir Nigel and Gerard Bartholomew will be here for the hand off. They will want their payments."

Joanna gazed at the stack of wool bags—evidence of the peasants' and farmers' hard work—and felt her indignation rise. "They have no right to this wool. We will not let them take it," she said.

Lukas smiled at the passion in her voice. "I agree," he said.

"Do you have a plan?" Slip scooted forward, eagerness shining in his eyes.

"We will quit this place as soon as the beach is passable," he said. "My horse is tethered behind Agnes's cottage. You and Lady Joanna must ride for the castle and have Sir Edwyn gather loyal men who can join me here to put an end to this smuggling operation."

"You are sending us away," he accused.

"You and Lady Joanna have shown more courage today than many knights do in a lifetime. It is time for others to take their turn."

Slip frowned, clearly disappointed, but Joanna understood Lukas's desire to have him safely removed from any possible violence. John's head injury at the shearing shed was sufficient testimony of what these men were willing to do to anyone who got in their way—no matter how young the victim.

"It would not be safe for me to return to the castle unaccompanied," she said, hoping to appeal to Slip's sense of valor once more.

Slip perked up slightly. "Might it be dangerous?"

"Undoubtedly," she said, all the while praying it would not.

Slip turned back to Sir Lukas. "May I carry one of Audric's knives to keep Lady Joanna safe?"

"That is an excellent suggestion," Lukas said.

A pleased smile crossed Slip's face, and he moved to examine the two knives more closely.

Lukas leaned closer to Joanna. "I thank you," he whispered. "He would not have agreed to go for any other reason."

Chapter 26

AUDRIC HAD STARTED MOANING BUT had yet to open his eyes when Joanna, Slip, and Lukas left the cave. Lukas took the lead on the narrow path, with Joanna next and Slip bringing up the rear. The rain had stopped, but the rocks were still wet, and the full moon reflected off the moisture, making everything glisten. The wind had also died down, and in the stillness of the night, every whispered word and shower of pebbles their feet dislodged echoed loudly off the cliff face.

By unspoken agreement, they kept their communication to a minimum. Slip stumbled once when his toe caught a root, but he righted himself with little more than a gasp. Joanna focused on following Lukas's footsteps, even though her knees threatened to buckle with every bend. She did not look down. The ever-increasing volume of the rushing waves told her they were getting closer to their destination, and the damp salt air seemed to feel colder the nearer they got to the water.

At last, Lukas slowed his steady pace. "We have reached the boulders at the end of the beach," he said softly. "Wait until my feet are in the water, then climb onto the rocks."

Joanna waited until she heard the slight splash of Lukas's feet entering the sea, then she scrambled onto the boulder. Her legs were shaking uncontrollably, and she sat, trying to draw the strength to enter the dark water and stand against the tide.

"Come," Lukas said gently. He was standing with his arms extended. "Let me carry you."

Joanna bit back a sob. "But you are injured."

He said nothing, but he slid one arm beneath her legs and placed the other at her back. Too exhausted to refuse, Joanna wrapped her arms around his neck and held on as he lifted her off the rock. The water sloshed as he stepped away from the rock and Slip climbed down.

"Not much longer, my love," he whispered. "You have been so brave."

Closing her eyes, she leaned her head against his broad chest and listened to the rhythmic sounds of his heartbeat and his feet whooshing against the receding waves.

"So. The missing archer is found." Sir Nigel's voice sliced through the air like a whip.

Joanna felt Lukas tense, his grip tightening around her as he stood and faced the man who had tried to kill him once before. She turned her head. Sir Nigel was standing about five yards away on the thin sliver of newly exposed pebbles where the woods met the beach. He held his horse's reins in one hand, but as she watched, he dropped the reins and exchanged them for his sword.

Lukas carefully lowered Joanna to her feet. Instantly, the cold water entered her boots and began rising up the fabric of her dress. He held her steady until she found her balance, then he let go and Slip stepped up beside her.

"Slip," he said without taking his eyes off the other knight. "I want you to take Lady Joanna back to the castle."

"No," Joanna said. "I will not leave you here alone."

"Lady Joanna seems to believe you need the assistance of a woman and a child, Sir Lukas."

Sir Nigel's mocking tone carried across the water, and Joanna saw Lukas's jaw clench.

Slip took one look at Lukas's face and reached for her arm. "Come, Lady Joanna."

Joanna stumbled backward. This was all wrong. "Sir Nigel, what are you doing?" she cried.

"Taking care of business that should have concluded over a week ago," he said, taking several steps closer.

"Of course," Lukas said. "I had forgotten that your code of chivalry includes attacking an unarmed man."

The moonlight caught the glint of Sir Nigel's teeth as he sneered, and he stepped even closer. "I will begin by relieving you of this," he said, placing the tip of his sword under the ribbon Joanna had tied to Lukas's arm earlier that day. With a flick of his wrist, he cut it in two. "Lady Joanna, Moreland Castle, and all its land shall be mine."

Muffling a cry with her hand, Joanna watched the ribbon bob once, then disappear beneath a wave.

Slip yanked on her arm again. "We must get out of the water, my lady." His insistence penetrated Joanna's terror, and she managed a few faltering steps.

"Sir Lukas! Your sword!" another voice cried out from the water's edge.

Joanna turned in time to see Sir Edwyn toss a sword directly into Lukas's hands.

Immediately, Sir Nigel lunged, and the ringing of clashing metal rent the air. Sir Nigel pushed forward, causing Lukas to retreat into deeper water as he parried each thrust. Their blades locked, and Lukas swung hard to the right, forcing Sir Nigel's arm upward. Thrown off balance by the diagonal movement, Sir Nigel staggered sideways. Somehow he caught himself, pivoted, and began his attack anew.

Joanna could not tear her eyes from the scene. She was vaguely aware of Slip's hand on her wrist, pulling her to stand closer to Sir Edwyn on the grass, and of his muted voice saying something to the older knight, but nothing registered over the deafening clang of steel and the pounding of her heart.

Suddenly there was a sound of ripping fabric, and a portion of Sir Nigel's white sleeve flapped loose around his elbow. Sir Nigel roared his displeasure and attacked with greater fury. Lukas deflected each thrust. Like a dance, the dueling men slowly rotated until Lukas's back was to the three spectators.

"Well done," Sir Edwyn muttered.

"What is it?" Slip asked. "What did he do?"

"He has turned the advantage," the senior knight said softly. "You notice who is backing into the deeper water now? Sir Nigel's anger is blinding him to Sir Lukas's strategy."

A large wave washed in, and Sir Nigel was caught unawares. He swayed, and Lukas seized the moment to thrust forward, wielding his sword with incredible speed and strength. Sir Nigel teetered backward, trying to regain his footing, but it was useless. He was almost waist deep in water when the tide pulled him under.

Lukas bent down and lifted Sir Nigel out of the sea by his collar. "Surrender," he said.

Sir Nigel coughed, water spewing from his mouth. He still held his sword, and he swung it wildly at Lukas. Lukas did not hesitate. Still holding the floundering knight by his shirt, he dropped him back into the water.

This time when Lukas raised him, he placed the tip of his sword under Sir Nigel's chin. "I said surrender."

Sir Nigel's coughing lasted longer, and when it finally slowed, his head lolled to one side, and he dropped his sword.

"Sir Edwyn," Lukas called. "Your assistance, please."

Sir Edwyn waded out to meet him, and Joanna watched as the senior knight recovered Sir Nigel's sword and walked behind as Lukas half dragged, half carried his opponent out of the water and stretched him out on the pebbly shore. Sir Nigel rolled onto his side, gasping for breath while even more seawater trickled out of his mouth.

"You will stand guard?" Lukas asked, returning Sir Edwyn's sword to him.

"Gladly." The senior knight took his position above the prostrate man, his weapon at the ready.

Lukas turned to face Joanna. He took one step toward her before she flew into his arms. She clung to him, burying her face in his shoulder. He held her close, his breath coming out in deep, ragged gasps. For several minutes, neither one spoke. Then Lukas raised his head. "We need rope, Slip. Can you fetch some from the cottage?"

"Yes, my lord," the boy said. "I'll go right away."

Slip took off at a run, and Lukas placed his hands on Joanna's shoulders. He pushed her a few inches from him. "Go after Slip," he said. "You are shivering with cold. See if you can find a blanket."

Joanna did not know whether it was the night air chilling her wet clothing or her reaction to Lukas's perilous sword fight causing her uncontrollable shaking. Either way, her teeth were chattering so badly she could barely form words.

Lukas lowered his hands and glanced worriedly at the path that led to the cottage. "Slip has already disappeared," he said. "Do you have the strength to travel that distance alone?"

Joanna nodded, not trusting her speech. Behind him, the pebbles rattled. Sir Nigel coughed and uttered an oath—a sure sign that he was reviving. While he was yet unbound, it was not safe for Lukas to leave him alone with Sir Edwyn.

"I will b-bring back a b-blanket f-f-for you," she said, already backing up. Then, hoping that her trembling, aching limbs would not slow her down too much, she hurried after Slip.

The moonlight made the path clear, and it was far easier to walk across the soft loamy ground than it had been to traverse the cliff path or negotiate the wet pebbles of the beach. Slip must have felt the same because by the time she had the cottage in sight, he was already on his way back with the rope.

"I found some out by the goat pen," he said, raising his bundle so she could see. "Sir Lukas's horse is there." He whistled. "He's a beauty."

"I'm going f-f-for b-blankets," Joanna stammered.

Slip's eyebrows shot up. "Is something amiss, my lady?"

She shook her head. "C-cold."

"The blanket on my pallet is the warmest," he offered.

She smiled. "Th-thank you."

He gave her a quick wave and sprinted off toward the beach. Joanna rubbed her hands up and down her arms and headed for the cottage.

The door creaked when she opened it. There was no welcoming fire because Agnes was at the castle, and Garrick was likely with her, but a single candle burned on the table. Joanna hesitated. Would Slip have left a candle burning after so short a visit? Didn't he say he'd found the rope outside? She took another step, listening. All was silent.

The candlelight allowed her to see the familiar layout of the simple cottage, and in the far corner was Slip's pallet with a folded blanket lying on one end. As she moved toward it, the door squeaked closed behind her, and as the latch clicked, an ominous sense of foreboding filled her. Joanna swung around. Gerard Bartholomew was blocking the door.

"You see." A woman spoke from the shadowy corner. "I told you she would come here eventually." Beatrice rose to her feet and joined the steward at the door. Joanna stared at her in shock. The older woman had completely dispensed with her wimple. She was wearing the same stained dress she'd had on earlier that day, and if anything, it was even dirtier than it had been then. Her gray, wispy hair was matted against her head, and she wrung her hands feverishly.

"What are you doing here?" Joanna asked, her shaking replaced by a calm, detached determination. She did not understand where the inner strength to face these two wrongdoers was coming from, but she accepted it gratefully.

"Waiting for you, my lady," Gerard said.

"And why would that be?"

He gave her an oily smile. "It would seem that my sister and I are in need of transportation to France. A boat will be here at midnight, but we fear your assistance may be needed to ensure our safe departure."

Joanna tried to grasp what he'd just told her. "Your sister?"

"Indeed."

With sickening surety, Joanna put another piece of the puzzle together. "You told Beatrice to poison Lord Gilbert."

Anger flashed through the steward's eyes. "I was ignorant of her incompetence," he said. "Lord Gilbert wanted to increase the guards at the shearing shed at a most inconvenient time. Beatrice was simply asked to give him something that would take his mind off protecting Moreland's wool for a few days." He gave his sister a scathing look. "The request was clearly beyond her limited skills."

"He may yet die!" Joanna said.

Gerard shrugged indifferently. "A regrettable mistake," he said. "But another will become Lord of Moreland, and things will go on much as they did before."

Joanna could scarcely believe what she was hearing. Had he forgotten that he was speaking of her father? She took a step toward him. She wanted to lash out, to hurt him the way he'd hurt her and her father and the poor people of Moreland, but she kept her fists tightly closed.

"You will answer for what you have done, Gerard Bartholomew," she said, conviction ringing through her voice.

At her words, Beatrice seemed to shrink, but Gerard did not flinch.

"I think not, my lady." He reached out and grasped her wrist.

Joanna pulled away. "Unhand me."

He laughed and tightened his grip. Dragging her across the room, he forced her onto a wooden chair beside a motionless wolfhound.

"Grey!" she cried. No wonder the cottage had seemed eerily quiet. There had been no welcoming bark from Grey. "What have you done to him?"

"It seems that Beatrice dispenses her potions more successfully to dogs than to humans—especially if it's hidden in meat. I fear he will not be coming to your rescue now, or ever again, my lady."

They had killed Grey. Gentle, blameless Grey. With a heartfelt sob, she twisted, trying to wrench herself free of Gerard's viselike hold.

"Pass me the blanket, Beatrice," he snapped.

The frightened woman scuttled over to Slip's pallet, grabbed the blanket, and handed it to her brother. Pinning Joanna down with one strong arm, Gerard wrapped the blanket around her torso and cinched it tight behind the back of the chair.

"Now," he said, stepping away so that he was facing her again, "we shall wait. And when midnight is here, we shall all take a walk to the beach together."

Chapter 27

By the time Sir Nigel's wrists and ankles were bound, Lukas and Sir Edwyn had endured more than enough of his vitriolic language. Lukas yanked off Sir Nigel's torn sleeve, placed it in the knight's venomous mouth, and secured it tightly behind his head. The ensuing silence was the only thing that made the unpleasant job of hauling their unwilling captive into the woods somewhat tolerable. Slip followed behind with Sir Nigel's and Sir Edwyn's horses, and while Lukas and Sir Edwyn situated Sir Nigel on the ground and made sure there were no rocks sharp enough to cut rope in the vicinity, Slip tied the animals to a nearby tree.

"The Frenchmen are expected at midnight," Lukas told Sir Edwyn when they returned to the beach. "I don't know how many there will be, but I believe reinforcements may be in order."

"I agree," Sir Edwyn said. He looked thoughtful. "You say Audric is in the cave?"

"Yes. He may be conscious by now, but he's tied up."

"He won't be as soon as his comrades reach him. And there's still a good possibility that Gerard will come. The guards were unable to find him or Beatrice in the castle."

While they had waited for Slip to bring the rope, Lukas had updated Sir Edwyn on the steward's involvement in the smuggling ring.

"Someone must go for help," Lukas said.

He looked back toward the cottage. He'd hoped Joanna and Slip would ride Shadow back to the castle, ensuring their protection along with delivering a message to the captain of the guard. But Joanna had been gone longer than he'd anticipated. Perhaps she'd decided to build a fire in the cottage to warm up properly.

"My lord." Slip was tugging at his elbow. "Do you hear that?"

Lukas gave his attention to the boy. "What is it, Slip?"

"A plopping noise, my lord. And quiet voices."

They stood perfectly still, listening to the sounds carrying on the night air.

"They're here," Sir Edwyn said softly. "That's oars we can hear. And there's at least two men on board."

Lukas turned to Slip. "Can you ride?"

"A bit," he said uncertainly.

"That will do," Lukas said. "I want you to take Sir Nigel's horse. Ride him straight to the guardhouse and tell the captain that Sir Edwyn requires his ten best men at the beach immediately. When you've done that, take the horse to the stable. One of the stable hands will take care of it for you."

"What about Lady Joanna?"

Lukas hesitated. He wanted her safe. Should he have Slip stop at the cottage so she could go with him? She would undoubtedly manage the horse better than the boy.

"We must act quickly." Sir Edwyn's urgency brought him back to their current predicament. "Slip needs to leave now if we are to have any hope of the guards reaching us in time."

The decision was made for him. "Ride straight to the castle," he said. "As fast as you can."

"Yes, my lord." Slip was already sprinting over the rocky beach and into the woods.

"Come," Sir Edwyn said. "We must get out of sight."

From the shelter of the trees, Lukas and Sir Edwyn watched the approach of the boat. At first it was nothing more than a dark shadow, but as it drew nearer, it was possible to make out the shape of the small craft and the silhouettes of two men.

"A couple of them," Sir Edwyn whispered.

"And the boat is small enough that there must be a larger vessel out at sea. They will need to make several trips to load all the wool."

There was a loud scraping sound as the boat made landfall on the rocky beach. That was followed by splashes and muted voices. They watched the men pull the boat to safety, then head across the pebbles toward the boulders that led to the cave.

The speed at which the men ascended the narrow path attested to the fact that they had made the trip before. When they reached the crevice, they disappeared, but it was not long before Lukas and Sir Edwyn heard their voices again. This time there were three silhouettes on the cliff, and each one carried a large sack.

"It seems that Audric is well enough to make the climb," Sir Edwyn said dryly.

Lukas watched grimly as the three men descended. They were moving more slowly now that they each had a load to carry. They reached the beach and moved quickly to the boat, their voices low but agitated. When they deposited their bags in the boat, they paused, turning to scour the edge of the woods. Lukas held completely still, sensing Sir Edwyn doing the same. Moments later, one of the men said something, and they all turned and hurried back toward the cliff.

They watched the men make two more trips before the Frenchmen pushed the boat into the water and Audric headed back to the cave on his own.

Lukas waited until the boat was well away before leaving his post to check on Sir Nigel. The knight was lying exactly where they'd left him, but now only one horse stood nearby.

"I know the frustration of having one's mount stolen," Lukas said. "But do not fear, yours was merely borrowed for a short time. It will be waiting for you at the castle." He raised one eyebrow. "Unless, of course, you bypass the stables and go directly to the dungeons."

Sir Nigel glared at him, his eyes expressing the fury his mouth could not. Heedless of Sir Nigel's obvious loathing, Lukas checked the integrity of his restraints before returning to Sir Edwyn.

"How long will it take for the guards to reach us?" he asked the senior knight.

Sir Edwyn shrugged. "If Slip made good time and the captain believes his story, they could be here soon."

He left the rest unsaid, and Lukas tried to push away thoughts of Slip being thrown from Sir Nigel's horse or being brushed off by the captain of the guard, just as he'd been trying to dampen down his growing concern over Joanna's absence.

"I'm going to the cottage," he said. "Lady Joanna should have returned by now."

Sir Edwyn nodded, but just as Lukas turned to leave, the older knight's hand shot out, barring his way.

"Someone is coming," he whispered.

The loamy ground deadened the sound of footsteps, but through the stillness, they could hear the distinct swish of fabric. Was it Joanna's long dress? Lukas started forward but froze as he heard the quiet but nasally tones of Gerard Bartholomew.

"Stop here," he said. "I hear the boat."

The splashing of oars was getting louder again.

"It's the steward," Lukas whispered.

Sir Edwyn nodded and pointed to the cliff. "Audric is back . . . with another bag."

Everyone was converging on the beach at once. The Frenchmen pulled the small craft onto the rocks and exchanged a few words with Audric, who dropped the bag he'd been carrying into the now-empty boat. Then, leaving the protection of the trees, Gerard stepped forward, flanked by two others.

"Who does he have with him?" Lukas asked.

Sir Edwyn strained to see through the branches. "It looks like Beatrice," he replied. "She's without her usual wimple, but her build and gait are those of the castle healer."

"And the other?"

Lukas knew the moment Sir Edwyn recognized her. Joanna. He pushed past Sir Edwyn, but the knight grasped him firmly by the arm.

"Wait," he said. "He has a blade to her throat. If we act in haste, it could cost Lady Joanna her life."

Trying to think past the pounding in his veins, Lukas pushed aside one of the branches to view the trio more clearly. The steward was leading the two women toward the boat. Beatrice shuffled a foot or two behind him, but Joanna was pressed to his side. The moonlight picked up the gold in her hair and the shimmer of her light-blue dress. It also highlighted the lethal weapon in Gerard's hand.

The Frenchmen and Audric were watching their approach warily, feet apart and knives in hand.

"Good evening, gentlemen." The steward's voice put Lukas's teeth on edge. "How many loads have you taken?"

One of the Frenchmen stepped forward and waved his blade between Beatrice and Joanna. "Why you bring the women?" Anger sizzled through his heavily accented English.

"This one"—Gerard jerked his head in the direction of Beatrice—"will travel with me to France. The other is my guarantee that we get there."

"There is no guarantee," the Frenchman hissed. "Ever." He stepped over to Joanna and looked her up and down, then reached out and fingered her long hair.

Joanna stood with her head held high, refusing to look at him.

"If I take you and you"—he used his knife to point at Gerard and Beatrice—"she is mine."

"Agreed," Gerard said. He pushed Joanna ahead of him to the side of the boat. "Get in."

"No." Joanna's voice was strong and clear.

Gerard raised his knife. "Get in," he repeated.

"If he forces her into the boat, we go after her," Lukas said. He'd already gauged the distance between his hiding place and the water's edge. He would be hard-pressed to reach the small craft in time should the Frenchmen decide to put to sea.

Sir Edwyn raised his hand, cocking his head as though listening for something. "A horse," he whispered.

"Yours?"

He shook his head. "It came from the path."

Hope surged through Lukas. "The guardsmen?"

Again, Sir Edwyn shook his head. "I think not. That many riders would make more noise."

Torn between discovering who else had joined them and monitoring the activity on the beach, Lukas's eyes went back to Joanna. The second Frenchman had moved to block Gerard's access to the boat.

"The wool goes first," he said. "Your lives"—he spat on the ground—"they are worth nothing." He pointed at the single bag of wool in the bottom of the boat. "This brings gold." He folded his arms across his chest. "The wool first."

The steward pointed to the cliff. "The wool is safe. Waiting on this beach is not."

The first Frenchman shoved Gerard. Joanna cried out, and Lukas tensed.

"Always you say no one is here. Why is it not safe now?"

Not far from Lukas and Sir Edwyn's position, the rattle of shifting pebbles echoed through the air. In unison, the men at the water's edge pivoted to face the new threat.

"Cedric Easton, collector of customs for His Majesty the King." The newcomer's voice boomed across the bay. "You're all under arrest."

Lukas waited no longer. Bolting from his hiding place, he raced past Sir Ivan and the two men who were with him. Out of the corner of his eye, he saw Audric take off toward the cliff. Ahead of him, Beatrice stood alone, petrified into immobility. The two Frenchmen had their shoulders against the hull of the boat, and it was moving rapidly across the rocks into the water.

Gerard hauled Joanna with him, and the moment the boat was bobbing, he tossed her inside.

"No," she screamed, scrambling to her feet.

The Frenchmen climbed in, one of them knocking her to the floor as they both reached for their oars. Gerard grabbed the side of the boat and heaved himself over and in. The small vessel listed heavily to the right, and the men already on board yelled at the steward, pushing him out of their way as they attempted to stabilize it.

Lukas heard the oars slot into position as he entered the water. "Joanna," he called.

Her blonde head rose above the side of the boat, and he could tell she was attempting to crawl forward. Gerard lunged for her, and the boat tipped again. The Frenchmen shouted, sliding one way, then the other to compensate for Gerard's erratic movement.

The water was to Lukas's chest. He kicked up his feet and started to swim. The boat was still rocking wildly, and he was within ten feet of the hull when he saw Joanna's face appear over the bow. She scanned the water, and he realized she could see nothing but blackness.

"Jump, Joanna," he called again. "I'm here."

She scrambled onto the bow's edge. Gerard reached out and grabbed her dress. She screamed, and there was a sickening sound of tearing fabric. Then she dropped into the sea.

Lukas pulled one arm through the water and then the other, stroking as hard as he could toward the area where he'd seen Joanna enter the ocean. Her dress formed a gray cloud beneath the waves. He dove, reaching out and finding her arm. He pulled, and their faces broke through the water's surface together.

"Can you swim?" he asked her.

She shook her head, clinging to him as she struggled for air. A wave rolled by, momentarily covering their faces, and she panicked.

"Easy," he said, working to loosen her iron grip around his neck while keeping them both afloat. "I won't let you go, but you must relax."

She coughed and took a shuddering breath. Then her stranglehold lessened.

"That's it," he said. "Now roll onto your back."

Slowly, with several stops to float and rest and to cough up seawater, he guided them back to shore. As soon as Lukas's foot scraped bottom, he pulled himself upright and placed his arm around Joanna to help her to her feet. She staggered against him, her breath rattling in her chest.

"You're safe now," he said, wrapping his arms around her.

At the sound of splashing, he looked up. Someone was wading out to meet them. Taking her hand, he led her through the thigh-deep water until the water level dropped below their knees and Sir Ivan reached them.

"I thought Lady Joanna might be in need of a robe," Sir Ivan said. He took the folded fabric off his arm, but instead of handing it to Joanna, he gave it to Lukas. Giving his friend a grateful smile, Lukas reached around Joanna's slim shoulders and attached the robe over her sopping dress.

"Thank you, Sir Ivan," Joanna said. She stopped to cough, then pulled the robe around her more tightly. "I am most grateful."

Lukas grasped Sir Ivan's hand and pulled him into an embrace. "You could not have timed your entrance any better," he said. "Were the customs officials very hard to persuade?"

Sir Ivan grinned and brushed at the moisture that had soaked onto his tunic. "I had only to mention Moreland's missing wool. Apparently the king is furious about that ever-increasing loss of revenue, so the collector of customs was eager for any opportunity to seize those who believe themselves exempt from import and export duties."

"But Gerard Bartholomew and the two French smugglers got away," Joanna said.

"I would not be so sure, my lady," Sir Ivan said. "Watch!"

On the beach, a torch flared and then traveled in a large arc from left to right. Seconds later, a matching light shone far out to sea. It illuminated the outlines of two ships and heralded the sound of a battle.

"One of the king's carracks was leaving port for London today. When the captain heard what was afoot, he agreed to anchor off the coast of Moreland until he received a signal from the controller." Sir Ivan gave a satisfied smile. "It should not take long for the king's men to board the smugglers' vessel. The smugglers will be apprehended and the goods confiscated."

"What of those who remained on shore?"

"Beatrice was taken without resistance," Sir Ivan said. "Audric made the mistake of returning to the cave, where Moreland's guards have him trapped."

"The guards came?"

"Yes. They are currently emptying the cave of its contents. Once the wool is removed, they will escort Audric, Beatrice, and Sir Nigel to the castle dungeon, where they will stay until Lord Gilbert decides their fate."

It was finished. Sir Ivan, Slip, and Sir Edwyn had all done their part, and now it was time for the castle guards and the customs officials to do theirs. Relief and fatigue seeped through Lukas's bones, and he knew he did not have the strength to do anything more, even if it were asked of him. He took Joanna's cold hand in his. "Come," he said. "It is time for us to leave."

Chapter 28

THEY RODE SHADOW BACK TO the castle. Lukas put Joanna in front of him in the saddle and kept his arms around her. Sir Ivan's robe helped protect her from the cool night air, but her wet dress clung to her skin and a deep chill was slowing her every movement and thought. She fought her heavy eyelids, jolting upright each time sleep threatened to overtake her, instinctively knowing that she could not let the cold lull her into unconsciousness.

Lukas, whose clothing was equally damp, could offer her little warmth, but he urged Shadow to greater speed, and they made the journey from Agnes's cottage to the stables in record time.

Leaving the charger in Peter's care, Luke took Joanna's hand and led her through the sleeping castle, up the stairs of the keep, through the great hall, all the way to the door of her bedchamber. He knocked, and Cona gave an answering bark. She heard the shuffle of Eva's feet moments before the latch lifted and the door opened.

Eva lifted her candle and peered at them. "Lady Joanna!"

Joanna was vaguely aware of Lukas placing his hand on her back and giving her a gentle push forward. Of Eva taking her hands with tears streaming down her face. Of Cona standing at her side, rubbing his head against her wet dress.

"She needs a warm bath, Eva," Lukas said. "Dry clothes and sleep. I will go for Agnes. She has wounds that need the healer's attention."

"Yes, my lord," Eva said, wiping her cheeks with her sleeve. "Thank you for bringing Lady Joanna back to us. I will take good care of her."

Then she drew Joanna into the room, and Lukas closed the door between them.

❧◦❧

The first thing Joanna was aware of was the sensation of a heavy weight pressing on her arm. Then it was warmth and the sound of rain hitting the window, a kettle singing, footsteps, and muted voices. And finally, it was pain radiating from her knees, fingers, and jaw.

"Lady Joanna."

She opened her eyes and blinked. Her bedchamber was filled with afternoon light. Cona was sitting at her bedside, his large snout resting on her arm, and when she returned his gaze, he raised his head and gave a happy bark.

"At last!" Eva placed her work-worn hand on Joanna's forehead and smoothed back her hair. "Merciful heavens, my lady, but you gave me a scare."

"Forgive me," Joanna said. Her voice was croaky, and she coughed to clear her throat.

Eva frowned. "Let me get some of the tea Agnes left for you." She hurried over to the fireplace, poured some steaming liquid from the kettle into a wooden cup, and carried it carefully over to the bed.

"Can you sit up?"

Joanna tried raising herself to a sitting position and moaned. Every part of her body hurt. Eva placed the cup on the floor and put her arm around Joanna's shoulders.

"That's it," Eva said, gently easing Joanna upward.

"What's wrong with me?"

"Well, let me see," Eva said, handing her the cup. "Apart from the fact that your knees are dark blue and have no skin left on them, your fingers look like you had a fight with a cat, you have a two-inch cut along your jaw, you climbed down a cliff, almost drowned in the sea, and caught a terrible chill—nothing much, I'd say."

Joanna wanted to laugh at her lady's maid's ridiculous list, but when the memories of her experiences the night before came flooding back, a tremor coursed through her instead. She'd never known such fear—fear of falling, fear of the water, fear of losing the man she loved. But despite it all, she'd survived. Lukas had survived. And the smugglers had been caught.

She took a sip of the hot tea, letting the soothing mixture glide down her scratchy throat, grateful for Eva and Agnes and their ministrations. She hoped Lukas was receiving similar care. His injuries and exposure to the cold sea had been just as brutal as hers. And he had earlier wounds that were still healing. Was he resting somewhere in the castle or had he gone to . . . ? Her fingers tightened around her cup as the appalling ramifications of sleeping through a goodly portion of the day hit her.

"Eva!"

Her lady's maid looked up in alarm. "What is it, my lady?"

"The tournament. Is it over?"

Eva's expression relaxed. She pointed at the window. "It has rained all day," she said. "The competition will not resume until tomorrow at the earliest."

Joanna closed her eyes and released a deep breath. Although her future was still unknown, she'd been granted another day before having to face it.

Cona barked, and the sound was followed immediately by a knock on the door. Eva hurried to answer it.

"Good afternoon, Eva."

Joanna recognized the voice immediately. "Agnes," she said, extending her hand to the kindly healer as she entered the bedchamber.

Agnes smiled warmly. "Well, now, that's what I was hoping to see." She leaned over the bed and dropped a soft kiss on each of Joanna's cheeks. "How are you feeling?"

"Sore," Joanna said.

Eva rolled her eyes, and Agnes gave a soft chuckle. "After what you endured yesterday, my lady, that is the least that should be expected." She placed her hand on the blanket covering Joanna's legs. "May I check the condition of your knees?"

Joanna nodded, and Agnes carefully pulled back the covers and lifted the lower portion of Joanna's nightgown to expose a wide bandage wrapped around each of her legs. The healer carefully unwrapped the first strip of cloth, and Joanna took a sharp breath. The damage was considerable. Dark-blue welts surrounded the badly grazed kneecap, and the entire area was puffy and swollen.

"I tried to remove all the embedded grit last night," Agnes said. "The wound will be angry for a few days, but if you keep it clean and apply the salve I gave to Eva, both legs should heal completely." She started unwrapping the other leg. "The seawater, cold and miserable though it was, likely did much to cleanse your wounds."

She applied a sticky salve to both knees, then rewrapped them and turned her attention to Joanna's hands. She took each hand in hers, turning them slowly as she examined them. "I do not see any sign of infection yet," she said. "But you must watch for any redness or swelling."

Joanna nodded.

"And this last wound," Agnes said, running a gentle finger along Joanna's jawline. "How did this occur?"

"Gerard Bartholomew's knife," Joanna said, only now remembering the sudden searing pain she'd felt when the Frenchman had pushed the steward away from the boat.

Agnes pressed her mouth into a firm line as though holding back words that wanted to spill out.

Eva had no such reservations. "Evil waghalter," she said, stomping across the room to retrieve a second jar of salve.

"How is my father?" Joanna asked, not wanting to think of Gerard anymore.

"He is much improved. The infusion of belladonna moderated his heart rate, and the hallucinations are behind him. He is weak but was well enough to bellow at me this morning." She smiled. "Sir Edwyn is with him now, and I believe he will make a full recovery."

Joanna squeezed her hand gratefully. "You are too good, Agnes."

"None of us are that, my lady." She rose from the side of the bed as though preparing to leave.

"One more thing," Joanna said. "Do you know how Sir Lukas fares?"

"I do," Agnes said. "But there are three young men waiting in the great hall who can tell you more on that score, if you are willing to grant them audience."

"Three young men?"

"More like two young men and one young knight," Agnes said, mischief dancing in her eyes.

Joanna's grip on the blanket tightened. She turned to Eva. "I should like to invite them in."

Eva nodded. "I believe that with Agnes and me in attendance, that is acceptable." She took a minute to pull Joanna's blanket up higher and to fuss over her hair, then she walked to the bedchamber door and pulled it open.

"My lord," she said. "Lady Joanna will see you all now."

There was a rattle of hurried footsteps, and Slip came hurtling through the door. "Lady Joanna," he said, staggering to a halt beside her bed. "I rode Sir Nigel's horse all the way to the castle, and I didn't fall off once!"

Joanna laughed. His joyful exuberance was the best possible medicine. "I'm so proud of you. You were a marvelous help to Sir Lukas and Sir Edwyn."

Slip positively glowed, and Joanna was reassured to see that the more traumatic moments of the day were not at the forefront of his thoughts.

"Hullo, Lady." Garrick came forward more slowly. He gave her a shy smile. "I missed you yesterday. Sir Edwyn and I never found Sir Lukas or Gerard Bartholomew. But we did find Agnes." He shuffled his feet. "I s'ppose being a good finder is harder in the castle."

"There are a lot more places to hide here," Joanna said. "But finding Agnes was the best thing you could have done."

His smile widened. "I think so too." He moved to one side and made room for Lukas beside the bed.

One look at him had her heart tripping over itself. His dark hair flopped over a bandage that wrapped around his head, covering his recent wound above his ear. Strips of cloth were also wrapped around his wrists where the ropes had cut him so badly. And in his hands, he held the biggest bunch of wildflowers she'd ever seen. He offered them to her.

"I wish I could claim that I picked these myself," he said. "Margery delivered them to the castle and asked that they be given to you." He gave a small smile. "It seems that word of the wool's recovery—and your part in it—has spread through Moreland faster than the plague."

"They are beautiful," she said, reaching for the flowers. His fingers lingered on hers, and warmth flooded her cheeks. "However, you, Sir Edwyn, Sir Ivan, and Slip deserve far more of the credit than I for discovering and reclaiming the wool."

He shook his head, his brown eyes claiming hers. "Most people will never know what you endured last night, my lady, but I will always remember your courage and grace."

Joanna knew there had been nothing graceful about her falls on the cliff or into the ocean, but she held her tongue. Something about the way he spoke made her feel that he was talking about much more. "And I shall always remember that you saved my life," she said quietly.

He held her gaze a moment longer, then he leaned over. Before she knew what he was about, he placed a kiss on her forehead, straightened, and walked back to the door. "Until tomorrow, Lady Joanna," he said. And then he was gone.

Joanna stared at the closed door, the wildflowers in her hands forgotten.

"Well, I never!" Eva dropped onto her wooden chair with a whoosh. "That, my lady, was completely uncalled for—and absolutely wonderful."

Chapter 29

THE NEXT MORNING, THE SUN rose into a cloudless blue sky. Agnes arrived early to tend to Joanna's wounds so that Eva had plenty of time to help her to dress and prepare her hair for the final round of the tournament. Joanna chose to wear her plum-colored dress and gold girdle, but she left her hair loose, hoping that the gentle waves that framed her face would mask the red scar along her jawline.

"Do you have a ribbon that matches this dress?" Joanna asked.

Eva gave her a knowing look. "Of course, my lady." She pulled a plum-colored ribbon from a box on the table. "Shall I tie it to your wrist?"

Joanna nodded and extended her arm. Would she have the opportunity to give the ribbon to Lukas? If another archer won today, it might be the last time they would speak to each other. A lump filled her throat. How ever would she survive that eventuality?

With the ribbon in place, Eva passed her a trencher full of bread and cheese. Joanna pushed it away.

"You have to keep up your strength," Eva said.

Joanna would gladly have gone without food until the tournament was over and, perhaps, depending on the results, forever after that, but Eva stood over her until she'd eaten a few mouthfuls. In Joanna's opinion, feeling ill after eating was no better than feeling weak from abstaining, but she refrained from pointing that out, not wanting to give her lady's maid any reason to send her back to bed.

"I must be on my way," she said. She rose gingerly, testing her knees before releasing her hold on the chair. "Come, Cona."

The dog was at her side in an instant, but he quickly moved from there to the bedchamber door, where he gave a warning bark just before a knock sounded.

Eva answered the door and immediately dropped into a curtsey. "Lord Gilbert," she said.

Stunned, Joanna watched as her father entered the room. She could not remember the last time he had visited her bedchamber. He stood tall, still emanating a sense of authority despite his loss of weight and the slight shake of his hand as he reached for hers.

Joanna took his hand and bent her head in greeting. "Forgive me, my lord," she said. "It is very difficult for me to curtsy at present."

"I heard you were injured," he said.

"My knees are painful," she said, "but Agnes assures me that they will heal."

"I am glad to hear it."

"And I am glad to see you so much improved," she said.

"I thank you." He cleared his throat. "I wish to attend the tournament. Perhaps, as we may both be a little slower of pace than usual, we could walk there together."

Joanna could not have been more astonished. Did Lord Gilbert intend to walk the entire distance to the south pasture in silence, or was he actually considering entering into a conversation with her? "I . . . I should like that very much," she said, surprised to realize that it was true.

He offered her his arm, and she took it. "Come, Cona," he said. The dog cocked his head to one side, as unsure as his mistress. But when Joanna snapped her fingers, he trotted to her side and escorted them both out.

Walking was a slow and painful process, particularly when they descended the stairs of the keep, but her father's arm steadied her, and after awhile, Joanna found that moving actually reduced some of the stiffness in her legs.

Most of the castle residents had already left for the tournament, so the inner bailey was unusually quiet. They walked in silence until they passed into the outer bailey. Here, the distant sound of the crowd gathering in the south pasture could be heard, and Joanna felt her tension rise.

"I have spoken at length with Sir Edwyn." Her father's voice startled her. "He told me of all you did to facilitate the return of Moreland's wool and the apprehension of the traitors among us." He paused. "I am proud of you, Joanna."

Joanna was dumbfounded. When had her father ever been proud of anything she had done?

"There were others who did far more than I," she said.

He tilted his head as though conceding the point. "I understand that a goodly portion of the credit belongs to a certain Sir Lukas of Cornwall."

"Yes, my lord. Without his efforts, the smugglers would surely have been successful."

"Why did he take this upon himself? He owes no allegiance to Moreland."

"He's a noble knight," she said. "A man who does not simply sit by when he realizes that an injustice has been done."

"A man of action," he said. "I like that."

"Being a man of action would be worthless if he were not also a man of compassion, who is honest and true," she said.

Lord Gilbert studied her curiously. "And I gather he is in the final rounds of the archery tournament?"

Joanna's stomach churned. "Yes, my lord."

He gave a pleased nod. "I look forward to watching him shoot."

They walked out the castle gates and took the path that led to the pasture. Music, voices, and laughter filled the air, but as they reached the lists, a stillness fell over the spectators. The men of Moreland bowed, the women curtseyed, and from somewhere at the back of the crowd, a young boy yelled, "Hurrah for Lady Joanna!"

A roar of approval filled the field, and as Joanna continued her slow walk toward the pavilion, peasants, farmers, and townspeople alike called out their thanks.

"God bless you, Lady Joanna."

Pink cheeked and overwhelmed by the reception she'd received, Joanna waved to the children lining the fence and limped up the stairs to take her position at the front of the stands.

From his seat beside her, Lord Gilbert leaned nearer. "You are very well loved, my lady."

"Only by some, Lord Gilbert."

A frown creased his brow, and he looked away.

On the other side of her father, Sir Edwyn rose to his feet and called for the competitors to approach the stands. Five men with bows in hand lined up, but this time, Sir Nigel was missing and Sir Lukas stood at the end of the queue. He was still wearing bandages on his wrists, but he had removed the one around his head. His hair hid the worst of his wound, but purple discoloration tinged his left temple and cheekbone. There was no startling evidence of what he'd so recently endured, but the people did not seem to need any. When Sir Edwyn presented each knight to Lord Gilbert, they clapped politely, but when Sir Lukas was introduced, their applause was deafening.

"By your leave, Sir Gilbert," Joanna said. "I have something I must do."

She stood, steadying herself, and the audience quieted, watching as she carefully navigated the steps that led down to the field. With a pounding heart, she walked along the line of waiting archers until she reached Lukas. "Sir Lukas," she said. "Would you do me the honor of wearing my favor?"

He stepped forward and dropped to one knee. Joanna pulled the ribbon from her wrist. It fluttered in her hand. With shaking fingers, she wrapped the ribbon around his arm and tied it in a knot. As soon as it was secure, Lukas raised his arm to his chest and bowed his head before her. The crowd cheered wildly, and Joanna fought back her tears. It had been only two days since she'd done this before, but so much had happened in the interim. The admiration she'd had for Sir Lukas then was nothing to the love she felt for him now.

"May your arrows fly true," she whispered once more.

He rose and backed away. He did not say a word, but he did not need to; the look in his eyes spoke for him.

By the time Joanna returned to her seat, the contestants had taken their positions across from the butts. Each archer was to have three shots. The scores would be tallied, and the men with the top three scores would shoot again. But from that point on, each arrow would count, and a poor shot could cause immediate elimination.

Joanna sat with her hands clasped tightly on her lap.

The officials bid the first three archers ready their bows, and a sense of anticipation mounted among the spectators.

"Nock. Mark. Draw. Loose."

The familiar calls rang out, painful in their slow and deliberate timing, and all at once, three arrows were airborne. Cheers and jeers followed as the spectators watched the archers shoot and the officials tally their scores. Joanna studied Lukas as he anchored his feet and steadied his arm for each shot. He made pulling the longbow's draw weight and shooting a bull's-eye at a 300-yard distance look effortless, and when all five men had taken their turn, Lukas was one of the archers through to the last round.

He lined up beside Sir Cuthbert of Dover and Viscount Maven of Winchester. Sir Cuthbert was a short, broad-shouldered man with gray hair and a gray beard. When he stood straight, his head reached Sir Lukas's shoulder. Viscount Maven, on the other hand, was tall and as lean as a reed. His young face was pockmarked, and before each shot, his Adam's apple bobbed up and down.

A hush fell over the crowd as the archers readied for the elimination round. Joanna wondered if her heart would beat right out of her chest. Beside her, she sensed her father lean forward in his seat, his eyes trained on the men on the field.

Sir Cuthbert took the first shot. A collective groan went up when it missed the bull's-eye by an inch. He stepped aside. Lukas took his place and readied himself. She listened for the official's call and watched as the arrow sailed right into the center of the target. The crowd roared. Joanna breathed again. Sir Cuthbert conceded defeat, and with a disappointed nod, he walked away from the butts.

Viscount Maven replaced Lukas. His Adam's apple wavered, and he let his arrow fly. It hit the bull's-eye. Cheers erupted, and Viscount Maven grinned. He moved away from the mark, making room for Lukas to take his second shot. Lukas stepped up. He rolled his shoulders and flexed his fingers. Only he knew how much pain he was suffering each time he drew back on the string. Joanna bowed her head and offered up a silent plea. Then she glanced to her left. Her father's face was tense, his eyes riveted on Lukas.

Lukas listened for the official's call and released his arrow. It sailed through the air, landing squarely in the center of the target once more.

"Nicely done."

Joanna barely heard her father's muttered words above the crowd's thundering applause. But she watched as once again Lukas relinquished his place to Viscount Maven. The tall young nobleman lifted his bow. His Adam's apple quivered, and he nocked his arrow. Silence fell over the crowd, and in the distance, Joanna heard a baby cry. It was instantly hushed. On the field, Viscount Maven lowered his bow slightly, then raised it again.

Lord Gilbert let out a hiss. "He shifted his stance."

"What does that mean?" Joanna asked.

"It means," her father said, leaning back in his seat, "that Viscount Maven just lost his foundation. A fraction of an inch off on his foot placement will affect his balance and the strength of his shot."

"Loose."

The official's voice reverberated down the lists, and everyone watched as Viscount Maven's arrow left his bow and landed in the second ring of the target. The audience gave a collective groan. Viscount Maven's shoulders slumped, and he dropped his head. Lukas walked over to him and clasped him by the hand. Joanna saw the tall nobleman nod a few times as they exchanged words. Then, with a small wave to the crowd, he slowly walked away to their appreciative applause.

As if in a daze, Joanna sat and watched the officials consult with each other before steering Lukas toward the stands. Had Lukas truly won? All around her, people were cheering and shouting his name. Her father rose to his feet and looked down at her, one eyebrow raised.

"It is expected that you join me in greeting the tournament champion," he said.

Joanna wasn't sure if her legs would hold her if she tried to stand. But this time, her fear of falling had nothing to do with injured knees and everything to do with overwrought nerves.

"Allow me, my lady." Sir Edwyn had moved to her side. He gently helped her to her feet and leaned a little closer. "I believe I am now qualified to give a sermon at church on the efficacy of saying prayers during tournaments."

Joanna fought back a smile. "I do not know what Father Jerome would say on the matter," she said. "But I would be most grateful to hear your thoughts."

Sir Edwyn gave her an almost imperceptible wink. "Come," he said. "Sir Lukas is waiting."

The men stood in front of the stands. The two officials who had managed the competition flanked Lukas and faced Lord Gilbert. One of the officials took a small step forward.

"Lord Gilbert," he said. "May we present Sir Lukas of Cornwall, winner of Moreland's archery tournament."

"I thank you, gentlemen, for overseeing the tournament so well."

The two men gave accepting nods, then they backed away, leaving Lukas standing alone. His bow was slung across one shoulder, his quiver over the other. He looked every bit the brave and fearless knight she knew him to be. But the elation that surely should have been present after such a hard-fought victory was unaccountably missing, and Joanna experienced a pang of misgiving.

"Sir Lukas of Cornwall," Lord Gilbert said. "I commend you on your skills with the longbow and congratulate you on winning this tournament. The competition was fierce, and your success not easily earned."

"I thank you, my lord," Lukas said with a bow of his head. "It was an honor to participate."

Lord Gilbert paused, and a flicker of something that looked remarkably like recognition crossed his face. "Your father," he said. "Did he serve under Richard, Earl of Cornwall?"

Lukas hesitated for only a fraction of a second. "No, my lord. His allegiance was to Moreland."

Lord Gilbert's eyes narrowed. "Who was your mother?"

"Her name was Katherine," Lukas said, facing Lord Gilbert's glare without apology.

Lord Gilbert's expression illuminated his intensifying outrage. Joanna felt herself pale, the sensation of icy whiteness quickly spreading all the way from her face to her fingertips. Beneath her hand, Sir Edwyn's muscles tensed, and she forced herself to keep breathing.

"Sir Edwyn." Barely suppressed fury simmered beneath her father's stately facade. "Would you care to explain the meaning of this?"

"My lord." Sir Edwyn kept his voice calm and low. "Sir Lukas's father died on the battlefield saving my life. His valor is undisputed. Only yesterday, Sir Lukas saved Lady Joanna from certain death and Moreland's wool from traitorous smugglers. No matter his past or his parentage, he has already proven his bravery and his loyalty. By winning this tournament, he has also confirmed his skill with the longbow. More than anyone on this field, he deserves to be named Moreland's champion."

Lord Gilbert's internal battle raged a few seconds longer before he turned his piercing look on Lukas once more. "You are no doubt aware of the reward that was posted for winning this tournament."

"Yes, my lord," Lukas said, a bead of sweat appearing along his hairline.

"I pride myself on being a man of my word, Sir Lukas." Lord Gilbert's tone was glacial. "The tourney prize will stand." Without looking at Joanna, he continued. "Step forward. I shall officially pronounce you the winner of the tournament and of Lady Joanna of Moreland's hand in marriage."

For over a week, Joanna had known that this moment would come, and yet her father's words still had the power to hurt deeply. With sickening surety, she knew that no matter which unknown knight the officials had brought to this point, Lord Gilbert would have congratulated him and then blindly placed his only daughter and her future well-being into that stranger's hands. A place, but for Lukas's skill and Sir Edwyn's prayers, she likely would have been even less cherished than she was now.

During their walk to the pavilion that morning, she'd harbored a faint hope that all that had occurred over the last few days had effected a change in Lord Gilbert's attitude toward her. It appeared, however, that her hopes had been in vain. Even if he were capable of showing her that he cared, he was not yet prepared to manifest it. She lowered her eyes, afraid that others would see her pain.

"Before that announcement is made, my lord, I would ask permission to speak with Lady Joanna."

Joanna's eyes flew open again. No one ever spoke to Lord Gilbert so boldly. And yet Lukas was standing firm, his determination unwavering.

Lord Gilbert pursed his lips, looking askance, first at Sir Lukas and then at Joanna. Still, Lukas did not move. From the seats behind them, whispers began to circulate. Joanna's grip on Sir Edwyn's arm tightened.

"You may have one minute," her father growled. "Then, whether you are ready or not, I make the announcement."

Lukas stepped forward. He was close enough to reach out and touch her. But he did not.

"Lady Joanna," he said. "When I first entered this tournament, I truly believed that there was nothing I wanted more than to make you my wife. But as my love for you has continued to grow, I have discovered a wish that is even greater." He paused, keeping his gaze on her. "I now realize that my greatest desire is to know that you are happy." Tears filled Joanna's eyes, but Lukas continued. "The very competition that gave me the chance to win your hand took away your opportunity to determine your future. And so, at the risk of losing something most precious, I want to offer that gift of choice back to you. If you wish to be free of a betrothal that was forced upon you, I will decline the tournament prize and release you from that obligation. If, however, you choose to accept my hand in marriage of your own volition, you will make me the happiest man in England."

Never before had Joanna seen her father stunned into silence. She relinquished her hold on Sir Edwyn's arm and stepped up to the wooden

bar that separated her from Lukas. Her heart was pounding, her tears
flowing, but she knew what she must say. "Sir Lukas of Cornwall," she
said, "I thank you for your chivalry, courage, and valor. But mostly, I
thank you for your love." She paused to wipe her tears. "Please accept
the tournament prize, not because it was offered to you as the best
archer but because I love you and because being your wife would bring
me more happiness than I can imagine."

Lukas's undisguised joy at her words brought a blush to her cheeks.

"Lord Gilbert," he said. "I would be honored if you would an-
nounce my betrothal to Lady Joanna."

"I should say so." Lord Gilbert's voice was gruff, but his eyes were
moist. "We have already waited too long by half."

Chapter 30

THE REMAINDER OF THE DAY passed in a blur. With the well wishes
of the tournament crowd still ringing in her ears, Joanna was saluted
crisply by smiling guards at the castle gate. In the great hall, servants
busily preparing for the banquet stopped their work to quietly offer
their congratulations, and when Joanna finally reached her bedchamber, Agnes and Eva greeted her with hugs and tears.

Only later, when Eva was preparing Joanna's hair for the tournament banquet and the room was quiet once more, did the reality
of her future with Lukas truly begin to distill in her heart and mind.
She was to marry the man she loved—and who loved her. Gratitude
and joy overwhelmed her.

That evening, she sat at the head table with her father at her right
and Lukas at her left and watched while Moreland's knights lined up
to welcome Sir Lukas into their ranks. Sir William gave him a somewhat sheepish acknowledgment, Sir Ivan offered him the warmest
greeting, and Sir Edwyn's was the most tender.

"Your father would be proud . . . both of the way you used his
bow and of the man you have become," he said.

Lukas murmured his thanks, but Joanna could tell that amid all
the joviality and celebrating that followed, Sir Edwyn's poignant sen-
timent had touched him deeply. He maintained cordial conversation

with everyone he met; he smiled and laughed at the banter of others. But all the while, he stayed close to Joanna. And when his leg brushed hers beneath the head table or their fingers touched at their shared trencher, she felt his nearness and wished for time together away from the confusion and noise.

Now that they were sitting in the great hall and the anxiety of the tourney and its outcome was behind them, a heavy blanket of fatigue was settling over her. She recognized tiredness in Lukas's face as well, and after awhile, she noticed that when her father reached for his goblet, his hand trembled far more than it had before.

The servants brought out one tray of food after another. Exotic meats, pastries, cheeses, and fruit arrived at their table in a seemingly never-ending parade of delicacies. Completing each course was a slow process, and by the time the minstrel began his performance, Lord Gilbert's face was ashen and Joanna was sure that his limited strength was spent.

"Let me walk you to your chamber, my lord," she said. "You must not undo all the good Agnes has accomplished."

When he responded with a compliant nod rather than a brusque rebuke, Joanna knew he was exhausted.

"I must escort my father to his bedchamber," she told Lukas.

"I will accompany you," he said, pushing back his chair and reaching for hers.

Joanna's knees were stiff from sitting too long, but it was Lord Gilbert who stumbled as he stood. Sir Lukas immediately took his elbow and steadied him.

"It is good to know you can act rapidly when called upon to do so, Sir Lukas," Lord Gilbert said. "As my advisor, you will need to be both quick thinking and decisive."

Lukas's eyes widened. "Your advisor, my lord?"

"Of course." Lord Gilbert looked at him as though he were addlepated. "You were the one responsible for having my former advisor put in the dungeon. I think it just reward that you take over his responsibilities."

If Joanna had not known better, she would have sworn her father was teasing him.

"Besides," Lord Gilbert continued, "how else are you going to learn how to run Moreland when I am gone?"

Now Lukas looked dumbfounded.

Lord Gilbert's lip twitched. He turned to Sir Edwyn. "I think he will do very well after all, Sir Edwyn," he said. "Very well indeed."

"I agree, my lord," Sir Edwyn said. "On most issues, he will speak his mind, but it appears that you still have the power to render him speechless."

Lord Gilbert slapped his hand on Lukas's shoulder, and for the second time in her life, Joanna saw her father smile.

"Come," Lord Gilbert said. "It is time for this old man to retire."

Joanna, Lukas, and Cona accompanied Lord Gilbert to his bedchamber and turned him over to Agnes's care.

As they walked back through the empty grand chamber, Lukas's steps slowed. He glanced at the large table standing on the dais on the other side of the room. "This is where Lord Gilbert conducts his private business," he said.

"Yes." Joanna slipped her hand into his, and he clasped it tightly. "This is where I first learned of Lord Gilbert's plan for an archery tournament. When I came to speak to my father, he was in counsel with Sir Edwyn, Sir Nigel, and Gerard Bartholomew." She looked up at him. "You may feel overwhelmed by the responsibilities that have been heaped upon you in so short a time, but after the abuse of trust that has occurred here, you must know what a blessing you will be to Lord Gilbert and the people of Moreland."

"Ah," Lukas said. "And are those the primary people who will benefit from my continued presence at Moreland?"

Joanna caught the twinkle in his eye. "Well, I do not see any benefit to smugglers or Frenchmen," she said.

Lukas chuckled. "No. None."

He pulled her closer and wrapped his arms around her. Instantly, Cona shifted from companion dog to guard dog, and a low rumble sounded deep in his throat.

Lukas did not flinch. "Sit, Cona," he said. "Become accustomed to seeing Lady Joanna in my arms." His gaze moved from Joanna's eyes to her lips. "Because from now on, it's going to be a regular occurrence."

Then, because Lukas had the power to bewitch Joanna's dog, Cona flopped to the floor, yawned, and rested his long snout on his paws.

Lukas gave a small, satisfied smile and slowly lowered his head. "I love you, Lady Joanna of Moreland," he whispered.

Before she could respond, his lips claimed hers. And when he finally raised his head again, any doubts Joanna had had over who would benefit most from Sir Lukas of Cornwall's presence at Moreland had fled.

Author's Note

THE LEGEND OF GELERT ACTUALLY originates in North Wales. The faithful wolfhound was said to have belonged to Llewelyn the Great, prince of Gwynedd, and was given to him as a gift from King John of England in the thirteenth century.

According to the tale, Prince Llewelyn went hunting and, upon his return, discovered his son's cradle upturned and Gelert by its side, covered in blood. Assuming that Gelert had killed his son, Llewelyn plunged his sword into the dog's heart. Moments later, however, a baby's cry alerted him to the fact that not only was his son alive, but his devoted wolfhound had also saved the baby from the attack of a ferocious wolf. Llewelyn was filled with such remorse over what he'd done, he buried the dog with much ceremony and was said to have never smiled again.

The small village of Beddgelert in North Wales is the site of Gelert's supposed grave. As a child, I visited the grave site on several occasions, and each time I read the story inscribed on the plaque there, I wondered how much of the legend was based on truth. My imagination took flight over how this experience may have impacted those involved. Did Prince Llewelyn really never smile again? How did killing Gelert affect his future relationship with his son? What if his son had been a daughter? Would that have made Prince Llewelyn even more protective?

I think those early childhood musings were the foundation for this novel. In *To Win a Lady's Heart*, I have moved Gelert into the fifteenth century, relocated him from the rugged mountains of Wales to the rolling pastures of England (I hope he will forgive me), and surrounded him by completely new characters. But notwithstanding these changes, I like to believe that the loyalty and courage Gelert exemplified so many centuries ago lives on through this book.

About the Author

Sᴵᴀɴ Aɴɴ Bᴇssᴇʏ ᴡᴀs ʙᴏʀɴ in Cambridge, England, and grew up on the island of Anglesey off the north coast of Wales. She left Wales to attend Brigham Young University, Provo, and graduated with a bachelor's degree in communications.

The author of several LDS novels and children's books, Sian has also written articles for the *New Era*, *Ensign*, and *Liahona* magazines.

Sian and her husband, Kent, are the parents of five children and the grandparents of three beautiful little girls and two handsome little boys. They currently live in Rexburg, Idaho, and although Sian has few opportunities to speak Welsh anymore, Llanfairpwllgwyngyllgo-gerychwyrndrobwllllantysiliogogogoch still rolls off her tongue.

Traveling, reading, cooking, and being with her grandchildren are some of Sian's favorite activities. Trying to do them all usually ends in chaos and laughter—which makes for the best days of all.